I opened the glass sliding doors and stepped onto the fragrant patio. I crossed the slate stones to the empty pool. Lying at the bottom, surprise fanning out over her exquisite face, dead eyes staring in stony sleep, was Leslie Ballard.

A scream filled my head, clogged my throat. When it stopped, I found I was on my knees. I swallowed with difficulty. I don't know how long I knelt, unmoving, breathing softly, waiting, watching.

Then a noise came from below, through the swaying grasses, from the direction of the steep wooden stairway that led up from Charles Cove. Struggling to my feet, I turned around. Hamm Hammett, his handsome face contorted, was charging toward me.

FINAL CLOSING

BARBARA LEE

WORLDWIDE.

TORONTO • NEW YORK • LONDON
AMSTERDAM • PARIS • SYDNEY • HAMBURG
STOCKHOLM • ATHENS • TOKYO • MILAN
MADRID • WARSAW • BUDAPEST • AUCKLAND

To Joan Machinchick

FINAL CLOSING

A Worldwide Mystery/March 1999

First published by St. Martin's Press, Incorporated.

ISBN 0-373-26304-X

Printed in U.S.A.

My thanks to the many people who generously contributed their time and expertise: Real estate agents Fran Haines, Mike Van Beuren and Carol Cross; Cheryl DePetro of the Sexual Trauma Treatment, Advocacy, and Recovery Center; Lieutenant Robert Jaschik and Officer Ron Hines of the Anne Arundel County Police Department; Kim Knapp of Artemis Self-Defense and Aikido for Women and Children; the information desk staff at the Howard County Public Library. And finally, my love and thanks to my husband, Bob Suggs, who makes books possible.

Although Anne Arundel County, Maryland, is real, Pines on Magothy, its inhabitants and their adventures are fictitious. They exist solely in the author's imagination for the purpose of this story.

ONE

HEADY AND SWEET, spring muscled its way into the dim church basement, through open doors and low windows hung with homemade curtains. There was no humidity yet, no fiery bruising air, just a gentle green promise floating on the breeze. Beyond the church parking lot, beyond the small bungalows and tall trees, the Magothy River—not a river at all but an estuary of the Chesapeake—flowed wide and blue.

Reluctantly, I turned from the open door toward the scene behind me. A hundred real estate agents, almost all women, mingled and buzzed, smearing bright stains on Styrofoam coffee cups and snapping at small pastries when they thought no one was looking. Two men struggled with the arthritic legs of a worn cafeteria table, wrestling it into place in front of rows of folding chairs. Friends greeted friends, then carefully staked out seats with briefcases and handbags. A church volunteer—his early-morning cheer hanging a little heavy—ran back and forth to refill the dented aluminum coffee urns.

It could have been any of a hundred events held in church basements all over Maryland. But it wasn't. No. Not this morning. This morning, we were going to learn how not to be killed by our clients.

The Art of Self-Defense, the workshop was called. An art—at least for female real estate agents in Anne Arundel County—that had suddenly become all too important. I looked into the faces of women chattering nearby. There was a certain tightness, matched by a whistling-in-the-dark quality to their laughter. And for good reason. First, a blizzard of calls reeking of sexual malice had descended upon us. Then, a week ago, at a secluded estate overlooking the Chesapeake Bay, an agent named Rose Macklin had

shown an unknown client a magnificent designer home. Today that
client was wanted for smashing open her head.

Pushing aside my grim thoughts, I watched with affection as
my seventy-some-year-old aunt, Lillian Weber, held court. A pair
of crutches leaned against a chair next to her. Two months ago a
bad fall had snapped a bone in her ankle almost in half, rendering
her homebound. Cursing the inconvenience, she had pulled herself
together and gone back to running the family real estate firm. With
my help. If what I provided could be called help.

The thought of a settlement that had fallen apart at the table
earlier this morning surfaced in my mind. There had been tears,
then yelling. The buyer wouldn't buy and the seller wouldn't sell.
And it wouldn't have happened, I thought, had Lillian been there.
People didn't like letting my aunt down so they rose to her level.
Like I was trying to. But selling real estate had proved to be harder
than it looked. Much harder than anything my twenty-odd years
in the New York advertising world had prepared me for.

"Hello." I turned to find a hand, its no-nonsense nails overdue
for the services of a nail file, thrusting in the direction of my
stomach. "You're Eve Elliott, I guess." I nodded and grabbed the
hand before it connected with my belt. A woman, built like the
masthead of a ship that had gained a few pounds, pumped hard
and long. She wore a white cotton turtleneck with tiny flowers and
a full denim skirt. Orthopedic sandals over anklets supported her
heft. She was of indeterminate age, maybe forty, or forty-five. Salt-
and-pepper hair fell straight and flat and short from a central whirl-
pool at the top of her head. I didn't know who she was, a fact
that wasn't lost on her.

"Joyce. Joyce Nichols," she said, resentment fighting with
courtesy for control of her face. Resentment, I could see, was
winning. My mind cast helplessly around for any frame of refer-
ence. Nothing. Though the voice was familiar, I was sure we'd
never met.

"I'm sorry...I...uh..."

"Gaylin Realty," she said. Her voice sounded familiar but
surely I'd have remembered her face. "We talk on the phone all
the time." I waited. "I fill in as a part-time receptionist at the

Annapolis office," she said, with exasperation. "Whenever Mitch needs someone to help out."

So that's why her voice was familiar. Gaylin Realty was owned by Mitch Gaylin, Anne Arundel County's newest and fastest-growing broker. In less than a year, he had opened two offices and attracted many of the best and most experienced agents. I glanced over to where he was chatting with a tough, small woman arranging objects on the cafeteria table. Today's workshop was his doing. And it *was* a good idea, I thought. Certainly, no one else in the county—police included—seemed to be doing much.

I became aware that Joyce Nichols was talking. Again, I realized I hadn't heard what she had said. She was looking directly at me, waiting.

"Sorry?" Another look of incredulity slid over her face as she discovered I didn't have a clue where we were in this conversation.

"Excuse me. Eve?" A dazzling woman, an explosion of dark wavy hair framing her small face, had come up behind us. Red lips echoed the color of her suit, fighting for attention with dark eyes and Mediterranean skin. Joyce sniffed loudly, then marched off to torment someone else. "I'm Leslie Ballard," said the woman. She glanced at Joyce. "Did I interrupt something?"

"No, not really."

"Good. With Joyce, it's sometimes hard to know." She turned back to spray me with the full force of her smile. "I was hoping to run into you here. I have clients who want to see your Charles Cove listing. Would tomorrow be okay? Around lunchtime?"

"Great." We struggled to exchange business cards. Hers had a tiny picture on it right next to the Gaylin Realty logo. Mine did not, a fact that exasperated Lillian, who believed that an honest face sold houses.

There was movement from the front of the long, low room. The microphone squawked briefly. People slouched toward their seats. We watched as Joyce dove for an empty chair in the front row, stamping on some feet in the process, if the face of one agent was any clue.

I turned to Leslie. "I think there are a couple of seats over there by my aunt." I pointed. Lillian was motioning us to the row in front of her. She leaned forward to greet Leslie when we sat down.

"Good morning, everyone. Can we get started?" Mitch Gaylin waited for the buzzing to die down, the milling to stop. His manner was relaxed, his clothes casual and expensive. I realized that the only time I'd seen him in a suit was on the real estate channel on cable. And I was surprised, as always, that he'd kept his tan. Despite the rotten winter we'd endured. Did he frequent a tanning palace? God knows, Anne Arundel County had enough of them.

"Before we begin," Mitch was saying, "Detective Simmons of the Anne Arundel County Police Department has kindly stopped by to give us an update on their investigations."

A plainclothes cop, his face pink and blandly puffy, as if he had a water-retention problem, stepped up to the mike. His hair was a halo of bright red fuzz driven back by a ferocious attack of male-pattern baldness. Eyebrows so light as to be invisible gave him a borderline albino look. Unsmiling, he thanked Mitch, glanced at the woman fiddling with things on the table, then scowled at us.

"Good morning. First, the obscene calls. To date the Anne Arundel Police Department has received complaints from seven real estate agents, all women." Surprisingly, his voice held strong traces of New York. The Bronx maybe. "Our crime analysis over the past month has shown that the calls are originating from pay phones throughout the county. There does not appear to be an established time or other pattern to them." He glanced at his notes.

"That's it?" asked a voice in the front row. "An agent is killed and your crime analysis..."

Some unhappy emotion trailed quickly over Simmons' face. "Miss Nichols," he said, "we have no evidence that the two crimes are related. If you do, I would appreciate your letting us know." A single titter came from the back of the room. I turned to see one of the church volunteers, a man in his early thirties, trying to pretend he hadn't laughed.

Simmons cleared his throat. "The Department obviously doesn't have the personnel to stake out every pay phone in the county," he said. "But that doesn't mean we've given up. Or that we think this is unimportant. Our next step is to put it out to the media and ask for the public's help. Perhaps someone has seen a stranger or a strange vehicle near these phones. We need a license plate number or a description."

Half a dozen hands went up. Simmons ignored them. "I'd like to go over with you the procedure for handling an obscene call. If any of you receive one," he said. Beside me, Leslie Ballard shivered.

"Have you?" I asked.

She shook her head. "You?"

"No."

"First and most important," Simmons was saying, "hang up. Do not engage in conversation. Do not interact with the caller, no matter how compelling it may be to do so. That's what he wants. He wants you to stay on the line and listen to him talk dirty. Or he wants to engage you in conversation. That makes him feel powerful. The victims describe his voice only as a low monotone. It may or may not be his real speaking voice. He may be trying to disguise it. And so far, he hasn't left any messages."

"So he's not actually interested in sex?" a large woman in the back asked.

Simmons tilted his head to see her. "He might be, or he might not be. We don't know in this case. The experts say that a caller will sometimes make calls for actual sexual reasons, perhaps to arouse himself as he masturbates. He might say sexual things to humiliate his victim. Or himself. On the other hand, he might be more interested in controlling his victim, perhaps by frightening her."

"But could the calls lead to a sexual assault?" the woman persisted.

"It's possible," Simmons said. "For some callers, fantasy is enough. Others get into sexual behaviors."

"Is this guy a peeping Tom?" someone asked. "Is he watching?"

"There's no hard evidence of that in this case," he said. "The caller has not so far demonstrated specific knowledge of the victim he is calling." He paused. "Although some of the calls have originated at pay phones near the victim's homes."

Leslie raised her hand. "What kind of specific knowledge?"

"For example, he has not referred to what the victim is wearing or doing at the time of the call. A voyeur with binoculars might do that. Or he might refer to something in her past or private life. To compel her to talk with him." Simmons' eyes scanned the room. "If you get a call, notify us immediately. We will, in turn, notify the phone company to have a trap put on your phone so that future calls can be traced."

"Oh, goody," said Joyce Nichols, "that should do it." I noticed a tiny muscle near Mitch Gaylin's mouth had begun to tick.

But Simmons ignored her, then shifted his weight to a different leg. "Let's move on. To the homicide. Unfortunately, I don't have anything new to report. More than what you know from reading the newspaper."

Rose Macklin, he said, had died of an injury from something slung at her head. That something—probably a brick or a sharp-edged rock—had not been found. She had not been sexually assaulted. Death, according to the medical examiner, was probably sometime between noon and 2 p.m. The estate's owner had found her body lying on a back terrace overlooking the water around 5:00 that afternoon. Her blue Mercedes was still parked in the gravel driveway and her handbag was missing. The house had not been entered. Nobody in the vicinity at the time had seen anything.

A hand in the back went up. Simmons nodded. "Do you think the motive was robbery?"

"That is one possible scenario. And we are watching the ATM machines in the event her credit cards are used." His eyes roved the room. "The victim apparently made an appointment to show the house to a client. We believe that the client gave a false name." Simmons glanced at Joyce, who sighed theatrically, but held her tongue. "As you may know, several real estate companies in Anne Arundel County have offered a special reward of fifteen thousand dollars for information leading to the arrest of the killer. If any of you have any information that you think might help, please call. It's part of the Metro Crime Stoppers program, so you don't have to identify yourself. Calls aren't recorded. And don't worry if you aren't sure if your information's related or useful. Let us make that decision.'' He rattled off a phone number. Next to me, Leslie Ballard wrote it down.

"Other questions?'' Curtains whipped in the sweetened breeze. The earlier show of hands had been replaced with a blanket of silence. Simmons waited for a few seconds, turned to Mitch, said something, and with a final glance around the room, left.

I studied the faces of the women chattering around me, wondering what fears lay yawning under the laughter and shop talk. There was safety here, yes. For the moment. But beyond the church basement? No one knew.

TWO

CHRISTINE MCGRATH had impressive credentials as a former Washington, D.C., cop who now made a living teaching people like us how to protect ourselves. On the table were a number of objects: guns and knives and a mobile phone, plus a few items I couldn't see. She smiled, a sour sort of smile. Probably the best she could do considering her line of work.

"Good morning, Ladies. And Gentlemen. I'm happy to be here this morning." Her voice matched the smile and made you wonder if she was all *that* happy about anything. "And given the circumstances in Anne Arundel County this past week, what I'm going to teach you today could save your life. So listen up, my friends."

"Tough, very tough," whispered someone in the row behind me.

The policewoman did indeed look that way, her small body thin and hard, uncomfortable in her serviceable navy business suit and white polyester blouse. Her hair had been permed in an attempt to soften her appearance, then bleached by a hairdresser trained in the Marilyn Monroe school of hair coloring. Perhaps that same person had instructed her in the application of makeup. The result was a slather of desperately pink lipstick and a heavy hand with the eyebrow pencil.

"I am," she was saying, "here to tell you that you aren't helpless. You do not have to be a victim." The crowd stirred, attentive. She was silent for a minute, letting her message sink in. "What I'm going to show you today will empower you. You can learn to be calm and resourceful. So let me repeat: You do not have to be a victim."

I looked around me. No one spoke. They were, I expect, thinking what I was: If this seminar had come a week sooner, would Rose Macklin have been alive and sitting here?

"First, I'm going to tell you a little about the people who may harm you. Some intend to, some do not. Some plan their malice, others grab opportunities. It does not matter. You can take measures to protect yourselves. It's up to you and only you. And it begins with common sense."

What followed was a stirring exhortation not to be stupid. Christine McGrath minced no words. I had begun to find her voice oddly thrilling, her message hopeful. Her eyebrows no longer consumed my attention and her body seemed to gather new strength. "You must not sit alone in model homes in new subdivisions," she said. "You must not. A phone is not enough. Anyone can come by, and if they have a gun, you may be raped, and you could be killed. No, my friends. You must never do it. Take another agent. Take your husband. Take a friend. Do not go alone."

I caught Mitch watching me from his position leaning on the wall between two open windows. His eyes, usually crinkly—laughing eyes Lillian called them—were somber. Only their potential to break his face into dozens of laugh lines remained. When he saw that I had caught him staring, the crinkles exploded, digging tiny trenches in a half-sunburst pattern.

"My friends," the policewoman was saying, "in your line of business, it is vital that you know your clients. I urge you to invite interested parties—your buyers and your sellers—to your offices first. To interview them. Ask clients for their driver's licenses, then copy those licenses." She paused. The crowd mumbled and rustled. "I know what you're thinking: that this is no way to inspire trust between you and your client. Well, too bad. Just too bad. Better you lose a client than your life."

The room quieted. She let the silence ride, then resumed. "Another thing. Make sure you know the value of things. Your life versus your handbag. Your life versus your car. Make sure you give your attacker what you value least." Still silence.

Then, after a moment, a hand went up on the right side of the room. The policewoman nodded, not quite pleased to be interrupted. A solid woman in a flowered silk dress with a big white collar like a bib stood up. "I don't know quite how to ask this, but...well, okay, I'll just say it. We are...I," she began, then stopped. She took a deep breath. "I am afraid of some young black men, but I don't want to appear prejudiced. How do I handle this?" She gasped slightly and sat down. I glanced around the room. A couple of African American agents, both women, sitting toward the front, looked a little uncomfortable.

The policewoman, on the other hand, didn't look a bit uncomfortable. "That's a very good question. And you handle the problem by inviting *everyone* back to the office first to interview them. I don't care if they are white-haired eighty-year-old grandmothers, you interview them, you copy their driver's licenses, and then...Are you listening, Ladies and Gentlemen?" Silence. "Then you pay attention to your feelings. If you do not feel okay about someone, you must not go out either alone or in pairs with that person. And I don't care if that person is your grandmother or an eighteen-year-old black man wearing dreadlocks." Her voice rose, a preacher's voice. "I don't care if it is awkward or embarrassing or whatever it is. This, my friends, can save your life. If you take nothing else away from this morning's seminar, take this."

She looked us over, then signaled a volunteer for a glass of water. There was silence as she drank it off, taking her time.

"I hate it that she keeps calling us 'my friends,' " said someone behind me on the left.

"Any other questions so far?" She waited, then listed techniques for driving in bad neighborhoods: windows up, doors locked, handbag on the floor under your feet, plenty of space between your car and the car in front of you at traffic lights.

The crowd in the basement room stirred a bit, restless. Anne Arundel County didn't have all that many blighted inner-city neighborhoods. And very few of these agents, I thought, would ever show a house in such a community.

"Oh, you don't go to neighborhoods like that, do you?" she jeered. "You live in the nice safe suburbs. You don't think that a carjacking could happen to you... Well, my friends, it could." She rattled off some stories, harrowing tales of people dragged out of their cars, or shot to death as they went about their daily lives in happy suburbia. "So listen up. It could be you and it could be in your nice water-privileged neighborhood. Right here in Pines on

Magothy, say. Or you could have just had a lovely evening at the symphony or the theater. Washington or Baltimore. You're coming home late, stopped at a light, your door unlocked..." A nervous laugh came from the back of the room. "All right," she said suddenly. "Now what can you do to protect yourself, if after all your precautions, you find yourself being attacked?"

She turned to the table in front of her. "There are a lot of defense gadgets out there. Some good, some bad. Some created by people who are making money off your fear." She picked up a mobile phone and waved it in our direction. "Good idea. Most of you have them in your cars and handbags. If you don't, get one. And use it if you suspect you are being stalked or followed. Don't wait until you are positive something's wrong. That may be too late. Use it if your car breaks down or something feels strange. Remember," she reminded us, "you are now paying close attention to your feelings." Putting the phone down, she picked up two small canisters, holding one in each hand. "Pepper spray. Sometimes helpful."

"Is it always legal?" came a weak voice.

"In Maryland it is and that's what we were talking about it, isn't it?" Her voice dripped ridicule, then quickly changed back to its normal gruffness. "Actually, I have mixed feelings about it." She suddenly touched one canister. Instantly there was coughing from the front of the room.

"What the hell," said Joyce, out of her seat sputtering and hacking and stomping, "was that about?"

I covered my nose and mouth, swallowing hard, fighting not to cough. Beside me, Leslie had fished a tissue from her handbag to cover her mouth. "I don't agree with Joyce very often," she said, coughing, "but this time she's got it right."

Lillian, behind me, her voice tight and low, echoed the thought. "I certainly don't know that I believe that was necessary." She hacked slightly as the spray made its way toward the back of the room. "To tell you the truth, I don't know how enamored I am of this woman."

The sporadic coughing died down, over as fast as it started, carried off by efficient cross-ventilation. The spray must have been absolutely minimal. I wondered if she had practiced her technique. "See what I mean?" she asked us. "There's a little problem of the wind direction. So maybe you don't want to rely totally on a spray in your handbag. Instead, you want to learn to use your voice to say loudly and clearly to anyone who might hear you: 'I am being attacked. Call 911 now.' " Her eyes panned slowly around the room. "It's okay to feel fear, but research studies show it is to your advantage to act confidently. Attackers always know who is vulnerable. And guess who that is, my friends? The person who looks like she doesn't know where she's going. The person whose shoulders are hunched, who looks at the ground. The person who acts indecisive or uncertain."

The policewoman was now fiddling with another couple of small objects. "Personal alarms. Not a bad idea if you are far from anywhere, I suppose. Although a phone is better. But you could keep an alarm in your car for emergencies, along with flashers and a windshield sign asking people to call the police. And don't be dumb and put the sign in the front window. No one can see your message there. And keep your car in good repair. More common sense. See how it works?"

She was down by the front row now, talking directly to Joyce, subdued apparently by the pepper spray attack and nodding fervently. The policewoman turned back to the table, suddenly spying what looked like some sort of large inhaler. Suddenly the room was filled with an ear-piercing blast. She smiled. "That, my friends, is a compressed-air foghorn. It'll cost you a few bucks in a boat-supply store. You could buy one for your car, your house, your neighbor. Let's take a break now."

THREE

MOST IN THE CROWD stood up, muttering in low tones among themselves, some still hacking, a few angry, most subdued. Others stretched and got up to fix themselves fresh cups of coffee. Leslie waved at someone across the room, then excused herself. I handed Lillian her crutches.

"Leslie Ballard has a client who wants to see the Hammett house."

"Well, hurrah for that," she said. "She say anything about the price?"

"No, but it's bound to come up again."

Lillian nodded, unhappy. We both knew the Charles Cove house was overpriced. But it was her listing, and the sellers, Elizabeth and Hamm Hammett, were her longtime friends and neighbors in Pines on Magothy. Which was part of the problem, I thought. After many years of marriage, Elizabeth had suddenly left, moving in with Lillian. That was weeks ago. Hamm was still living in the Charles Cove house. They agreed only that the house needed to be sold. Or so Lillian said. I was just trying to stay out of the whole mess.

"I'll talk with both of them again." She didn't sound very hopeful that it would help.

"Leaves an impression, doesn't she?" Mitch Gaylin said, coming up behind us. He nodded in the direction of the former policewoman, who was standing alone by the refreshments table.

"I wonder how she'll demonstrate what guns can do," said Lillian dryly.

Mitch grinned. "Hard to know. Particularly since I don't think she believes in the public relying on guns."

Lillian merely shrugged, then turned away as two real estate agents I didn't know enveloped her in an awkward group hug.

Mitch grew serious. "You know, I think half my agents are carrying guns or planning to get them." He shook his head.

"We are probably the only two people in Anne Arundel County who think they are a bad idea."

It was a touchy issue with me. After Rose Macklin's murder, Lillian had been adamant about buying a handgun. My normally serene aunt had become surprisingly contentious when I refused to drive her and her broken ankle to the gun store. To keep peace in the family, we had chosen not to discuss it. I had no idea what she had done, but Lillian was notoriously resourceful. And she had a lot of friends.

I suddenly realized for the second time this morning that I wasn't listening.

"You'll work with me on this?" Mitch asked.

"Uh...I..."

"Wasn't listening?" Unlike Joyce, he smiled, then bailed me out. "I was talking about an ad hoc committee to draw up standardized safety guidelines."

"Not me. Get Lillian." Mitch's mouth pulled back at the corners slightly. Brown eyes registered what looked to be disappointment. Then he shrugged, dropping the subject. I knew that Mitch Gaylin usually got what he wanted. I decided I didn't like him the less for it.

"Is Lillian back at the office yet?"

I shook my head. "The doctor doesn't want her to put weight on her ankle."

"And you're still picking up the slack?"

"For whatever that's worth," I said.

"Bad day?"

"Not your problem." Mitch Gaylin's eyebrows shot up, but he chose not to comment. We stood in silence, each of us thinking our own thoughts, oblivious to the hum of voices around us.

"I'm sure Lillian will join your committee," I said finally, then changed the subject. "What's with Joyce Nichols and Detective Simmons?"

Mitch shook her head. "Oil and water. No, incomplete analogy.

Spark and tinderbox. Fertilizer and fuel oil. I have no idea why, but he just sets her off."

"I gather they'd met before."

"After Rose Macklin was killed, Simmons spent a fair amount of time in the Annapolis office, asking questions and going over our office procedures. True, he was a little heavy-handed, but I can't say Joyce made his job any easier. Or mine for that matter."

"So why did you hire her?"

"Because she needs the work," he said simply. "And I needed a part-time receptionist who knows the business." We watched as Joyce ate a jelly donut in two bites, then spoke to an agent pouring coffee beside her. The agent smiled weakly, then looked around for an escape. Mitch sighed. "She means well, I know, but the constant talking..." He glanced at the back of the room. "I'd better get this thing started again, if we're going to finish before tomorrow. I just found out the pastor wants to say a word or two." He turned his full attention in my direction. "Look, if you won't be on my committee, at least have dinner with me instead. It's been a while."

"Sure, fine, sometime."

"Said with such enthusiasm," he said, the eye crinkles detonating into widening circles.

"So what do you think so far?" I turned to find Leslie Ballard drinking a fresh cup of coffee.

"Very scary stuff," I said. "Clearly the police have no idea who's making the calls. And the murder investigation doesn't sound like it's going anywhere either. Did they interview you after Rose's death?" Leslie nodded. "What did they want to know?"

"The usual stuff. Sort of like on TV. Did she have any enemies? Had she said anything unusual or acted strangely the previous week? Had I seen her that day? What were her habits in the office?" Leslie looked with distaste at the coffee, then deposited her cup, almost full, on the table. "I wasn't much help. We didn't travel in the same circles. Detective Simmons really grilled Mitch, Joyce, and Nancy, the full-time receptionist, and all the other agents who'd been there since the office opened last fall."

"And no one knew anything?"

"Not really. Rose wasn't personally close to anyone." I watched as Leslie applied lipstick. "And apparently she made the appointment with the client herself and then left a message on the seller's answering machine. The name in the appointment book was fake, so nobody even knows if it was a man or a woman."

The mike chirped. Joyce headed to her seat, ignoring us. We took our seats as the policewoman took up her position behind the table. Mitch then introduced Jack Hardwick, the pastor of the Church in the Pines, who welcomed us ad nauseam. Behind me, I could hear chairs scraping against the linoleum and pages rustling as people fidgeted. Somewhere up front, a pager went off and an agent hurried away, gratitude written all over her face. Behind me, Lillian sighed deeply. He was her pastor, but it didn't blind her to his dullness. A sigh of relief went up when he surrendered the mike.

"Ladies and Gentlemen," said the policewoman, "we have a lot to cover in the next hour." She had fluffed her hair and applied fresh lipstick. After passing out pamphlets, she leaned against the front of the table, relaxed now, in the homestretch. "I'm going to show you a few techniques, but I warn you that each situation is different. And nothing is a match for a knife or a gun. But these tips may just help in other circumstances. Now, I need a volunteer."

No one moved or spoke. Third grade again, I thought, all of us scared to death we'd be called upon. After a long pause, a male agent in his fifties bravely stood up. Another day there might have been laughter or jokes. Not today.

"Good," she said. "Now, let me begin by saying that the first few minutes are crucial. You must stay calm and determine how you will take care of yourself." She was holding the rest of her pamphlets rolled up in her hand. Suddenly she turned on the man and feigned an attack in the direction of his head and neck, then quickly backed away. His hands were in front of his face protecting himself, his eyes narrowed with concern.

"You real estate agents are very lucky," she said to us. "You always have something in your hands: newspapers or papers of some kind, a pencil or pen, keys. Keys and pens are good. Use them to jab upward into the neck, into the Adam's apple." She put down the pamphlets and picked up a key chain and held it over her head. On it was a small metal instrument with finger holes and pointed blades, sort of a mutant scissors. "Another gadget. It goes directly into the eyes. But like all gadgets, it may not be within reach. So you can use your fingers like the beak of an angry bird. You can," she said, deliberately, "kill a person by putting out their eyes."

Several people in the room sucked in their breath. I looked around to see Lillian shaking her head in disbelief that she had lived so long as to have to know this.

"Keep your head for those minutes..." Her sentence hung in the air, unfinished. "Now," she said, "some self-defense experts will tell you not to fight back. But, my friends, studies show that it may be even more dangerous to go with your attacker, so try not to get in a car with him."

By now the policewoman had positioned the male real estate agent in front of her and showed us a couple of ways to slip out of the attacker's grasp. The trick, apparently, was not to beat and pound the attacker or pull backwards as he'd expect, but rather go toward him, slipping under his arm to get away or using the force of twisting hips to spin out of his grasp.

Then she pushed her increasingly reluctant volunteer behind her and told him to attack. "If someone grabs you from behind, you grab their two pinkies and you snap down. Hard." She demonstrated, pretending to give his little fingers a snap. She then maneuvered the man directly in front of her again. "Here's another technique if someone grabs at you from the front: you step on their feet, then go for the genitals. But"—she turned back to the crowd—"you don't kick, you grab and twist as hard as you can." She mimed how. The agent jerked away, fearful and embarrassed. She thanked him and he sat down, sorry he'd ever gotten out of bed this morning.

Christine McGrath looked at her watch, then held up an assortment of knives and handguns to show us. "Knives and guns." Picking up a large handgun, she walked slowly around the left side of the room toward the rear. "Oh, they work. They work really well. The trouble is..." She stopped to see if we were listening. "The trouble is you may not be able to bring yourself to use them, so here is my advice. Ignore it at your peril: Do not carry a gun or knife if you are not prepared to use it. It is the worst possible thing you can do. Because, my friends, it may well be used against you." There was silence.

Lillian shifted a little in her chair, refusing to look in my direction. Actually, knowing my aunt's steely determination in most things, I thought she just might be able to use a gun.

The policewoman was wrapping up now, talking again about common sense, about knowing when to fight, when to negotiate and run, when to give up cars and handbags. There were a few questions, mostly from someone I couldn't see asking about self-defense classes. A polite round of applause. A couple of younger women rushed up to ask questions.

I looked around the room. Which one of us, I wondered, will need to know these things?

"Well, that was just horrible," said Lillian, behind me. I nodded, then followed her glance toward a tall, elegant man standing near the back of the room. "Oh, God," she said, "how long has Hamm been here? He and Elizabeth had an argument on the phone this morning. She hung up on him. Now, I'll bet dollars to donuts that he's come by to try to finish whatever they were talking about." She turned to look at me directly. "You know what Elizabeth does all night? When she can't sleep?" I shook my head. "She vacuums. I have a very clean house." My aunt sighed and struggled to her feet. "Well, let me go see if I can mediate. Or throw my crutches at them. Or something. I do wish they'd work this out."

"Maybe they won't be able to." Lillian shook her head, more in sorrow than disbelief. My beloved Uncle Max had died about eighteen months ago, after a rare and felicitous forty-year marriage. She didn't talk about him much any more, I noticed, preferring finally to keep her memories for herself. "Lillian," I said, "we could find a place for Elizabeth to live, until things are settled."

Lillian grabbed the crutches I handed her. "Only if she wishes.

In the meantime, she is welcome to stay with me as long as she wants. I just hate taking sides, you know. Both Hamm and Elizabeth are my friends. Here, hold this thing.'' She shoved her handbag in my direction, then put both crutches awkwardly under one arm, grabbed back her handbag, and hobbled off to find Elizabeth.

Leslie Ballard sat with her back to me, her head down, fiddling with something on her lap. She took a deep breath, her shoulders raising slightly. Then, snapping her briefcase closed, she turned halfway around in her chair. Her face was tight, black eyes serious. ''Could you actually poke someone's eyes out with that appalling scissors thing she showed us?'' she asked.

''God, no. Could you?''

She shook her head violently. A ray of sun caught and shook blue glints off her undulating mass of hair.

''So what does that leave people like us?'' I asked.

''Prevention, I guess.'' She smiled suddenly, making all the talk of mutilation seem absurd. ''Well, I've got an appointment. I'll call you later about the Charles Cove house,'' she said.

Lillian, I saw, had lumbered to the kitchen door and was chatting with Elizabeth Hammett. I joined them. Inside the kitchen, the other volunteer, his back to us, was bagging the garbage.

''Elizabeth's got some errands,'' said my aunt. ''Can you give me a ride home?''

I nodded. Elizabeth smiled at me, mouthing her thanks, then glanced at the far end of the room. Her smile faded. Hamm Hammett was making his way in our direction.

''I don't want to talk to him right now,'' she said to Lillian. ''This morning was enough. I'm not going back, but he doesn't seem to understand that yet.'' She gathered her handbag and headed toward the open door. Hamm was faster. We watched as husband and wife faced one another, the spring light melting them into silhouettes in the church doorway.

FOUR

WARM, HONEY-SOAKED BREEZES spilled into the car through the open windows. Lillian was staring straight ahead, lost in her thoughts as we drove. I could feel my spirits lift with each mile, each bend in the road.

There had been no scene between the Hammetts, just a poisonously quiet encounter between two people trapped in a marriage that wasn't working. Elizabeth's face had been stony, Hamm's more animated. After a few minutes, he'd shrugged, then left. She had followed shortly.

I parked the BMW in Lillian's driveway. "Damn," she said. "Wait a sec. You know what I hate most about all this?" I shook my head. "It takes me forever to do anything, that's what." Hanging hard on my arm, she grabbed the crutches I thrust in her direction. "Lord, this car is small." She looked meaningfully at her garage door. Behind it was her beloved Cadillac, undriven now for many weeks.

"How's your ankle feel?"

"I could dance if anybody asked me, but oh no."

Half an hour later, with tuna sandwiches and glasses of iced tea in front of us, we were settled in Lillian's comfortable home office. Piles of paper marched along every available flat surface, each with a multicolored note to remind her what to do with it. A computer and printer and fax machine took up two-thirds of her rosewood desk. The fax began cranking.

"Look at the length of that," she said, her mouth half full, "it must be twenty pages."

Selling real estate often seemed like the worst of all worlds: tricky, angst-filled negotiations between sellers and buyers, last-minute disasters, and enough paperwork to take out a stand of forest. And it was getting worse. Every week and month the list of required and suggested forms and contracts grew longer. We watched together in silence as the fax flowed in long curls over the rug, then settled down to talk business. Lillian had taken news of the morning's disastrous settlement in stride, vowing to bring buyer and seller together again.

"I want you to see something," she said suddenly. She fished around the strewn desk, found the TV remote, and aimed it at a small set in the far corner. Channels flicked by until we were watching the cable real estate channel. Pictures of properties alternated with pictures of well-dressed listing agents. A silky announcer read the script describing houses. Suddenly, Rose Macklin's face appeared on the screen, her honey-streaked hair perfectly cut and styled around a blazing smile.

"Oh, Lord, they haven't taken that off," Lillian said. "I'm going to call them." She picked up the phone. I lowered the sound, continuing to watch as the announcer's voice droned on. I recognized some of the properties. Quite a few were under contract. Television advertising worked. Which, I knew full well, was why Lillian wanted me to watch: Weber Realty was going to advertise on cable. I glanced at my aunt, who was hanging up the phone.

"Never occurred to them," she said, again absorbed in the cable channel.

"I'm afraid to ask what you are thinking."

"I think we should give it try." She watched the repeating tape. Leslie Ballard's likeness appeared between various pictures of a large colonial on a windswept hill. White fences enclosed several horses munching in the surrounding pasture.

"I swear," said Lillian, "half of Gaylin's agents advertise here. Mitch must have worked out some sort of deal with the cable company." I turned off the television. "Oh, nuts," she said suddenly. "I forgot to give Mitch the contract for that parcel of land in Crownsville. This ankle business has made me lose my mind. It's here somewhere." She fished through the rubber-banded piles, uncovering a stack of brightly colored corporate reports and a few less flashy investment newsletters. "I don't know why I keep these. I never read 'em," she said, depositing them on the floor under the desk. "Here, hand me those." I set another pile in front of her. She unearthed a wad of sheets from it and handed it to me. I stood up and turned to go.

"And Eve?" I waited, knowing what was coming. "Get your picture taken. Here's the photographer's number." She handed me a business card, then grabbed it back. "Wait, if you're going to Annapolis, maybe he's free this afternoon."

I watched helplessly as she dialed, said a few words, smiled at me, and hung up. "Done." She handed me back the card. It had a tiny map of Annapolis on the back. But no picture.

CALLING DAN LLOYD'S studio a studio was a stretch. It was, in fact, a garage hidden deep in the historic district. A tall, skinny man with an awkward manner, he didn't smile when I rang the bell of his bungalow. Instead, he motioned me to follow him to an ugly cinder-block structure behind his house. Inside, amid the cobwebs and the lawn care clutter, he had placed an old kitchen chair against a sheet of seamless white paper. A 35mm camera stood on a tripod. The sum total of the amenities was a small, dirty mirror hung near the door. Well, you get what you pay for, I thought. And Dan Lloyd charged a ridiculously small price. Lillian had told me every real estate agent in Anne Arundel County had made the trip to his garage at one time or another.

"You want to fix yourself or anything?" I nodded, then ran a comb through my chin-length hair, wondering if I needed a haircut. I applied fresh lipstick. He watched without interest, then pointed to the chair. In five minutes we were done. I got out my checkbook.

"Nah," he said. "Later, when you pick them up. Be ready tomorrow. I'll give you twenty prints of the best one."

I sighed, deciding that making Lillian happy was more important than insisting on choosing the pose myself. "Can you make a living at this?" I asked.

For the first time he grinned, a strange event that had little effect on anything but his mouth. "Yup. You real estate agents are a vain lot. Got pictures on your business cards, in the newspaper, on cable TV. You got 'em on plaques in your office, on your flyers, in your magazines. Some of my clients get new pictures every few months. All good for me.'' Abruptly, the grin vanished. ''Pictures be ready tomorrow.''

I promised to call before I came. He shrugged, abruptly pointed to the garage door, then turned back to the tripod to unload the film. I got in my car. I hoped Dan Lloyd's pictures were better than his social skills.

MITCH GAYLIN'S office in West Annapolis was a happy mix of newly renovated interiors in an odd, multilevel complex of buildings. Small stores—selling coffee, used clothes, mystery novels, and New Age paraphernalia—lined the rest of the street. Unlike most of the rest of Annapolis, there was parking which, I thought, must have been why Mitch had chosen the location.

Joyce Nichols, sitting behind the tall reception desk, didn't see me come in. A wall of open mailboxes and a fax machine didn't leave much room for her. In front of the desk, a couple of wing chairs and a long couch coordinated with the gray-flecked carpeting. Polished end tables offered real estate magazines, some with newsprint pages lined with rows of tiny black-and-white pictures advertising properties for sale, others in full color. I picked up a slick magazine. At the top of each page was the name and logo of the agency and a small photo of a smiling agent who'd be very pleased to sell you a nice little million-dollar waterfront home.

I cleared my throat. Joyce, her considerable breasts forming a shelf in her turtleneck, abruptly rose from behind her computer.

''Oh, it's you,'' she said. ''Lillian called to say you'd be here. Take a load off,'' she said pointing to a chair. ''Mitch'll be off the phone soon.''

''No need to bother him. I'm just dropping this off.'' I held out a manila envelope.

She ignored it. ''He'll kill me if I don't tell him you're here,'' she said, wiggling her eyebrows at me. She launched herself out of her chair and headed for the back reaches of the office.

What the hell did that mean? I was still holding out the manila envelope. I started to lay it on a pile of signed contracts on the reception desk. A very big pile. Gaylin agents did well. And Mitch himself must be rich as Trump. Glancing at the top contract, a

familiar address jumped out on me: Round Bay, a waterfront community on the Severn River. The house was a large new contemporary, with a long expanse of waterfront and all amenities. And
pricey. I had shown it several times to some clients of Lillian's.
They'd seemed interested, then, abruptly, they had stopped returning my calls. Lillian merely shrugged when I told her. Some clients, she said, needed lots of time.

So what did it sell for? I scanned the familiar small print, stop-
ping dead when I got to the buyers' names. Richard and Davina
Canin. Lillian's buyers, the very ones who had professed to love
Round Bay, and had, I thought, been near to making an offer.
Holding my breath, I searched for the name of the selling agent.
Rose Macklin.

"Find something interesting?" Joyce asked, reading over my
shoulder. Her voice was intensely curious. She shoved the pile out
of reach.

"Uh, nothing really. I just wondered who...er...finally bought
that wonderful contemporary in Round Bay."

"Dunno. Rose Macklin sold it." A trace of some emotion flitted
over Joyce's face. I tried unsuccessfully to hand her the manila
envelope for the second time. "Mitch'll be out pronto," she said.
I sighed as she sat back down. "You get anything out of that
workshop this morning?" she asked from behind the desk.

"I guess. Interesting and scary stuff."

"But no surprises. We gotta be careful these days. I don't even
like being here during the evenings. And taking people out alone
to show houses, well, no way, Jose," she said, standing up to grab
a pile of papers on the counter. "You and Lillian going to take
all the precautions that female cop suggested?"

I nodded. "Some of them, at least."

"Good. Hate to have anything happen to you." She abruptly
sat back down, having apparently done her duty in the small-talk
department. I could see only the top of her shiny salt-and-pepper
bob.

"Joyce," I said. She stood up. "Joyce, you worked with Rose
Macklin."

"Yes."

"What kind of clients did she bring in?"

"Rich ones, hon, rich ones." She sat back down. "And lots of 'em."

"Joyce?" Up she popped, her eyebrows flown north to give her face a now-what-do-you-want look? "Did you like her? Personally, I mean."

The eyebrows made their way back to where they were supposed to be and then some. "Like her? Well, no, to tell the truth, I didn't much like her, God rest her soul." She started to sit down, then changed her mind. "She attracted every man from here to eternity, you know. If it wore pants, it swarmed in her direction." The phone rang.

I sat down and picked up the real estate magazine again, thumbing through the pages, wondering why I'd asked. It fell open to a double-page spread with the Gaylin Realty logo. Rose Macklin smiled out at me from the masthead. Speak of the devil, God rest her soul, Joyce would probably have said. I studied the small picture more closely: the mane of long, tawny rich-woman hair, the perfect makeup, the large earrings, the high-necked white blouse and dark, well-cut suit.

Though we'd only met once, I remembered her perfect nails and expensive fragrance. Its name escaped me but years ago someone had given me a bottle. Too sweet, it had made me sneeze. I looked again at the picture of Rose. She was a knockout.

"Many's the time," said Joyce, putting the phone down and standing up again, "when Rose would come back to the office after..." She glanced around behind her.

"After what...?"

"Well, you know..." She hesitated, lowering her voice. "She tested the beds in the houses she showed, if you know what I mean. Not to speak ill of the dead, but we all know it improved her sales." Her eyebrows were now doing a regular boogie all over her wide face. "Men of all sizes and shapes, as long as they had money, it didn't matter to Rose. Flashed that head of hair their way, sprayed on more stuff, and you know what?" I shook my head. "I think she wanted everyone to know she did it."

Is this what had happened with the Canins? Had Rose met Richard Canin...? Then another, more deadly, thought flew through my mind: Is this why Rose Macklin was killed? Had she slept with a client who then killed her? But surely Detective Simmons had checked her clients out.

Mitch joined us by the counter. "Hi," he said. "Joyce, I need these faxed, please. And eight copies of these, when you get a chance." She rolled her eyes at me, nodded, then lumbered resentfully over to the fax machine behind the desk. Mitch pointed the way to his office, grabbing a couple of pink message slips from his mailbox, shaking his head. "We continue to take half of our messages by hand. People still hate voice mail."

I followed him down a corridor, past what must have been a dozen cubicles separated only by chin-high dividers. Most were filled with agents chatting on the phone, or fiddling with computers, or shuffling papers. I hardly noticed, still getting over the initial shock of Rose Macklin's duplicity. I could feel my anger beginning to flow.

Mitch pointed around a second, shorter corridor and down a few steps into what must have been another building. I walked into a huge office, a light-filled room that looked out onto a serene vista of green and stately trees. Heavy carpet muffled our steps. Unlike Lillian's office, there were no piles of paper, no clutter on the blond credenzas and wide desk. Well-organized bookshelves lined the walls. Mitch put the messages on his desk, then pointed to a soft couch slipcovered in some expensive white fabric made to look casual, the kind of couch that made me want to take a nap. At the other end was an enormous sleeping black cat. I sat down, resisting the urge to sink in too deeply.

"Lillian forgot to give you the contract for that lot over in Crownsville." I nodded in the direction of the manila envelope I'd handed him.

"Thanks. Something wrong?"

"Uh, no. Not really. Mitch, what happens to Rose Macklin's contracts?" I asked. "The ones that haven't gone to settlement."

"I'll personally herd them through. Then her part of the commission will go to her estate. Why?"

"Just curious."

I thought again about the property at Round Bay. Lillian was going to blow a gasket when she discovered that Rose had grabbed her clients. But there was no way I was going to whine about the lost sale to a dead woman. Worse, a murder victim. I got up to go.

"Eve?" Mitch touched my elbow suddenly. "Do what Christine McGrath suggested. Okay? And get someone to stay with you. Or move in with Lillian until the cops find whoever killed Rose."

FIVE

THE SUN WAS A RED BALL through the trees by the time I reached my rented cottage on Weller's Creek Road. Its elderly owner had died last summer, leaving behind an estate that included two large dogs and an exceptionally lovely and secluded cove. For now they were my responsibility. On most days, I could see a sliver of the creek from the pine-needled clearing in front of the house. Usually my spirits rose at the sight. Not this evening.

I'd spent the best part of the half-hour drive from Annapolis brooding on what I had just learned at Gaylin Realty. If things were as they seemed, Rose Macklin's ethics stunk. Not that she'd done anything illegal—since the Canins hadn't signed an exclusive agreement with Lillian or me. So how do you extract justice from a dead woman, I thought. One murdered for God knows what reason. You don't, and that was that. Still, the thought of the Canins' signatures on the contract lying on Mitch Gaylin's counter made me see blood. How many houses had I shown to them, singly and together? A dozen? Fifteen? Twenty?

I wasn't surprised to see Will St. Claire's elderly red pickup parked in front of the cottage. He lived rent-free in a small bungalow on the property, in return for help with maintenance. It was an arrangement begun when Ray Tilghman was alive and it continued after his death. Will and I had found each other last summer, during a crossroads in each of our lives.

As I pulled into the clearing, he opened the screened porch door. The dogs poured out, swarming me as I got out of the car, managing to upend my briefcase in the process. The Labrador's pink tongue made long joyful swoops at my face. And Lancelot, the red-brown Chesapeake Bay retriever, usually dignified and intense, wagged until his whole thick body was in motion.

I looked up as Will himself came down the steps and stood

silent and waiting in the sweet evening air. He was wearing jeans and a khaki workshirt. I felt the usual pleasure at the sight of him. He was compelling with his black Irish coloring, his dark hair, damp and curly when he worked, blue eyes changeable as sky and water. A kind of intensity surrounded him, making him seem older than his twenty-five years. As I watched, he rotated his arms above his head, first one, then the other in a stretching, loosening move. It comforted me to watch this unconscious exercise to smooth out the knots from long days of physical work.

We stood back as the dogs chased each other in a fit of unrestrained joy, across the yard and through the underbrush. Will leaned down to stroke Lance, then straightened up, his face revealing traces of some emotion he didn't want me to see.

"Your phone's been ringing off the hook," he said.

"Anyone interesting?"

"Depends on what you call interesting."

"Someone who wants me to find them a ten-million-dollar house." Actually, I didn't even care. This day made me feel all of my forty years. "So who called?"

"Lillian. An agent named Leslie Ballard. Some guy in New York. Weller Church. And your lawyer in New York, Peter somebody. Oh, and a client who hated the mortgage broker you recommended and wants to talk about it. That enough?"

I tried to sort it out. "Peter Fox called?" Will nodded. We were still standing on opposite sides of the clearing, making no move toward each other. I was no longer surprised at his reticence. Lately, he'd been broody, keeping his distance. I had had trouble getting used to it. "Did he say what he wanted?"

"Something about your divorce. And..."

"And?" I walked toward him, putting my arm through his. It felt a little artificial, a little strained. I was glad for the boisterous dog dancing at my side. "And what?"

"He's got a job offer for you. In New York. An amazing offer." I turned to look up at him. His face was noncommittal.

"An amazing offer?"

"His words, not mine."

"I see." We were both silent. "And Weller?" I asked finally. "What did he want?"

"For you to call back." I nodded, a tiny prickle of dread running down my spine. I knew all too well what the elderly Annapolis lawyer wanted, and it wasn't something I wanted to deal with this evening.

"I was over at Charles Cove earlier today," Will said. Underneath his casual tone, there was an undercurrent of tension. "I saw your sign on the property across the cove from the Hammetts."

"So? Mr. MacAfferty's daughter came up from Florida to put it up for sale. Her father died of pneumonia a couple of weeks ago. The open house is Sunday."

"That's smart." His casualness was gone. "Some psychopath is making obscene calls. Then an agent gets killed, and you are still holding open houses for any maniac who happens to come by and see your sign."

"Will, get real. What am I supposed to do?" He pulled away, stuffing his fingers in the small front pockets of his jeans. "Look, I went to a self-defense seminar this morning," I said. "I know to be careful. I promise to take out only people I know or go out with another agent."

"Well, that's a relief."

"I can't very well hire a full-time bodyguard to protect me from my clients," I said. "And I also can't argue about this tonight."

I walked past him and up the steps to the screened front porch, dropping my briefcase and handbag onto the low table. At Will's whistle the dogs abandoned their game and lunged up the steps, falling to the floor in cheerful slobbering exhaustion. He followed them in and then wordlessly wrapped his arms tightly around me. It was a smothery hug, too tight for breathing.

"I could use something to drink," I said, pulling free.

A month ago Will and I had been a lot happier with each other. Then some strange impatience had taken hold of me. He had responded by retreating into a dark, brooding world I didn't share or even want to. It sometimes seemed we did nothing but argue. And I could see tonight was going to be no different.

Returning to the porch from the kitchen, he handed me an open bottle of beer.

"I bought food," he said.

"Thanks. Later."

He nodded, sitting down across from me, slouching as he always did, legs apart, feet flat on the floor, slumped with his neck pressed along the back of the wicker chaise. Somehow he managed to make it look comfortable. Black Zeke came to sit beside me, leaning his weight against my leg, his silky head in my lap, brown eyes shining forth love. Lancelot, oily curls damp from play, was already half asleep.

Stroking the black Lab, I looked up to find Will watching me. "I'm sorry but I just can't argue tonight," I said. "Not about my safety or anything else. It was just too lousy a day." I started to tell him about Rose Macklin and the Canins, then stopped.

"You hear there's a big reward for information about whoever killed that real estate agent?" he asked. I nodded. "And police are warning women in Anne Arundel County not to walk alone at night or in isolated places."

"They saying anything else?"

He shook his head, then stared into the darkness beyond the porch. It concealed a wide path that led to a half-circle of perfect waterfront on Weller's Creek. "Eve, you gotta be careful." His voice was earnest now. "There's someone out there, doing these things. You could be on his list."

I shivered a little, then shoved away my uneasiness. I could feel the beer beginning to do its work, melting the tension in my brain, then heading for my arms and legs.

"Will, I can't talk about all this tonight. I just can't."

"Suit yourself," he said. "But if..."

"Look, I just want to forget the whole damn day right now. Okay with you?" Surprised, I found I was nearly shouting.

"That's right. Just forget the whole damn day," he said. "Forget to be careful, forget to lock your door, forget..."

"Cut the patronizing crap," I said. I stopped, seeing a shadow fall over his eyes. "Look, I just need some space right now."

We'd been over this a thousand times before. "It doesn't make you less important to me."

"But I am, aren't I? Things were fine until recently. Or don't you remember?" he asked.

"Yes, I remember." I watched his face. The status quo suited him: the long days of hard work as he built his landscaping business, followed by our long nights together. I, too, had loved the deeply cold, intimate winter months, but now something in me was getting ready to move on. I hadn't wanted to admit it to myself, or to him, but it was there. And he knew it, too.

"If we are just going to argue, you better leave." I got to my feet.

I could have eaten my words as soon as I said them, but the damage was done. For both of us. Will stood up silently, his eyes a bitter blue. My words had given him no choice. I had with just a few words pushed him away, denying us both a chance to find comfort and sleep.

"Fine," he said. "Have it your way. I don't need this either."

He hesitated only a moment longer, shook his head slightly, and, without looking back, brushed by me. The porch door slammed. I listened as the pickup rumbled to a start, then stared into the dark night. I was so tired. Maybe he was wrong. Maybe there was no one out there.

SIX

THE DOGS followed me out into the spring night, bewildered by Will's abrupt departure. A night breeze was coming up and off the water. In the darkness, Weller's Creek wasn't visible from the clearing, but I could hear water lapping faintly. Was there something to fear here? I could almost hear the policewoman's words: "Some plan their malice, others grab opportunities." A faint tickle of apprehension crept through my exhaustion, unfolded in my mind, and made the nerve endings on my arms prickle.

I stood for another minute, resenting my fear but too tired to fight it. Reluctantly, I went back inside, locking first the outside door, then the door between the screened porch and the living room. Across the large, open living room, on a rolltop desk, the message light on my answering machine flashed blast after red blast. Will had left my messages.

I grabbed a pencil and pushed the play button. The whiny, high voice of a client fumed about the unfairness of mortgage lenders. She needed to talk, she said, really needed to talk. Next Weller Church's kindly baritone greeted me and asked me to return his call. At my convenience, of course. I wrote down his home number, then listened as Lillian told me the rescheduled date for the aborted settlement that had kicked off this wonderful day. No need to call her back. Leslie Ballard wanted to show the Hammett house tomorrow at noon. I could call back up to 11 p.m. Her message clicked off. Peter Fox, my lawyer in New York, had a question and more important, news of a job offer. The last message was from someone named Lawrence Schoenfeld. Name and phone number only. Area code 212. I put my pencil down as the machine clicked off.

I knew Lawrence Schoenfeld. He was the boy wonder who had opened a stunningly successful New York ad agency just three short years ago. I also knew what he wanted. But how had he known to call me here? I swiveled around in the old office chair.

The phone rang. "Eve, Peter. Sorry about the hour, but I needed to talk over a couple of things before a breakfast meeting with Ben's attorney tomorrow," he said. "I figured you'd rather talk now than tomorrow morning."

After reassuring him that I had nothing better to do than talk with him, I listened as he recited figures and dates. It was a blur, this dissolution of my marriage. Distributing the tangible goods that Ben and I had acquired over the years just didn't seem all that important tonight. There was a long pause. "Huh? Peter? Can you say that again?"

"Eve, is everything okay?"

"Sort of," I said, struggling to pay attention. I momentarily longed to pour out all the details of this rotten day, then caught myself.

"We really could talk about this tomorrow morning," Peter said.

"No, no, it all sounds okay. Just do what you have to do. Ben's being very cooperative. I really don't have any trouble with any part of his offer." Something occurred to me. "What's the date this finally happens, anyway? The divorce, I mean." He started to say something. "Peter, wait a sec. I just dropped my pencil and I can't remember anything without writing it down."

He made the obligatory joke about the mind going when one reached forty. I shuffled around in the top desk drawer until I found another pen. Then I wrote down July 23 on a pink pad, tracing the number over and over until the letters were dark and thick. It was just a date, I thought. Like a wedding date, there was a divorce date. Would Ben celebrate? Somehow I doubted it. The last months had brought a softness to his voice, a husky concern that hadn't been there a year ago, as if he too had begun to understand the meaning of what we were about to do. Despite our renewed friendship, things were hurtling irrevocably in a new direction. It was, I thought, almost more disturbing than outright animosity.

"One other thing, Eve," Peter was saying, "a guy named Lawrence Schoenfeld called for your number. You know him?"

"We've met. He's some sort of insufferable boy wonder advertising genius. He could sell anything to anybody. You know, umbrellas to fish," I said.

"You interested in returning to New York?"

"I don't know." I could feel my anxieties rising. I was being offered a chance to take back my old life. In advertising. In New York. A chance to be good at something again, I thought. Zeke's cold nose pushed its way into my hand.

"Call him," Peter said shortly. "He outlined what he had in mind and it's rather impressive. No, make that downright indecent."

"Don't tell me. I can't deal with it tonight. How did he get your name, anyway?"

"Joe Lister," Peter said.

Joe was my first and only boss, the man who had introduced me to advertising, then helped me navigate its rough waters for almost twenty years. However angry he'd been when I hadn't returned to Lister, Klein, and Andronucci after a leave of absence last fall, he apparently wasn't holding it against me. In fact, he was giving his competition my phone number. I smiled. It was hard to know if this was a compliment or not.

I hung up, sinking back in the creaking, swivel desk chair. It was almost nine o'clock. Picking up the phone, I called Leslie Ballard. She wanted to show the Hammett house around twelve-thirty tomorrow. Fine with me. An electronic lockbox—which held the house key—hung on the doorknob so I wouldn't need to get her a key.

"Who's your buyer, anyway?" I asked.

"A relocation. Roger Fawcett. Actually, he's an old client," she said. "I sold him a house in Arnold maybe six, seven years ago. Then his company moved him to Denver. And now they're moving him back."

"The pleasures of corporate life," I said. Leslie Ballard's laugh echoed lightly.

"The well-paid pleasures of corporate life. He's looking for waterfront this time," she said. "I met with him when he was in town a month ago, but he wanted to wait to house hunt until his wife was out here with him."

We chatted a little more before hanging up. She hadn't mentioned price and neither had I. Then, taking a deep breath, I called Lillian to ask her to call Hamm. And to tell her about the Canins' contract on the house on Round Bay. There was a moment's silence. I could almost see a thin white line forming around her mouth.

"From now on," she said slowly, "don't show property—any property—without a contract." Her voice was barely audible, a sure sign she was furious. "If no one has any ethics anymore, we'll protect ourselves with more paper."

"Okay." I knew what this cost her, how much she hated the distrust, preferring to work on the basis of a handshake. But what had that trust gotten her? She coughed once, then changed the subject. Case closed, I thought, hanging up a few seconds later.

I shuffled through the phone messages. The unhappy client would have to wait until tomorrow when I could find another mortgage broker. I dialed Weller Church. It was his mother's family who had given their name to Weller's Creek, which had in turn loaned him back his given name. I could picture him at home, dressed in baggy chinos, a gin and tonic in his hand as he surveyed the waterfront scene in front of him on Arundel Island.

"Weller," I began, "I haven't made a decision yet."

There was a low grunt on the other end of the phone. Several weeks ago, as the executor for Ray Tilghman's estate, he had called to say he had a buyer for my rented cottage, one able and willing to abide with the unusual demands of the will.

"Is money a problem?" he asked. "If it is, I'm sure..."

"No, money's not the problem."

"Well, you know the thirty-day period is almost up," he said. "The other buyer is anxious."

"Weller, who is this buyer? Who in their right mind other than me would sit still for Ray Tilghman's crazy conditions?" More silence. "You can't tell me anything?"

"I'm sorry."

"I'm sorry, too. I'll let you know, Weller." I thanked him and put the phone down.

I had long known that this day could come, but somehow I hadn't really believed it ever would. I sat thinking about Ray Tilghman. He had lived like a pauper although he was not, not worrying about the house or small comforts, perhaps because of age and illness, perhaps because he couldn't be bothered. I would never know. Last August, during a savage summer storm, he had drowned in the protected cove along Weller's Creek, his body dragged to shore by his powerful Chesapeake Bay retriever.

Now I lived in his house, cared for his beloved dogs, and wondered each day how long I would stay. Weller had written rights of first refusal to buy the property into my rental contract. But now I had to make a decision sooner than I wanted to. By the end of May. The days were closing in.

I had told no one, not Lillian, not Will, not Peter Fox in New York. I wasn't sure why. Instead I found myself conferring with Ray Tilghman's spirit, one that became more powerful the longer I lived in his cottage. I found it generous, almost kindly—unlike the old man himself. Looking down at the dogs, I knew why. Ray, old and sick and in pain, had loved them, depended on them. Now I did, too. Lance thumped his meaty tail on the wide floorboards.

Hunger was getting to me. I padded into the small, old kitchen, the dogs at my heels.

"Forget it," I said. "You're not getting another dinner out of me." In response, Lancelot lay down, blocking the doorway to the living room. Zeke sat solidly in front of the elderly refrigerator, looking forlorn and hungry. "You're working together, aren't you? One begs and the other guards the door so I can't leave? Right?" Tails thumped. I handed each a large biscuit from a bag open on the counter. Zeke ate his in two large crunches, crumbs scattering over the floor. The Chesapeake Bay retriever carried his off to enjoy on the living room rug.

Will had left red grapes, oranges, a box of linguini, a long loaf of good bread, and stuff for salad. In the refrigerator, a roasted chicken, faintly indecent, took up most of one shelf. On the table were a couple of bottles of red wine. I considered, decided I was too exhausted to face a regular meal. Grabbing a handful of grapes, the bread, and another beer, I carried them to the front steps. The dogs sat down on either side of me. They were, I soon discovered, much hungrier than I was. Dividing the rest of the bread into two pieces, I forked them over. Then I finished the beer, looked around the clearing, closing my eyes. The clean smell of pine was nearly overwhelmed by the suffocatingly sweet honeysuckle that grew wild along the narrow road to the water.

The dogs were quiet beside me. I reached down to scratch Lance's ears and then lean deeply into Zeke's fur. He smelled fresh and salty from swimming in the creek. Abruptly, angry tears boiled over. I didn't want to have to decide to stay or leave. I didn't want to be afraid every time the phone rang, or live behind locked doors, too scared to walk down by the water. I didn't want to think about self-defense techniques. The dogs drew closer.

In a couple of minutes, my anger changed to sadness: for my marriage which was over, for Will who could not stay, for myself who could not let him. The tears slowed, then stopped. Feeling oddly better, my mind clearer, I went inside.

Sitting at the rolltop desk, I looked around at the modest room where I had lived since late last summer. Just a few months ago, with the clearing in front of the cottage under a foot of snow, Will and I had sat in front of the fire laughing and drinking bottles of red jug wine he bought at the local drugstore when the liquor store was too far to go. It had been a time to read and listen to music, to trudge happily to the cove with the dogs in the freezing air. But February, then March, had come, the snow had melted, and some unkindly spirit had taken up residence at the foot of our bed.

The phone rang. I grabbed the receiver. No one. No breathing. No noise. I put the receiver down. My skin had turned suddenly crawly.

It rang again. Zeke whined once, the solitude of the cottage faintly menacing now. I picked up on the second ring. Mitch Gaylin's easy voice greeted me.

"God, you scared me to death." A stream of air rushed from my lungs, surprising me.

"Sorry, I know it's late," he said. "I'm still at the office and

I wanted to ask you about something." His voice had grown a shade tight.

"What?"

"Eve," he began, "that contract you were looking at today. For the property at Round Bay. What was wrong with it?"

I didn't answer right away. Nor did he try to fill the silence. Then I told him, my words slow and careful at first, then gaining in volume and speed as the day's frustrations raced to the surface. In three minutes, I was done.

His voice was low when he spoke. "I'm very sorry to hear this. There's no chance that..."

"That Rose didn't know that I'd shown the Canins a bunch of houses?" I asked. "Seems pretty unlikely."

"I wish I'd known earlier," he said. "Maybe..."

"Mitch, just forget it. Lillian already has. I'm angry and she's angry, but there's no recourse. Neither of us is going to take a dead woman—no, make that a murdered woman—to court."

"If you like, I can call, uh..." I heard him shuffle papers. "Richard and Davina Canin."

"Mitch, no. There's nothing to do. Fair is, as my old boss Joe Lister used to say, a four-letter word." He laughed, a cramped, unfunny little laugh.

"Okay."

"Good."

"About dinner sometime..."

"Mitch," I interrupted, "did you phone me just before you phoned? I mean, did you ring me, then hang up for some reason before I could answer?"

"No, why?"

"No reason." I said good night and hung up. Somewhere in the night, a pine bough scraped against the house.

SEVEN

A CONSIDERABLE BREEZE had kicked up overnight. The car windows were open, whipping my hair across my face as I drove along a narrow stretch of road. The Beatles, booming from the BMW's expensive sound system, wanted to hold my hand. Last night's fears seemed remote, even ludicrous.

I glanced at the Anne Arundel County map book that lay open across the steering wheel. Somewhere along the eight thousand miles of the Chesapeake's meandering shoreline lay Wildwood Bay and Sassafras Lane. I hoped it wasn't one of those awful developments, named with excruciating cuteness by some real estate developer's daughter or wife. Maybe there would be actual sassafras trees. Not, I thought, that I would know a sassafras tree if I drove into it.

I glanced at the clock. Being late had become a way of life with me. Not one I much liked. And it wasn't great for business. House hunters, as Lillian had once pointed out, were often on their lunch hours. Some just plain weren't inclined to wait. Or if they did, their mood turned sour. It was certainly no way to begin the intricate dance that selling a slab of real estate demanded.

Sassafras Lane appeared on my right. Turning, I inched down a cramped road, its pavement pitted and chipped from the hard winter. The inland side of the street was unexceptional: small bungalows, big yards neatly kept, sailboats, some still covered in the ubiquitous blue plastic tarps that recently had begun to dot the landscape. On the waterfront side, the houses were set farther back on narrower tracts of land. A few lay unseen behind trees half a hundred feet tall. I began to catch glimpses of a blue cove.

There were still no cars, no signs of life on the street, only the smells and chirps of spring. I crept along in first gear, braking suddenly as 407 Sassafras announced itself on a rusting mailbox.

Turning right through a weathered shadowboard fence into a secluded driveway, I parked my BMW beside a blue Oldsmobile,
then got out. Most buyers could amuse themselves for a short time:
walking about the property, peering in windows, and making un-
flattering remarks about the owner's taste in furnishings. And since
this was waterfront, I would probably find my client—actually a
friend of a friend of Lillian's—at the water's edge, admiring the
view and dreaming. My watch said 11:40 a.m. Ten minutes late.

The house at 407 Sassafras Lane, like many in the waterfront
communities near Annapolis, was a weekend home. Vines and
weeds grew over the doorstep. I shoved my keypad into the electronic lockbox, then punched in my personal four-digit code.
Somewhere a computer kept records of who had shown the property and when. Clients liked the system, and so did real estate
agents. The lockbox fell open. It was empty. Footsteps within told
me the house wasn't.

The door opened. "You startled me," said Leslie Ballard, her
dark hair wild, lips brushed with fire. "I'm afraid that all the talk
yesterday..." She took a deep breath, her shoulders relaxing as
she exhaled, the smile I remembered overtaking her face. "But
come in. I was expecting you."

"You were?" Glancing at the property listing in my hand, I
looked for the name of the listing agent. Marsha Rowen. Lillian
had called her earlier this morning. "I thought Marsha..."

"She is." Leslie laughed. "We often help each other out. Since
I was going to be nearby, she asked me to drop in and straighten
up." A vase of flowers sat on the drain board. "The place wasn't
too bad today, but if the sellers are in a hurry, it can look like a
war zone." She held the door.

The bungalow wasn't much more impressive from the inside
than it had been from the street. The kitchen had been installed
long before dishwashers or microwave ovens. Sitting in the shallow enamel sink were a few dishes, left by owners who lived in
D.C. and spent occasional weekends here, dashing off on Monday
mornings. A breakfast nook had just enough room for a small
painted table and two chairs. The living room wasn't much better,
filled with odds and ends. I again glanced down at the listing.

"They want two hundred sixty nine thousand for this?" I asked.

Leslie Ballard laughed, a glad sound, a sound as wild as her hair. "Forget the house. You should see the property." She pointed. Beyond the living room, an enclosed sunporch with wraparound windows—called a Florida room by agents ever alert for an enticing image—opened onto a wide, new deck overlooking Wildwood Bay. An unexpected expanse of fence-enclosed lawn led to a long covered pier with an elaborate pulley-like apparatus. Beyond that was what must have been a thirty-foot sailboat.

"The requisite boat and lift," I said, turning back to her. "I don't get it. I look at sailboats and all I see is sunburn and housework."

Her ringing laughter came again, bouncing off the low ceilings and winding me in a cloak of good spirits. "Try night sailing on someone else's boat," she said. "That should eliminate both problems."

"Yes, I guess it would."

"There's a wildlife preserve over there." She pointed again. "So if your clients don't love sailing, maybe they will love ducks." Heading for the door, she straightened the chairs, like most real estate agents preoccupied by neatness. She glanced at the clock on the wall. "I should be off if I'm going to make my appointment at the Hammett house."

It was my turn to look at the clock. Almost noon. There was no sign of my client. Leslie was watching me.

"Real estate's a numbers game, you know," she said. "You make a hundred appointments, seventy-five show up. Fifty are interested, ten are qualified." She was collecting her briefcase and handbag. "And one buys. Buys big." She handed me the house keys. "And if you believe that, you're probably self-deluded enough to be in this business." Her mouth had thinned to a narrow red line, her laughter gone. "I swear, some days I'm ready to pack it in."

"I thought it was just me."

She shook her head, then sat down at the edge of one of the small chairs. "No. Things are definitely harder than they used to be. Everybody fighting over clients, agents moving from office to office trying to get a better deal, brokers themselves looking the other way in order to make even more money." She sighed deeply. "You're lucky it's just you and Lillian. Agents in our office are having such a tough time that you could cut the competition with a knife. Everybody's fighting over cold calls and walk-ins." She glanced out the window, then sighed.

"I...I thought everybody at Gaylin did pretty well."

Leslie glanced sharply at me. "Where'd you hear that?"

"I guess I just assumed it." Her red mouth opened slightly. "When I dropped by your office yesterday, there was this huge pile of contracts on the counter. So in my own depressed state, I assumed that everybody was making sales left and right."

Leslie snorted, a weird out-of-character sound. "Mitch and a few others may be, but most of us are still feeling the effects of the recession last year. Even those of us who have done well in the past." She shook her head of dark curls. "Mitch's a whole lot better than most brokers—honest, accessible, and all—and he hires good agents. But there just aren't enough buyers to go around. Could be worse, I suppose. Working for a broker who sets quotas." She looked again across the cove, thinking of ducks, perhaps, or, more likely, of how to survive. "And if we're not selling in May with these improving mortgage rates, how are we going to...?" She looked at me. "Don't mind me. I've got a teenage kid to feed."

I didn't know what to say, so I picked up the flowers and put the vase where buyers would see them as they entered.

"There is so damn much money to be made in real estate. How is it a few people always seem to make most of it?" Leslie seemed to have forgotten I was there. "Sorry. I know this isn't your problem, but I lost a sale this morning. Because I didn't return a message, my buyer thinks she lost the house of her dreams. Never mind that I showed it to her over three weeks ago." She squared her shoulders and took a deep breath. "And you know why I didn't return that call? Because I didn't get the message."

She looked over for my response. But I was still reeling over the idea of quotas. If Lillian had them, I'd be bagging groceries at the local supermarket. "So what happened?" I asked finally.

"The client blew up and complained to Mitch, who let her out of her contract with me."

"Does he know that you didn't get the message?"

"He does now. There was a scene with Joyce. Who's got some sort of persecution complex, I think. Mitch hired her part-time to help her out. So what does she do? Talks on the phone when she's supposed to be greeting clients. It happened again this morning: She's chatting away in a cubicle in the back while this buyer is tap-dancing out front trying to get her attention." She pulled out her mirror and reapplied lipstick that didn't need reapplying. She threw the tube back in her bag and looked at me directly. "I know I'm overreacting. Mistakes happen. I suppose I'm a little to blame, too, since I can't stand wearing a pager. I'm just a little...I got a call last night."

"Oh, God." We stood quietly in the small house.

"What did he say?"

"Called me a slut and told me in exquisite detail what he'd like to do to me. How I belonged to him. All in about two seconds before I could hang up. It was exactly as that cop described." She shuddered. "I keep thinking about Rose. The police may think she was killed for her credit cards because her bag was taken, but..."

"But what?"

"Nothing really, just speculation. It's just that...that the...I don't know really, but robbery seems far too easy somehow."

"Well, maybe Rose resisted."

"Yeah, but would someone go to all the work of setting up an appointment under a fake name to rob someone of their handbag? I don't think so."

"Maybe they had planned to ransack the house."

Leslie considered this. "Well, I suppose. But how would someone know which agent he'd get when he called the office?"

"Good question. In that case, the guy must have asked for Rose herself. He could have called her at home."

She nodded. "Well, if we can think of these things, so can the police." She glanced at her watch. "I really have to go," she said. She turned back to me. "Thanks for listening to me vent. It's hard to be upbeat all of the time.'' She turned on her radiant smile, as if trying it out, to see if it still worked.

I watched her smooth her dress before getting into her car. Gold buttons caught the sun and glittered. Then, with a sureness I admired, she maneuvered around the BMW and onto the road. The house was quiet and empty. I decided to look around.

The small bathroom was clean, but a little messy. Toothpaste and brushes, a tube of bronze-colored makeup, a heavy ring entangled with a chain and bunches of earrings, and bottles of expensive moisturizers and makeup cluttered every square inch of the sink between the old-fashioned hot and cold water faucets. I touched the shiny chrome with white enamel labels inscribed with black letters and resisted the urge to open the medicine cabinet.

Returning to the living room, I found an uneven flight of fold-down stairs led to an unfinished attic through a door cut out of the ceiling. I climbed up. Two cots separated by a chest of drawers just fit under the dormer. The room was suffocating, but pleasant light poured through the windows. Downstairs, I found an even scarier set of steps to the basement. The temperature was cooler here, but the grimy furnace and rusting hot-water heater didn't exactly inspire confidence.

Drawn back to the deck a last time, I took deep breaths and studied the cove encircled by deep woods. In Maryland, real estate agents often advertised waterfront homes with pictures of the view rather than the house itself. I had scoffed until I found that vistas of water moved properties, brought in the big dollars. I went back inside. With some wicker furniture and deck paint, the cottage would be charming. Still, $269,000 bought deep water and a view. A few ducks. It did not buy much house.

It was almost 12:30 p.m. I might as well admit I'd been stood up. Dialing an old-fashioned black phone I found in the bedroom, I called Weber Realty to find out if Shirley had heard from Lillian's client. She hadn't, so I called my aunt. Listening to her phone ring, I wondered how she with her forty-odd years of real estate experience handled weeks like this.

Lillian had just heard from her apologetic client, an hour late, stuck in construction traffic on the Washington Beltway with no way to call. Not, I discovered, that my aunt was in any mood to much care.

"We got an offer for the Hammett house," she said, her voice low and controlled, a sure sign of anger, "from that big dumb agent at Merlin Realty in Annapolis. The guy who showed it about three weeks ago. And guess what it is?" I couldn't guess. "Seventy-five thousand below asking price. Can you even imagine?"

"Lillian, it's overpriced," I said. "Not seventy-five thousand maybe, but thirty or forty." I could hear Lillian shuffling papers. "Look, I know it's waterfront. But you can barely dock a rowboat in that swamp. So even with the pool..."

"Okay. Okay." My aunt sighed deeply. "Maybe this offer will knock some sense into Hamm."

"What about Elizabeth?" I asked. "I thought she was anxious." 'Owner anxious,' I had discovered, was real estate code meaning make an offer, any offer.

"Anxious doesn't describe it by half. I think she'd practically give it away, but since the two of them aren't talking...," said Lillian. I heard her other phone ring. "Hold on."

My aunt hadn't sounded very optimistic. Knowing Lillian, I guessed that she was probably blaming herself for not selling her friends' house at the price they wanted.

"I'm back," she said. "I've got an idea. Since Hamm, not Elizabeth, is the problem here, rather than my calling him later with that offer, why don't you stop at the house after he gets home from work. Tell him about the offer and then show him the listing for the house across Charles Cove. You know, the MacAfferty house. It's priced much better. Maybe if he has the listing in front of him in black-and-white..." Her phone rang a second time. She was back in thirty seconds. "Listen," she said, "I almost forgot. I faxed the newspaper ad for your open house Sunday. I started to call you last night about it but then my other phone rang and then I forgot to call you back." Her phone rang for the third time. "This is crazy. Call me later." She hung up.

So Lillian had been my mysterious caller just before Mitch. Thinking about my fear last night left me feeling more angry than relieved. Was I seeing malice where there wasn't any, needlessly scaring myself to death? I noticed a smudge from the cellar door and went back to the bathroom to wash my hands. Gingerly, I turned on both taps, half expecting hot water to pour from the cold tap, and cold from hot. It didn't. In Ray Tilghman's bungalow, I still occasionally forgot about the reversed faucets and burned myself when the C tap spewed scalding water. Looking in the mirror over the sink, I saw deep bluish circles under my eyes, circles carved from weeks of fitful sleep. Maybe, I thought, it was time to admit defeat selling real estate and go back to New York.

EIGHT

THE TOWN OF PINES on Magothy lay serenely between the Magothy River and Weller's Creek, a modest old beach community radiating out from one main street. There was little traffic, probably because the parking lot of the Lido Beach Inn, the Pines' only bar, was jammed. I parked on the street instead, behind a pinkish-brown Detroit aircraft carrier. One bumper sticker read Practice Random Kindness and Senseless Acts of Beauty. Sure. My sentiments exactly today. Grabbing a folder of documents for Marian Beall, the Inn's owner, to notarize, I headed inside.

The Lido Beach Inn was full, the lunch crowd washing their sandwiches down with drafts as fast as Marian and her assistant could replenish them. Workers needed to be back on the job by one o'clock. Even now, some were leaving. I found an empty stool at one end of the horseshoe-shaped bar and began to sort papers. Thoughts of my conversation with Leslie kept popping into my mind. A sandwich and a mug of coffee appeared in front of me.

"Hi, Hon," said Marian. "I can't do that for a few minutes so, since you gotta eat, you might as well eat here."

Marian, I had long since discovered, sort of took things for granted. I put the papers aside. This time she was right: I did have to eat. I gingerly lifted the white bread to discover pale neat circles of something. Mayonnaise oozed in all directions. I bit down gingerly, chewed, and, with a shiver, swallowed. When it didn't kill me, I took another bite.

The Lido Beach Inn was part of the glue that held Pines on Magothy together. It served one kind of sandwich, coffee thick with caffeine, and beer. Hard liquor if you needed it. Gossip. Cigarettes in the machine near the door. Marian had recently expanded her menu to include small bags of potato chips that she yanked off a display behind her. I watched her work. There were no wasted movements and a certain grace to her stumpy body as she retrieved plates, poured refills, and made easy conversation with her regulars.

A young man I had never seen before, blond hair hanging long-ish around a delicate face with tiny blue eyes, stared at me from down the bar. I was no longer surprised that everyone seemed to know who I was. It was a mixed blessing, being Lillian Weber's niece. Made me long sometimes for New York's anonymity.

"Hear you real estate agents gettin' some pretty sexy calls," he said.

"Some have," I said, wishing water was on Marian's menu. It wasn't, unless accompanied by something stronger. With some effort, I swallowed again, then drank coffee to cut the grease. "How do you know about the calls?"

"TV news." He took a long pull at his beer, draining the glass and waving it in Marian's direction.

She plopped another in front of him, foam cascading down the side. "That's it, Kevin," she said. "You're done." He nodded, not offended. Feeling for a roll of bills in the small front pocket in his jeans, he peeled off a ten and put it on the bar.

Watching him hook a deviant lock behind one ear, I thought how odd it was that only blue-collar workers now had long hair. Sort of reverse 1960s. I also found myself fervently hoping he wasn't operating heavy machinery this afternoon. Like a car. As I watched, he picked up his glass and half sat, half leaned on the stool next to me.

"You don't mind, do ya?" I shook my head. "About them calls. I can think a plenty a guys who'd try stuff like that. Sorta as a joke. Did it myself in high school."

How reassuring. What could I possibly say? It didn't matter. He and everyone else at the bar were now following the adventures of a grossly large fly, shimmering blue and drunk with spring. It buzzed with rage and frustration as it ricocheted off the bar into whatever was nearby. Marian suddenly swatted at it with a rolled newspaper, sending it glancing off my mouth and onto the bar. I recoiled. Others at the bar laughed, then grew quiet as Kevin lifted his hand and finished the massacre, wiping his hands on his pants.

There was a round of applause from the other side of the bar. He bowed deeply from the waist, his face red when he righted himself. I shivered again, wishing I could scour the memory of the fly off my mouth.

When the ovation had died down, Kevin settled back on the stool and grinned in my direction. "Death comes to a fly," he said. "That's how police oughta handle murderers, if you ask me, kill 'em like flies."

"And whoever is making obscene calls?" I asked. "What should the police do about them?" He finished his beer and held his glass up for Marian's assistant to see. From the far end of the bar, Marian shook her head ever so slightly. "Maybe," I said, deciding to see where it got me, "you should tell the police if you know who is making obscene calls."

"Sure would, if I knew who. But, didn't say I know who. Besides, ain't the end a the world, you ask me. Police oughta be lookin' for that murderer, not some dickhead makin' calls." He looked me over carefully, got no response, shrugged, and headed for the door.

Marian was standing in front of me on the other side of the bar, pen in her hand and notary seal in the other. "You think he really knows something?" I asked.

"Nah, he's blowin' smoke, doesn't know what he's talkin' about." Too many years of tending bar had given Marian the same speech patterns as her customers. Despite a couple of college degrees. Or just maybe, I thought, she found it helped business. She walked around the bar and pulled up the stool Kevin had just deserted. Her assistant attended to the slackening lunch trade. "Kevin's just like the rest of 'em. The Pines' gift to the world," she said. "Works hard, drinks hard, talks too much. Not one of the lot of 'em would recognize an actual thought if it jumped up and bit 'em on the butt." We watched as several more young men, their jeans tight and dirty, left money on the counter and returned to pouring cement and cleaning septic tanks.

I grinned. "But they pay the bills."

Marian grinned back. "Damned right, they do."

I handed her the papers to notarize. She got busy, expertly running through them, signing and sealing, and slapping them back into piles.

"So. Done," said Marian, handing me several bunches and sitting back on her stool. "That detective, Simmons, was here yesterday, asking questions. The boys there"—she nodded in the direction of three old men still blathering on the other side of bar—"gave him the benefit of their best theories. Which I gather is about all he's got to go on." Marian was fishing. Which, I thought, was useless since I always knew far less than she did. "Well, then, I conclude the police haven't got anything and are waiting for someone to make a stupid mistake. Or someone to come up with a tip. Which, since there's fifteen thousand bucks riding on it, someone will." She waited for me to say something. When I didn't, she leaned closer. "Mitch Gaylin is gonna miss Rose Macklin. Ten-million club or something. Twenty-million, for all I know."

I stopping paper-clipping sheets together. Real estate agents quantified their success in millions of dollars of property listed and sold. Marian was still fishing. But I had to admit she did try harder than most to get her facts right. It made her, I thought, a very reliable source of all kinds of information, information she wasn't above using to liven up the bar whenever things got dull. But, then, everybody in Pines in Magothy already knew this.

"How's Lil?" she asked, when she saw we weren't going anywhere with the topic under discussion.

"Chafing at the bit. Wants to dump the crutches."

"You tell her," said Marian, "that I said she has to follow doctor's orders this time. Besides, with Elizabeth there, it's got to be easier on her."

"Yes and no." Marian was stuffing her notary seal back in a small velvet pouch along with the twenty dollars I'd handed her. "She hates taking sides between Hamm and Elizabeth."

"Well, she shouldn't," Marian said. "If Elizabeth had any sense, she'd have left Hamm years ago. He's been running around on her forever." I watched as Marian suddenly stood on the front rungs of her barstool and threw her short body across the bar in an attempt to fish something out from beneath it on the other side.

Her assistant, a skinny middle-aged man I didn't know, came to her rescue, handing her a package of cigarettes and a lighter.

My cue to move on, I thought. Besides, I wasn't sure I wanted to get into a discussion with Marian about infidelity in marriage. It was a subject all too close to home. I packed my papers and left a few bills under my plate for lunch.

"Got to go, Marian. Thanks for lunch."

She nodded, drawing on the cigarette and blowing smoke out with deep satisfaction. Fortunately for Marian and the owners of other small bars and restaurants, Anne Arundel County didn't seem to worry too much about smoking and non-smoking sections. The Lido Beach Inn and others like it were usually blue with smoke.

I left Marian deep in thought and headed out into the breezy sunlit afternoon. By the door, a honeysuckle bush in full bloom ambushed my senses. The parking lot was all but abandoned. The street was also empty, the BMW waiting alone in the sun. Everybody had gone back to work. I glanced at my watch: almost two-thirty. It felt later. Sunlight glinted across the dashboard and into my eyes. In the distance the Lido Beach Inn's jukebox suddenly came to life. A country and western singer bitched about something. Unconsciously, I again tried to rub the sensation of fly from my mouth. What was wrong with me? Why was this sweet and breezy spring day making me so itchy and irritable?

NINE

It was almost three o'clock when I sat down at my desk at Weber Realty. After pushing paper around for a while, I gave in to full-blown ennui and watched Shirley Bodine do ten things at once in the front office. At four-thirty, I picked up the phone, dialed Lawrence Schoenfeld in New York, then hung up before anyone could answer. By five-twenty, I couldn't stand it any longer.

Dread settled over me during the short drive to Charles Cove. I wasn't looking forward to telling Hamm Hammett that a buyer valued his house exactly $75,000 less than he did. All you have to do, I told myself, was present the offer, hand him the listing for the MacAfferty house across the cove as Lillian had requested, and be on your way. Let her suggest how much he should lower the asking price for their house.

The Hammett house was on the Magothy River side of Lido Beach Road, on a steep semicircle of land that dropped down to a cove of swampy water. Long wooden stairs connected the properties to docks half hidden by tall clumps of feathery marsh grasses. Homes here were not the modest bungalows of Pines on Magothy's main street. They were newer and larger, concealed from the road, and closer to their neighbors than they first appeared to be. Hundred-foot trees, dense shrubbery, and natural ravines gave privacy, as did the wetlands that were preserved by law. The trees and interesting terrain should be the selling points for Charles Cove, I thought. They were certainly more attractive than the grassy swamp that masqueraded as waterfront.

I pulled into the Hammetts' long gravel drive, beyond the low spreading pine which half blocked the entrance. Two cars were parked near the house, one of them Leslie Ballard's blue Oldsmobile. If she was back for a second look, maybe her buyer was actually interested, wanting to see it again before returning to Denver. I tried to keep a lid on my hopes. In the distance, a dog barked twice, forlorn or edgy, I couldn't tell which.

The Hammett house was a colonial, stolid and unremarkable. The lockbox hung open and empty. I knocked on the front door, then knocked again, feeling my resentment rising. How many times this week, I thought, had I stood in front of other people's houses, knocking on doors that weren't answered? Nearby, the ever-present honeysuckle grew over thick hedges, broadcasting its oppressive perfume into the spring air. After the mayonnaise sandwich, the stuff was beginning to make me sick.

"Hello? Leslie?"

I rang the bell again, waited, then twisted the knob. Locked. Leslie had probably secured it from the inside and then taken the Fawcetts out to the patio and pool, maybe even down the long steps to the water. I studied the bushes blocking access to the backyard, then walked to the sunroom at the side of the house near the driveway. Relief unfolded inside me as the knob turned easily.

"Leslie? Hello?"

The house was completely still, a quiet so resonant that my pulse sounded in my ears. Everything looked exactly the way it had the last time I'd been there. Past the cheerful sunroom, I could see a formal living room. Chinese rugs covered polished hardwood floors. The fireplace with its brass andirons didn't look like it got much use. Elizabeth's taste ran to the English country house look of Laura Ashley. Tasteful, I thought, if a little conventional. I suddenly wanted to laugh. I was no better than my clients: making nasty cracks about the choice of furnishings.

"Hello? Anybody home?" The formal living and dining rooms opened at the back of the house to a huge country kitchen, its cabinets and appliances spotless. Not so much as a single tumbler defiled the sink. At the far end, the breakfast nook—its round table free of all the debris that dogs all but the most tidy among us—opened onto a flagstone patio. From the window I could see the looping handles of the ladder at the deep end of the swimming pool. It was set into the sharply sloping contour of the land. The Hammetts, Lillian had told me, had sunk a fair chunk of change into the pool. They'd never get their money out, I thought. But, then, everybody knew pools made notoriously lousy investments.

I opened the glass sliding doors and stepped onto the fragrant patio. The rickety stairs that led to the shallow water below weren't visible. Somewhere, not far away, came the sound of a car, then a roar as a lawn mower came to life on the other side of the cove. I crossed the slate stones to the empty pool. Lying at the bottom, surprise fanning out over her exquisite face, dead eyes staring in stony sleep, lay Leslie Ballard.

A scream filled my head, clogged my throat. When it stopped, I found I was on my knees. I swallowed with difficulty. I could see Leslie's radiant dark hair spread out against the peeling blue of the pool. Heavy waves hung over one side of her face, nearly obscuring it. The other side of her face was bruised, with darkened marks defiling the flawless skin beneath the eye. Her bright mouth was slightly open, as if speech were still possible. Suddenly, I could almost hear the glad laugh that had wrapped me in good cheer this morning. I don't know how long I knelt, unmoving, breathing softly, waiting, watching. Beyond me, the clement breeze and the sounds of life in suburbia belonged to any other spring day.

Then, a noise came from below, through the swaying grasses, from the direction of the steep wooden stairway that led up from Charles Cove. Struggling to my feet, I turned around. Hamm Hammmett, his handsome face contorted, was charging toward me.

AN HOUR LATER, cops talked of death in calm tones, doing their unhappy jobs with a matter-of-factness hard for me to fathom. Through a front window, I could see that police cruisers and unmarked cars had spilled out of the driveway and onto the road.

Hamm and I sat in silence in his formal dining room, led there by a young policeman with a blond crew cut. The young cop had been the first to arrive after my call to 911. He had called for backup, then herded us into the dining room before quietly asking questions. His name was Scott Lisle. I had met him once before, under circumstances not much happier than today's. He had shown kindness then and now, for which I was grateful.

My mind raced back and forth between the horror of finding Leslie Ballard's body and the disturbing necessity of reliving the experience for the police. I thought about Rose Macklin. Two women—both real estate agents—murdered within a week, within a couple of miles of one another. Who was doing this? And why real estate agents? Across the mahogany table, Hamm Hammett was sitting in a dazed, artificial calm, head lowered. Only his hands nervously picking at each other gave away the extent of his emotions. Detective Simmons, I gathered, had grilled him pretty hard.

My racing thoughts were interrupted by the detective himself. His red hair was cropped more closely than I had remembered from the self-defense workshop, his pale face and nearly nonexistent eyebrows blending into each other. He had questioned me earlier, too, writing slowly and carefully as I described what I had seen. His eyes, chilly blue and aloof, had at first focused on me like a bug at the end of a pin, softening slightly when he found out that I, too, was a New Yorker.

Now as Simmons pulled up a chair, Scott Lisle returned with the glass of water Hamm had requested. The detective hissed something under his breath at the young cop, who blanched noticeably, then left.

"Miss Elliott, I'd like to go over a few things again, to make sure I have them right."

As he read his notes back to me, I found the words strangely numbing, the scene vivid but no longer real, like something remembered from a movie. These were just words, I thought, unrelated to the woman who lay at the bottom of the pool. A part of my mind had separated itself off from the meaning of the long moment in which I knelt and watched.

"So you entered the house through the sunroom, walked through the living room and dining room into the kitchen," said Simmons. "Did you touch anything?"

"I don't think so." I shook my head. I found he was staring at me. "What? Did you ask me something else?"

"I asked what you were doing here?"

"There was an offer for Mr. Hammett's house. I was dropping

it off.'' Hamm Hammett, his head still bowed, showed no interest in this bit of news.

"Mr. Hammett,'' said the cop, turning to face him. "Is that right? Miss Elliott is your real estate agent? Mr. Hammett?''

Hamm looked up, his eyes deadened from what he too had seen at the bottom of the pool. "Yes.''

"Mr. Hammett, why was the pool dry?''

"I was going to have it repainted.''

Simmons barely nodded. I wondered if he had a pool. Or even a house. "Mr. Hammett, I want to go over a few things again. Where were you all day?''

Hamm sat up straighter, his face haggard. "At an engineering conference.'' He named a hotel at the edge of Baltimore's Inner Harbor. "I left there about four-thirty p.m. Came directly here. I saw the blue car when I turned into the drive, and pulled in beside it,'' he said. "I guessed it belonged to the real estate agent who was showing the house today. I unlocked the sunroom, then walked through the house, and out to the patio. Her body was...was at the bottom of the pool.'' His voice was tightly controlled, in contrast to his twitching fingers. "Then I went down to the cove to see if anybody was there.''

"You really thought you might catch someone by the water? What, swimming away?'' Hamm didn't appear to notice Simmons' sarcasm. "Then what?''

"I heard a cry and ran back up the stairs and found Eve by the pool,'' said Hamm. "She was getting up from her knees.''

Through the window, past the spreading evergreen, a police van was pulling around the other cars and onto the grass. I was grateful I couldn't see the scene on the patio at the back of the house.

"Her knees?'' Simmons looked at me with renewed interest. "What were you doing on your knees, Miss Elliott?''

A wave of anger rocked me. I took a sip of water, buying time to control my temper. "I don't exactly know, Detective. I just sort of fell down when I saw the body. I don't spend my days looking at dead people. I was frightened. I was surprised. I was horrified.'' I stopped, daring him to say something. "I still am.''

"Take it easy, Miss Elliott. Being angry doesn't help.'' Looking out the window, he noticed the mobile crime van in the front yard. "Wait here."

I looked over at Hamm. I was suddenly anxious to talk. "You must have arrived just minutes before me." He nodded, his graying dark hair perfectly cut, his face with its even features, nearly unlined. Except for the slight shadow of a beard, he looked like he'd just stepped from the shower. I hadn't much liked him when Lillian had first introduced us. And Marian Beall's comments earlier today hadn't helped any. But there was no doubting the misery on his face. I watched as he stood up and strode to the front window, his bearing reminiscent of the naval officer he used to be.

From the hallway came snatches of conversation, punctuated by the sound of police radios. Paying closer attention, I gathered that Leslie Ballard's handbag was missing. Like Rose Macklin's. I tried to remember if I had seen her handbag or briefcase, either in the house or at the bottom of the pool by her body. I hadn't. Maybe whoever had done this had grabbed Leslie's bag, then shoved her into the empty pool. The killer could have gone back through the house, locking the door behind him.

I forced myself to picture Leslie's body at the bottom of the pool. The surprise on her face. The bruises and black marks under one eye. There had been no blood. Had the fall killed her? Or had something else? Unlike Rose Macklin, she didn't appear to have been hit with something. Was it possible, I wondered, that she had gone outside to breathe in the honeysuckle, perhaps to wait for the Fawcetts? Could she have simply slipped and fallen into the pool, hitting her head? I tried hard to remember if I had seen a puddle of water or a garden tool at the edge of the pool. I hadn't. But where was her handbag? And what did the black marks mean?

Hamm sat back down. "I'm glad Elizabeth isn't here," he said, to no one in particular. Some painful emotion I didn't recognize briefly flowed over his face before he could control it. "I wouldn't want her to see this."

"Miss Elliott," said Simmons, from the doorway. "I'd like to talk to you again. Alone. While Mr. Hammett goes through the house with Detective Clarke to see if anything is missing. In the other room, please." He pointed toward the living room.

"Miss Elliott," he began, settling heavily into a flowered wing chair, "can you give me a list of agents who have shown this property?"

"Leslie Ballard was the only one in the last week or two, unless someone came and went without telling me. A central computer records the identification number of any agent who uses her key-pad to open the electronic lockbox. And the time and place."

Simmons grew noticeably more interested. "Go on."

"I think it's very unlikely you'll find anyone has shown it, since it's a courtesy to call the listing agent if you want to show a house. Besides, if you don't, the seller may be there or there may be a mess."

He made notes as I spoke, not looking up. "Just a formality, Miss Elliott, but I need to know your whereabouts all day."

I told him, hour by hour, watching his small mouth turn fretful when I mentioned running into Leslie at Wildwood Bay. I repeated our conversation, told him about Leslie's lost sale, her depressed mood. He made more notes, interrupting me when a member of the crime lab team approached him.

"Sounds like I need to talk with Mr. Gaylin again." He said it like a question, then waited for my reaction. I nodded, which appeared to make him happy. "You know the name of the clients Miss Ballard was showing the house to?"

"Fawcett. They're relocating here. She'd worked with them before." He wrote it down, then looked up.

"That's all for now, Miss Elliott, but I'm probably going to need to talk with you again. Make sure we have your phone numbers. You may have been the last person to see Miss Ballard alive." I shivered. He got out of his chair. "Oh, and Miss Elliott, I want to remind you that you are not to divulge anything that you saw here today. No details. Nothing. Not to relatives or friends, and especially not to the media. Clear?" He nodded, then turned to go. One vent of his sports jacket was caught in his pants. He pulled it free, not looking back.

"Detective," I said, "I almost forgot; there's one more thing." Simmons turned around. "Leslie told me she got an obscene phone call last night. I don't know if she called the police."

TEN

TENSION, thick as air pollution, hung over Lillian's normally serene living room. Elizabeth had answered the door. Behind her, I could see my aunt looking tired and too thin. Across from her, the pastor of the Church in the Pines, Jack Hardwick, fidgeted. His perpetual smile looked a little forced tonight. Several ledgers and a large business checkbook lay forgotten on a nearby end table.

"Thank God, you are here," said Lillian. "And that you are okay. You *are* okay?" I shrugged, wondering if there were a right answer. "Hamm called a while back. To tell us what happened."

Beyond the fieldstone fireplace that commanded most of the far wall, I could see the dining room. Chairs had been pushed away from a table cluttered with dishes, the meal unfinished and forgotten. A platter of something was hardening to grease.

"We were eating," said my aunt, following my glance. "Then Jack and I were going to try to get the church finances in order. Though God knows..." Her voice trailed off and her body sagged in a favorite Queen Anne armchair, her bad ankle propped up on an ottoman. I pulled up a side chair. She grabbed my hand and squeezed. "This is just awful about Leslie Ballard. And you know what scares me? What I am so afraid of..."

"Now, Lillian," said the pastor, "you can't let yourself give in to fear." He had risen to his feet and was moving in Lillian's direction. Then something stopped him. I turned to see Lillian almost imperceptibly shaking her head, her eyes dangerous. He stood motionless for an instant, shrugged, and folded himself back into an overstuffed chair across from her.

"What a horrible horrible thing. Everyone was afraid of something like this," she said. "Marsha Rowen called me earlier when she heard. She said that Leslie got an obscene phone call last night. It scared the wits out of her."

"Nobody," I said, "knows if the murders and calls are related." I wondered if I believed this. A cordless phone lying on a side table rang.

"I'll get it," said Jack. He turned away from us to talk, his voice low, the conversation punctuated with nervous laughs.

"Jack? Who is it?" said Lillian. "Jack?" She said it louder the second time, her voice harsh. I was surprised. My aunt rarely sweated the small stuff, but the pastor was on her nerves tonight. Or maybe, I thought, everybody was on everybody's nerves. He handed her the phone, his hand large over the mouthpiece.

"It's Howard Lucas. He just heard about Leslie Ballard's murder on the news. They are talking about a serial killer." The pastor's voice was low and thin.

As Lillian took the phone, he turned to me, shaking his head. "God help us, a serial killer." He was still whispering. Then he shook off the words and composed himself, retreating into stilted drawing room small talk to fill the void. "Do you know Howard?"

"No."

"Good man. Volunteers a lot. Had a rough year. First, his mother moves to Florida, then she dies. A month later he loses his job at Westinghouse, then..." He watched as Lillian put the phone down.

"You don't have to whisper anymore, Jack," she said.

I looked over at Elizabeth, wondering what she made of all this. I wasn't sure she had even heard the phone ring. But she noticed my glance and dragged herself from her torpor.

"I keep thinking about Leslie Ballard. Who could do something like that? And now who will buy the house?" She blew her nose and looked around at us. "Sorry, it's selfish of me to even think about that right now."

"But perfectly natural," said the pastor. Elizabeth stared at him, as if she couldn't remember who he was.

Lillian turned to me. "Tell us exactly what happened."

"I can't. That cop, Simmons, told me not to talk about any of it." Lillian's mouth pulled back at little.

"I keep thinking," said Elizabeth, "how strange it is that as this terrible thing was happening, we were all going about our lives as if nothing were happening."

There was a sharp knock on the door. I opened it to find a plainclothes cop, his badge open, standing on Lillian's front step. I had seen him earlier conferring with Simmons. His name was Clarke and he looked drained, as if what he had seen earlier had sapped his strength. "I was told Mrs. Hammett is staying here. I need to take a statement from her."

I opened the door wider. There was silence as he took in the scene, his gaze moving from Lillian to Jack Hardwick, resting finally on Elizabeth.

"Mrs. Hammett?" She nodded. The pastor stood up, hand outstretched, then sat back down when the detective didn't notice. "I need to ask you a few questions. Is there somewhere private we can talk?" Elizabeth glanced nervously at Lillian.

"Mrs. Hammett is feeling a little shaken, Detective," said Jack Hardwick. "As we all are. I think it's better if you talk with all of us in the room. I think Mrs. Hammett could use our moral support."

"And you are?"

The pastor sprinted across the room, hand out, for the second time. The detective shook it reluctantly, then motioned for him to sit back down. He pulled out his notebook. "Okay, Mrs. Hammett, this is all routine. But I have to ask where you were all day."

Elizabeth's mouth opened, then closed. She took a deep breath, then another.

"She was at the church office, from this morning until late afternoon," said the pastor. "She was working on the church newsletter. We both were." Clarke looked annoyed, but said nothing.

Elizabeth nodded. "Yes. He's right. I was at the church. In the office. From late morning..." She turned to Jack. "I got there, at what, about ten-thirty or so?" He nodded agreement. "I worked most of the day, then went to Marley Station Mall to pick up a few things. That must have been about four."

"Did you know the deceased?" I could feel my skin crawl.

How could Leslie Ballard, so full of life, be reduced to this? But Elizabeth didn't flinch.

"No."

Clarke wrote rapidly, then asked about her present living arrangements. Lillian sucked in her breath, but Elizabeth's voice was again calm when she answered. The detective took phone numbers, snapped his notebook shut, and with a warning that he might need to question her again, was gone. I closed the door behind him.

"That hardly seemed worth his time," said Lillian. "But I guess since it's your house, he had to talk with you." Elizabeth nodded, gloomy again.

"Just a formality, I imagine," said the pastor. He was stuffing ledgers and the big checkbook back into a cardboard box. "Well, I'm off. Sorry about the ledgers, Lillian. Can you meet next week?" She nodded and told him to call. With a few more words of what I supposed were meant to be comfort, he, too, left.

Lillian sighed and shook her head. "God knows, Jack tries," she said, "but..." The rest of her thought hung in the air, unfinished.

I found exhaustion was dropping over me like a blanket. It was getting harder to focus on the present, harder to push away the awful image of Leslie's broken body, black hair, and vivid lips against the crumbling blue pool. I needed to go home, to the dogs and a night's sleep. If I could sleep after what I'd seen.

Elizabeth stood up, smoothing her cotton skirt, looking around, waiting for something. No one seemed to know what. Finally she spoke. "I wonder if Hamm is staying at the house tonight." She turned to me. I shrugged. Simmons had again been questioning him when I had left. I glanced at Lillian, who was suddenly studying her perfectly manicured nails with great interest. Was she wondering the same thing I was: Would Hamm seek refuge and comfort in the bed of the woman he was currently sleeping with?

Elizabeth excused herself, then headed for Lillian's expansive deck overlooking the dark Magothy. I could hear light rain as she closed the sliding doors behind her.

"Did you talk with Hamm or did Elizabeth?"

"I did, but she's worried about him," said my aunt. "And I know he cares for her." I thought back to the scene at the workshop yesterday and wondered. Lillian made her ankle more comfortable on the ottoman.

"Marian Beall thinks that Elizabeth should have left him years ago."

Lillian snorted. "Marian should mind her own business."

"Lillian," I said, "Elizabeth is right about having trouble selling their house. It's already overpriced and now a murder."

If my aunt was surprised at the change of topic, she didn't let on. Instead she sighed deeply, something I noticed she'd been doing a lot of tonight. "Maybe," she said slowly. "We'll just have to hope that since this awful thing happened outside the actual house, people won't be so put off."

"What about the price?" I asked. "Why is Hamm so stuck on getting his price? Why not lower it thirty thousand and just sell it and move on? I thought both he and Elizabeth agreed that since their kids are grown the house is just too big. Even before Elizabeth left, they wanted to sell and move into something smaller. So what's his problem? Do they need money?"

My aunt shook her head. "I'm not sure," she said. "Hamm is usually the most rational of men, but he's not rational about this. If it were up to Elizabeth, we'd get the house sold in a few weeks. With Hamm, who knows? Maybe it's a matter of pride, that he wants the house to be worth what he thinks it's worth. Or..." She tried again to find a comfortable position for her ankle. "Or maybe he doesn't really want to sell it. Elizabeth seems to be getting ready to move on in her life. Maybe Hamm isn't."

"Of course he isn't. Why should he? He's got all the advantages of both..." I was rewarded with a dirty look.

"They are both my good friends." My aunt's voice was quietly fierce. "And they've been rocks in this community. Hamm has raised buckets of money for the Anne Arundel Council of Churches over the years. He tutors children who need academic help. And he chaired the hospital's fund-raising drive. Elizabeth...well, I could hardly begin tell you all she has done from— getting the community center built to keeping the Chesapeake

Light Opera Company afloat.'' Lillian leaned in my direction. ''So don't start with me about what Marian Beall thinks. She ought to mind her own business.''

I stared. This was a rare mood.

My aunt pushed a thin strand of blond hair back into its carefully teased helmet. Baby-pink scalp showed through. ''I'm sorry,'' she said. ''First, I eat Jack alive for accidentally bringing the wrong ledgers and then I nearly hang up on poor Howard. Now I'm barking at you.''

''No apology needed,'' I said. ''I'm going home, Lillian.''

''Home? Why don't you just stay here tonight? Call Will and ask him to take care of the dogs. I'm sure he wouldn't mind.''

''I'll be okay.''

''I don't like you going off by yourself.'' She eased off her chair and onto the footstool, feeling around for her crutches on the floor underneath. ''Whoever did that to Leslie Ballard and Rose Macklin is still out there. And you don't have any protection.''

''I have dogs. And Will is just next door.'' I kissed her. ''Say good night to Elizabeth for me. And don't worry. I'll call you tomorrow.''

She nodded, unhappy but aware she couldn't say anything to make me stay. I closed the door. To my surprise, I was hungry. Life went on for the living, I thought.

ELEVEN

IT WAS RAINING lightly by the time I reached the car. Usually the damp organic smell, rich with ozone, pleased me. This evening was different. The rain came down harder as I drove, with an occasional bellow of thunder in the distance. A long vine, unmoored from its supporting tree by the beating rain, scraped along the side of the BMW. I turned down Weller's Creek Road. On my right, I could see Will's truck parked close to his bungalow. From his window, light spread dimly outward into the damp thicket.

The dogs burst down the steps when I opened the front door to the cottage, glad to be loose in the sodden world beyond the screened porch. After a few minutes I whistled them in, then set out bowls of dry food. Oddly ravenous, not remembering when I last ate, I pulled out the roasted chicken Will had left in the fridge. With a salad and the rest of the grapes, I was soon full. The companionable sounds of hungry dogs wolfing kibble filled the small kitchen.

I listened to the messages on the answering machine. Mitch offered to talk. Marian Beall and Joyce Nichols fished for information to feed their gossip mills. Finally, Will, his voice concerned, told me to call when I got in. It was almost nine o'clock. I wanted sleep. I'd talked enough for today. Walking into the bathroom to brush my teeth, I stopped short at the mess.

Will had been working here today. Last winter's heavy snow and ice had seeped through the bathroom's ceiling and into the walls, ruining them beyond hope of minor repair. I'd had the roof replaced, but plastery chunks were still falling daily into the tub and sink. The floor was marked where melting water had created rusty stains like Rorschachs. The toilet and sink looked as if they might work, but the rest was a mess.

I wanted to fill the footed tub with sudsy water and sink deeply into the foam. To let the warm water soak away the vivid memory of what I had seen. But the tub stood apart from the wall, waiting for Will to reattach it. Depressed and exhausted, I trudged up the steep stairway and slumped onto the bed in the darkening bedroom, closing my eyes to doze for a couple of minutes.

Without warning, a grotesque specter appeared before me, her mouth red and wailing, her face bruised and shredded by thin black marks, her teeth gleaming and belligerent. Then the wailing stopped and with a sigh, the savage mouth closed. A low hum filled my ears. The specter reached out for me, the damaged face close to mine. Frozen, clutching the sheet, I awakened to find my clothes twisted and damp, my heart whipped into a sickening rhythm. For a terrible instant, I couldn't remember what had happened. Then the nightmare moment kneeling on the Hammetts' patio came back in a rush. The bedside clock said just 9:30. It had, I thought, taken that monstrous apparition just minutes to find me.

Overhead the low ceiling pushed down. I fled the bed, stripping off my clothes, rummaging for jeans and a sweatshirt and sneakers. I dressed, lunged downstairs, called to the dogs, and ran up the wet winding road to Will's bungalow.

The wedge of yellow light from the window was gone, replaced by the eerie purple glow of grow lights. At the back of the kitchen was the large single room that served Will as both living room and bedroom. I stood on the flagstone at the front of the house. It lay even with the doorjamb, its dull surface dappled with shallow puddles of water. The rain was turning to mist, refreshing and clean and filled with ozone. Zeke and Lance, delighted by the walk, danced around me as I knocked. There was no answer, but inside I could hear movement. I knocked again.

The door opened and Will stood in the damp evening, his body silhouetted from behind by the lavender light. Without any greeting, he wrapped his arms around me. The dogs swarmed through the open door, dashing around us in frantic circles. Lancelot showered us both with a long, slow whole-body shake.

Behind Will, I could see the usual clutter: long flats of small plants, paper bags empty and lying sideways on the floor, half-open sacks of topsoil and peat moss dribbling onto his work table. A couple of bananas were ripening on the edge of the sink.

"I heard what happened," he said. "Are you okay?"

I freed myself from his embrace. "Sort of. It was awful. She was just lying there, so alive looking. Then Hamm Hammett comes up from the swamp. The police think he knows something, I think. The lead detective—a guy named Simmons—was pretty awful. He kept asking the same things over and over. Though he was a little nicer to me when he found out I was from New York. When he was through with me, I went to Lillian's house and she and Elizabeth and that pastor were all sitting around like zombies. Then, when I came home, I had this horrible dream." I shivered, aware that I was babbling and not much caring. "It's just so senseless."

Will pulled me close for a second time.

"I need a shower." He nodded, making no effort to hang on. I walked past him into the messy, plant-filled kitchen, the smell of dirt almost as pungent in here as outside. Oscar Peterson's effortless, elegant version of "Night and Day" played in the other room. Will's stereo system, I knew, was worth about five times more than his truck.

The bathroom was tiny and spartan, with only a tin-can shower. The mirror had peeled a bit around the edges. I ran the water until it was blisteringly hot. It soaked my body and sedated my mind. By the time I had finished, the small window overlooking the yard was opaque from steam. From the living room came a sweet, biting smell and the voluptuous piano of Keith Jarrett, with its driving melodies and groans of rapture. I studied my reflection in Will's mirror, looking into the eyes of someone I used to know. I had to keep toweling off a semicircle in the mirror to see myself. The smell, like the music, was picking up strength.

"What's that?" But I needn't have asked. I would have known it anywhere: the agreeable, singular smell of marijuana. Will was lying on his bed. In his hand was a joint. Wordlessly he offered it to me.

"Are you out of your mind?"

"Actually," he said slowly, a smile nudging the edges of his mouth, "I am beginning to be." He sat up, making room for me to sit. "It's not bad."

"Where did you get it?" But I knew the answer to that, too. The purple grow lights in his kitchen and the dense wooded copse behind the cabin would make growing marijuana child's play for someone who landscaped the grounds of the rich for a living.

He opened his mouth to say something, couldn't find any words, and instead formed his lips into a radiant smile. Resentment began to rise in me. I had come here to be comforted. To share the terrible red-mouthed apparition who had chased me in sleep, scaring me awake. And the all-too-real horror of finding Leslie at the bottom of the pool. But Will wasn't really available now, here only in body. His mind, I knew, was far away, amusing itself along the convoluted roadways of his brain, enjoying the twists and turns of the slow, pointless journey.

"It was awful, seeing her like that," I said. Simmons' words of warning came back. No details, he had said. Zeke moved uneasily toward me, his black shining bulk hovering close, eyes turned anxiously upward. Will took another deep drag, then stared, his eyes dilated, uninvolved. I felt a flame of anger shoot up through me. "Do you hear me?"

"You found the woman who was murdered." The words were right, I thought, but nothing else was. He smiled again, not interested really. With a rush, I remembered that feeling, the relief of not being interested. I remembered music separating into melodies and rhythms, the saxophone apart from the piano and bass. Melodies more beautiful than ever before imagined. Ben and I had smoked night after night one long hot New York summer during college. We had been living in a West Seventy-Sixth Street sublet then. I could almost see it: a basement room filled with someone else's stuff. One room had been enough that summer. We had dreamed and dozed and laughed.

I watched from a distance of years as Will stood up and walked toward me. He handed me the joint. I took it carefully, its homemade roughness and spitty paper at once revolting and appealing and familiar. The smoke stung my throat, harsher than I remembered. Holding my lungs tightly closed, I waited, looking up only to find Will had gone somewhere. After a few more deep drags, and who knows how long, I looked around for an ashtray, feeling the smoke begin to work its magic.

Would I recognize an ashtray? I wondered. Maybe not. After all, I thought, what is an ashtray? There is a certain ashtrayness about many objects. I slowly wandered the room, holding the joint in one hand, picking up and examining objects with the other. An antique fountain pen, seed catalogs, a paperback copy of *Hundred Years of Solitude,* a spray mister, an empty juice glass. The glass seemed the most promising, I thought, studying it further: too deep to be an ashtray perhaps, but better than the book, which could hold only words. Only words. Words of shock. Words of death. Words of anger. A kind of murky sadness took hold of me. Words were useless and I was tired of words.

Will was there now. In his hand was a saucer. I laid the joint down carefully. Our laughter mingled and spun with the rhythms of the piano, the pounding bass finally rescued by the floating melody just when I thought I couldn't stand it a moment longer. The horror of the day evaporated, sealed off in some other part of my brain, hidden by the spell cast by the marijuana. From a distance, I heard the sound of a car as it droned in the night.

Wordlessly, we lay down on Will's rumpled bed, the cool mist rising through the low, open windows to blow across our bodies. Reality became nothing but hot, damp skin, the piano swirling around us, my hair wet and burning on my neck. My mind was empty of murder, of dark dreams and predatory ghosts and hurtful, useless words. And no apparition stood at the foot of the bed.

"I'm going to get some..." Will said, when we were done. I briefly wondered what as I watched him throw off the sheet. He got out of bed, then stumbled over Lancelot in the dim purple light. I watched him lean down to touch the dog, then leave the room. I waited, not knowing what I was waiting for, dozing a little. When I came to, the music had stopped. I got up. Tiny misgivings stabbed around the edges of consciousness, pricking the calm. An image of Simmons, his hair rising red, his eyebrows almost white, sped across my mind. Odd, I thought, that I should think of him and not of Leslie Ballard. The curtains flapped as a gust came up. I stood at the window and looked into the darkness. Somewhere outside, in the low bushes, an animal ran for cover.

I got dressed slowly, with difficulty and regret. Will returned to the bedroom, in his hand a can of something cold.

"We need to talk," I said.

He was still naked, thin, graceful, and utterly relaxed. "Sure." His voice was distant, unhurried. He drank deeply. I looked at the sweaty can, craving the sweet, biting liquid.

"Are you growing grass here?" He shook his head. I could feel relief fall over me. The clouds in my mind began to part. "Why smoke, Will?"

His voice was stronger this time, closer to what I knew. "To hear the music," he said.

He walked past me into the living and bedroom. "Please, Will." He turned, his eyes dark, filled with some emotion too complicated for marijuana, something we couldn't talk about this night.

"Yes," he said.

"I'm going," I said. I called the dogs and opened the front door, turning to see him kneeling, fiddling with the CD player, already having forgotten me.

The night air was cool and damp, shocking in its pungency. The ever-present honeysuckle overpowered the pine. I stood quietly for a minute, trying to assess the distortions in my brain. Zeke and Lance ran down the road in front of me, then back up, waiting and wondering what was taking me so long. The drug was lifting now, though like the residue of the day's horror, it still circled my body, ebbing and flowing. Underfoot twigs snapped as I walked. A crescent moon was beginning to rise in the distant sky.

I stopped and shook my head. The joint had been so strong, clogging my brain in seconds, after just a few drags. I stumbled a little on a large rock half buried in the rutted road. Ahead of me Lance barked once. Zeke sped to his side, then stopped and waited for me to catch up.

The narrow dark driveway from Will's bungalow opened into the pine clearing in front of Ray Tilghman's cottage. I stopped and looked around me. This house, the distant waiting cove, the water, dark and secret, the dense pines, they could all be mine. I had only to sign some papers. Did I want them? And the dogs and my life here?

Then I saw the car, its dim bulk half hidden in the dense low foliage along the wide path that led past the clearing to the cove and Weller's Creek. A wave of fear ran up my body, cutting crisply through the haze in my mind. Christine McGrath's words echoed in my head. "Some plan their malice, others grab opportunities."

TWELVE

ZEKE AND LANCE rushed toward the car, giving away my presence. I tried to focus: a real car, not some image circling in my mind. Fear sliced through my thoughts. This was not some fantasy caused by the powerful joint. I ran for the cottage, then whistled. The dogs came reluctantly, eyes pleading with me to allow them to go back and find who or what had broken the calm night. I locked the front door, then stood in the dim light. Lance slumped at my feet after a long drink in the kitchen. Zeke stood waiting, listening.

Suddenly, both dogs sprang to their feet by the door, barking hard and steadily. There was an impatient bang on the screen door, then another. Shit. Killers don't knock. Was I imagining this? Zeke threw himself at the door, falling backward from the effort.

"Miss Elliott? This is Detective Simmons." He was standing on the stoop, hand up to rap again. Relief and irritation surged through me in one massive wave. "Miss Elliott. I need to talk with you."

By the time I opened the door, Simmons had retreated to the soft pine-needled clearing below the steps. He was standing a few yards back, giving me a moment to take in his presence. Holding Zeke and commanding Lancelot to sit, I held open the screen door to the porch, then the main door.

What the hell did he want that couldn't wait until tomorrow? Surely I told him everything I knew. My head ached, my mind reeled from the residue of the powerful joint. My throat was dry. I hoped my clothes didn't reek of sweet smoke. Zeke growled deep in his throat. I tugged lightly on his collar, pulling him toward me as Simmons walked in. Lancelot rose to his feet, but didn't move. The detective looked around, then back at me.

"I see you are well protected," he said, nodding at the dogs. "Not a bad idea."

The anxiety in me suddenly surged, scattering the clouds in my mind. "What's wrong? Why are you here so late? Did something else happen?"

He made a big deal of pulling back his jacket cuff and looking at his watch. "It's only just after eleven."

Eleven? It was only eleven o'clock? What had felt like half the night with Will had been less than two hours? My body still felt warm and good from the sex. Traces of the joint floated through my brain, slowing my thoughts, alternately causing anxiety, then amusement. I have to keep Simmons away from me, I thought. The smell must be strong in my still-damp hair and clothes.

"Sit down." I gestured toward the couch at the far end of the room. Commanding Lance to lie down again, I pulled Zeke with me into the bathroom, then quickly brushed my teeth. Had it been less than a couple of hours ago I'd been staring into Will's mirror? I looked down at my own mirror, grateful it was on the floor, resting against the wall. I didn't want to see my stoned eyes. I returned to find Simmons was standing where I had left him.

I pointed for a second time toward the couch, then collapsed in the musty old armchair next to the fireplace. With luck, the chair might smell stronger than I did. "What do you want?

"We've both had a long day, Miss Elliott," he began. "But I need you to answer a few more questions."

"You scared me to death, you know? Leaving your car down by the path like that."

"I waited for you for some time," he said. "While you were out." I tried to imagine him sitting silently in his car while Will and I... Oh, Lord, had Simmons actually been in his car or had he been wandering around? How long had he waited for me? Had he smelled the unmistakable sweet odor of marijuana drifting in the night air? Had he looked in the window? I had to talk with Will again tomorrow.

"What do you want?" I asked again. Exhaustion had given my anxiety a shove. Zeke positioned himself next to me by the chair, still on full alert.

"Miss Elliott, how well did you know Rose Macklin?"

Rose Macklin? In my mind the sound of Keith Jarrett's pounding piano solo revolved, then dissolved. I concentrated with difficulty, forcing the music to retreat.

"Miss Elliott?"

"Uh, not well." Where was he going with this? "The only contact I ever had with her was to make arrangements to show her properties. On the phone. Oh, and I met her in person once or twice at some real estate seminar. Months ago. That's it."

"And there's nothing else? You don't know anything else about her?"

I took a deep breath. "Well, there is one thing. A month before she was killed, I showed a house to a couple named Richard and Davina Canin. My aunt's clients actually. They live in Washington and were looking for a weekend and summer place." I stopped. "I need a drink." I got up, returning with a half-empty bottle of cranberry juice, wishing there was something to eat with it. Like brownies, I thought. Oh, God, had I said that aloud? For one bad moment I wasn't sure. Simmons was watching me. Should I have offered him something to drink?

"You were telling me about the Canins," he prompted. "What happened?"

I made an effort. "They appeared ready to buy a property in Round Bay. Rose Macklin was the listing agent. It was a big, new contemporary, right on the water. You know the kind, sort of gray weathered wood—that's cedar, by the way—with lots of decks and cathedral ceilings and clerestory windows..." I was babbling. "I'm sorry. I'm very tired. You really want to hear about clerestory windows?"

"They were prepared to buy this house?"

"I thought so, but then they suddenly stopped returning my phone calls." I drank the rest of the juice and put the bottle down on the floor by my feet. Zeke knocked it over and stuck his tongue in the wide mouth before I could move it out of the way. Simmons, I noticed, looked a little repulsed. But the tart juice had helped some, cleared my head a little. "I never talked to them again. We didn't have a contract, so...

"Contract?"

"For me to act in their behalf exclusively as their agent. To help them find and buy a house." I hoped he wouldn't ask me to explain the practically unexplainable real estate practices of buyers' and sellers' agents and dual agency. Who works for whom and who pays what to whom. Lillian, I thought, was absolutely right. Never work without a contract, as long as there were Rose Macklins and Richard Canins. I suddenly remembered Simmons, sitting on the couch waiting for me to continue.

"Well, anyway," I said, "at first I thought something had come up, but then after a few days I realized that something had gone wrong. Or they had changed their minds and didn't want to tell me or Lillian."

"What happened?" he asked.

"Nothing. That was the end of it. There was nothing I could do. If they weren't returning our calls, neither Lillian or I could very well go to their house in Kalorama and sit on their doorstep." He looked puzzled. "Kalorama. In D.C."

"And then?" He had taken a small pad from his inside breast pocket.

"I found out yesterday that the house in Round Bay had a contract on it." He sat, his hands searching pockets for a pen. "The Canins."

He was writing intently now. Then he looked up. "You think that Rose Macklin did something illegal to make the sale, Miss Elliott?"

"Well...no, er...not illegal since there was no contract between Weber Realty and the Canins." I tried to think carefully about my words. "I gather Rose Macklin was too smart to do anything illegal."

"How much would your commission have been?" Simmons asked suddenly.

I thought for a second, my mind sticking, refusing to do the math. I got up and walked across the room to get a calculator. Zeke watched Simmons with care. I named a figure. He whistled.

"That's a lot of money, Miss Elliott. It must have been hard for you and Weber Realty to lose that sale."

I sat down again. "It happens all the time. Nobody likes to lose one like that, but sales fall through for all kinds of reasons." Wow, listen to me, I thought. Must be the grass. I could feel faint bubbles of laughter forming in my throat.

Detective Simmons was watching me closely. I squelched the laughter. A faint thought crept through the mist in my brain. "You think I had something to do with Rose Macklin's murder?"

The fatigue in his face lifted a bit and he almost smiled. "No, I don't," he said. "I already checked you out. In case you don't know it, you have a perfectly good alibi." He named a home inspector I'd been with at the time, going over a house in Severna Park. I stared. How on earth...? "Mrs. Bodine in your office was kind enough to let me look at your schedule. The home inspector confirmed your appointment."

"Oh." I tried to focus my thoughts. "Well, then what do you want from me?" Suddenly, I suspected that he'd known all along about the Canins. "You knew all along about that sale in Round Bay, didn't you?"

"Yes. I just wondered if you had anything more to add."

I shook my head. "And what about Leslie Ballard? She wasn't stealing clients. In fact, she said she was having trouble making ends meet. Where does that fit?" A sharp twinge of irritation cleared my head. "Haven't you got any real evidence who did these murders? Blood, hairs, or fingerprints? What happened to whatever the killer used to bludgeon Rose Macklin to death? How did Leslie die?"

He ignored my outburst. "What else can you tell me about either Rose Macklin or Leslie Ballard?"

"You mean personally?" He nodded. "Not much since I'd never met Leslie before yesterday at the self-defense workshop. Rose, I told you about." I felt like I'd been saying the same thing over and over for days. I glanced at the clock and was stunned to find it was only eleven-fifteen. The joint was still doing its time-slowing work.

Simmons' pager went off. He glanced down, then looked around. I pointed to the phone on the desk, then leaned down to pat Zeke.

Simmons dialed, his back to me. "They done?" he asked. There was a pause as he listened. "Noon to two? How certain of it are you?" He was nodding. Leslie had died at the same time as Rose. "Bruises. From what?" Pause. "Any other marks?" Another pause. "Semicircles? What's that about?" He listened. "Really? Interesting. But she wasn't raped?" He listened. "Head injuries? From the fall?" He suddenly turned, realizing I was standing nearby. "Okay. Okay." He wrapped it up and put the phone down.

"So she wasn't raped?"

"No. She wasn't." I breathed, deeply relieved. Zeke nudged his shiny black head into my hand. Simmons was watching me. He fished a card out of his pocket and threw it on the desk. "That's it for tonight. If you think of anything, call me." The dogs were quiet, watching him. "And Miss Elliott, if I were you, I wouldn't go visiting friends at night on foot for a while. As a New Yorker, I should think you would know how to be more careful."

I heard his car engine turn over as I sunk into the chair at the desk. My head was completely clear now. I thought about Simmons' conversation. Leslie hadn't been raped. Bruises and marks had been found on her body, but she had died from head injuries from her fall.

I double-checked the front door lock and went upstairs, falling into the unmade bed. Thoughts receded, sleep hovered near. Suddenly, I was wide awake. How had Simmons known about the house at Round Bay? Mitch Gaylin, I thought. Simmons had had one busy night.

THIRTEEN

I AWOKE to birdsong. A deep calm saturated the morning, carried by sunbeams seeping through the stand of pines and the hundred-foot tulip trees that commanded the dense woods behind the cottage. The dogs frolicked as I sat on the steps with a second mug of coffee. Yesterday was still all too real. Sleep hadn't shaken the horror of finding Leslie's body. Somewhere in the woods, a twig snapped, making me jump.

I went inside and sat down at my desk, then flipped the pages of the calendar. Six more days. To decide to stay or leave. I dialed Lawrence Schoenfeld at home in New York.

"You must be one busy lady," he said. He had taken the call on a speaker phone. Our voices echoed. There was giggling in the background. What else he was doing? And with whom?

"Yes."

"I don't know what Peter Fox told you," he began. I told him, then tried to listen with an open mind. He talked about the agency, about a new account for breakfast cereal, or maybe it was lipstick or laundry detergent. No, I thought, it was cereal. He had said cereal. I was sure of it. I tried harder to listen.

"Of course," he was saying, "I can't make this offer formally until we get the account. But we will. In a couple of days, a week at the most." Behind the echoey voice, he had the confidence of all of his twenty-eight years. "So, Eve Elliott, have I got your attention?"

I wasn't sure he had. I swiveled back and forth in the office chair trying to remember Saturday mornings in New York. This guy wants me to sell kids cereal shaped like bicycles or sharks or something, I thought. For enough money to buy Ray Tilghman's house in an eye blink. The trouble was that with Schoenfeld's offer came the impossibility of spring mornings like this one. And no more damp, love-besotted dog trying to get in my lap.

"Zeke, down."

"What?"

"Nothing. That's a rather amazing offer," I said. "But..." There was someone speaking low in the background. I had a picture of a woman slowly, voraciously moving her hands over him.

"I gotta go," he said abruptly. "I'll let you know when we get the account. Be before the end of the month. We need to meet to discuss the details. Next week would be good. You set up an appointment with my secretary." He laughed then, a kind of embarrassed twitter. The phone went dead. Did I want to work for this guy, even for that sum of money?

I got dressed, found my shoes, and headed for Lillian's. Will's pickup was gone when I drove by his bungalow. My aunt was in her office, expertly sifting through piles of papers and trying to pretend this morning was like any other. The tension from last night still blanketed everything.

"How is Elizabeth?" I asked. "Or should I say how are the Hammetts, singly and collectively?"

"I talked with Hamm this morning. He's putting up a good front, all very hearty, although it's terribly strained. He stayed at a hotel last night," my aunt said. "Elizabeth, though, is a different story. I'm worried about her. She was up all night again, pacing back and forth. Then out to the deck and back inside."

"You hear anything more about the investigation?"

"Nope. I think the police are trying to be real low-key. In order not to get the serial killer stuff going." My aunt gazed out her office window, across the wide lawn that wove its way around tall trees, finally dipping down to the Magothy.

"Simmons stopped by at eleven o'clock last night," I said. "Had a bunch of questions about our losing the Round Bay sale to Rose Macklin." I sat back. "Mitch must have told him."

Lillian abruptly swiveled around. "I don't particularly like where that's going. Maybe I'll have a little talk with Weller." She reached for her crutches. One caught on the underside of the rosewood desk. She swore, really bad words, but not at all like the angry mood of last night.

The *Baltimore Sun* was open on the dining room table. Elizabeth was making a late brunch. She deposited a bowl of strawberries, then went back to the kitchen for toast and scrambled eggs and coffee.

Lillian pointed to a chair. I pulled it out for her, then filled my plate, and, like last night, ate ravenously. Elizabeth drank coffee. Lillian picked. Conversation didn't exist.

"Can you pick up your pictures from Dan Lloyd today and drop them at the cable station?" asked my aunt suddenly. "I want to make the deadline for this week."

I nodded, unable to think of anything else to do. A colored photo in the newspaper had grabbed Lillian's attention. "Oh, Lord, it's June Week. What with all the...uh, the...I forgot...And..." She put her folded napkin down on the tablecloth and turned to me. "Traffic will be awful."

"June Week? It's May. What is June Week?"

Lillian chuckled. "My mistake. It's the week of the Naval Academy graduation and the festivities that go with it. Actually it's now called 'Commissioning Week' since it's in May."

"How bad can the traffic be?" I asked.

"Bad beyond your wildest dreams. Annapolis will be crammed. Parents and friends. There are a lot of events the next few days, right up until graduation and then some."

Elizabeth had said nothing yet, concentrating apparently on Lillian's elaborate window treatments. She looked older than her years, I thought, her face puffy and sagging. Maybe it was the lack of sleep.

"Hamm and I got married right after graduation," she said. "In the Naval Academy Chapel. You remember, Lil? It was lovely, but..."

"But what?" my aunt asked.

Elizabeth shook off her lethargy. "Would I do it again? Get married to a mid, that is?" Lillian looked uncomfortable. She opened her mouth to say something, then decided against it. "No.

The answer is: I wouldn't. The Navy is a bad place for women. Any women. Even wives."

"Tailhook?" I asked.

She nodded. "Among other things. Did you know that several years ago a female midshipman was chained to a urinal and photographed by her fellow midshipmen?" My aunt was shaking her head. "Go ahead and shake your head, Lillian, you've never had to live in a culture that believes women are second-rate," said Elizabeth. "You and Max were equals, in business and in your marriage." Her voice held surprising rancor. "Did you know that Hamm still secretly believes that women shouldn't be allowed at the Academy? And for years, he did everything but forbid me to work?"

Lillian's dining room was suddenly suffocating. I yearned to be somewhere else. My aunt was lining up plates, saucers, and silverware with the edges of her placemat, but said nothing.

"I'm sorry I snapped, Lil. Yesterday..."

My aunt smiled faintly, then patted Elizabeth's hand.

"I guess...," I began, "I guess I'm kind of surprised you feel so strongly about this." Elizabeth nodded a little. "I thought that...that." I stopped, embarrassed.

"That I was a good Navy wife." She pushed away her half-eaten eggs. "Well I was, but those days are long gone."

Lillian reached across the table to take another slice of toast, dropped it on her plate, and leaned back in her chair. Elizabeth swept crumbs from the table. There was only the ticking of a wall clock. She let out a long sigh. "I was a good Navy wife. Hamm swept me off my feet. He was so handsome in his uniform. Still is. Handsome, that is. And it was all so romantic. I moved when he moved, waited for him when he was at sea, raised Brian and Mark, made a home for us." She appeared to be talking more to herself than to Lillian and me. "None of that is bad, of course."

The phone rang. I brought it to Lillian.

"Yes, Howard," she said, then listened for a very long time. "Oh, I'm so sorry. I know it's hard, but you have to believe that your luck will change. Firms will start hiring again. Just keep the temporary job at Office Giant." She listened some more. After another round of encouragement, she put the phone down, shaking her head.

"Howard Lucas. Poor man, he's lonely, I guess, but I swear he calls me about three times a day. Between him and Jack, I'm beginning to feel like a surrogate mother." My aunt stuck a bite of toast in her mouth, chewed, swallowed, then turned to me. "Howard's mother died a few months ago. In Florida, where she was living with her sister-in-law. He was devoted to her, though, God knows, she was a controlling type. And he's always been such a shy boy. It's not helping him in his job search." Lillian sighed deeply. "I think sometimes he doesn't quite know what to do with himself without Irene telling him. So he calls me."

"And the pastor?" I asked. "What's with him?"

"Oh, Jack. This is his first church. He wants to do the right thing, but he, too, needs a lot of direction." She shoved away her plate, the toast gone. "I am just getting old and grumpy, I guess."

"Only sometimes," I said, smiling. I studied my aunt. Half of Pines on Magothy leaned on Lillian, I thought. Myself included. I got up, cleared the dishes to the kitchen, and began to load the dishwasher. I could hear low voices in the dining room. Elizabeth apologized again.

"This murder or whatever it is, on top of the separation, has unhinged me, Lil," she was saying. "And I...I don't want to impose on you any longer." My aunt said nothing. I could almost see her shaking her head. "All I can think of is starting my new job and then finding a place to live."

"All in good time," said Lillian.

"I have something else to tell you." Elizabeth's voice was controlled now, almost shy. "I found out yesterday that I was accepted for a graduate program in psychology at College Park." Then she laughed, a happier sound than I had heard before. "It's a long haul. So you think I'm crazy to do this, Lil? At my age? Hamm does."

The dishwasher drowned out my aunt's answer. I suddenly had a mental picture of Hamm Hammett, his handsome face distorted, lunging up the steep steps toward me. Marian Beall's words echoed in my mind: "She should have left him years ago."

FOURTEEN

TRAFFIC IN ANNAPOLIS was just as bad as Lillian predicted, maybe worse. And my parking karma wasn't working. I found myself waiting at a traffic light in Church Circle for the fourth time. Historic St. Anne's Episcopal Church squatted serenely amid the swirling cars. I went around again, then took a right on Duke of Gloucester Street.

On a side street, a man was getting into his car. I zipped the BMW up behind him, leaving him just room to maneuver his car out of the space. He threw me a dirty look as he drove off, furious that his neighborhood had been invaded by outsiders. I wasn't one of them, I wanted to say. But it wasn't true, of course. In Annapolis, in Pines on Magothy, I was an outsider and I always would be.

Fifteen minutes later, I was ringing Dan Lloyd's bell for the second time in two days. The photographer was wearing the same brown polyester flowered shirt that he had worn yesterday. This time he wordlessly stepped back into the house and pointed to a card table set up in the middle of what passed for a living room. Brown manila envelopes, neatly layered and alphabetized, with black magic marker names showing at the top of each, were arranged carefully. He pulled mine out and handed it to me.

I opened it and gasped. The pictures were good. Very good. As good as any I had ever had taken by a pricey New York portrait photographer on West Fifteenth Street. Maybe better. And there were twenty prints of the very one I would have chosen.

"These are great." His curious grin appeared. I used a corner of the card table to write my check. "Dan Lloyd Studio?"

He nodded. As I ripped the check off, I saw an envelope with Rose Macklin printed at the top lying on the table. Quickly, my eyes moved upward to look for Leslie Ballard. It was there, too, along with envelopes for several other agents I knew from Gaylin Realty's Annapolis office.

I glanced up to find him watching me. "Mitch Gaylin's going to pay for them," he said. "Since they can't, can they? Too beautiful, that's my theory."

"What? What did you say?" I moved a little closer to him. "Just now, what did you say?"

Abruptly, the grin vanished. "You're asking me about my theory about who is killing real estate agents?"

"Yes."

"A killer who only goes for the pretty ones." He let this sink in for a few seconds. "The others can rest easy." We stood awkwardly. "You better watch your step, Miss," he said. I stared at him. "Remember that." It would, I thought, be hard to forget.

Once outside, I stood for a minute on the sidewalk, trying to make sense of what I'd just heard. Was Dan Lloyd right? Should I tell Simmons?

Everywhere around me there was traffic, both on foot and in cars. I began to walk. Beneath my shoes, I could feel the ruptured sidewalk, the bricks propelled skyward by tree roots grown big and aggressive. Here, as in much of Annapolis, the houses were tight on the street. Behind them lay hidden gardens. The noonday sun beat down. I shivered.

In the distance, I could see the Naval Academy Chapel's dome. I turned down Maryland Avenue, which radiated outward from State Circle, toward it. Small stores selling antiques, pizza, and children's books ran the length of the street. Across from me there was an Art Deco movie theater which hadn't seen audiences for a while. And somewhere a laundromat emanated warm dryer smells. Nearer the Academy, the historic Hammond Harwood and Chase Lloyd houses faced each other. Groups of tourists stood in the sun, shuffling their feet and trying to get their money's worth. Behind them a plump female guide in eighteenth-century dress, her mop cap pinned to her hair, flat basket over her arm, was spewing facts. It was a tour I'd never taken.

What had Dan Lloyd meant? Only half-conscious of where I was, I walked toward the chapel, nearly knocking down an elderly couple standing exhausted and confused on the sidewalk. Too many cars inched along the tight cobblestones toward the gate-house. Whole families streamed in the same direction, here to watch proudly as their sons and a few brave daughters become officers later in the week. A stiff young Marine at the entrance, secretly alert, pretended he wasn't interested in any of them. Or in me.

The Naval Academy Chapel was on my right. John Paul Jones lay entombed underneath. Or so I'd heard. Another time I'd go see, but not today. Instead, I headed down a diagonal walkway, dodging cars and foot traffic, past an obelisk-shaped monument on my left. Yesterday, I knew, the monument had been bathed in lard, or whatever the Navy used to grease its monuments. Then in some rite of Naval Academy passage, members of the plebe class swarmed to the top to hang a midshipman's cap. Scaling the Herndon Monument marked the end of the first year, Lillian had said. There had been a picture in her *Baltimore Sun*. I stopped for a moment and tried to imagine Hamm Hammett greasy and smelly and scrambling. It wasn't possible. Like so many military rituals, the whole thing seemed colorful, but impossibly dumb. Maybe you had to be there, I thought.

A limo crept along the curved path in front of the chapel and stopped. Across the street, standing near the bandstand, a small crowd had gathered. I joined them, turning to watch the chapel steps just as the door broke open and a photographer backed out, followed by guests and then the wedding party. The organ strained powerfully in the distance. From the left came a party of mid-shipmen in full dress, carrying swords, their feet moving in unison. Arranging themselves on the chapel steps in two rows, they crossed their swords as the bride and groom came blinking and laughing into the sunlight. The couple ducked under the swords, stopped amid the teasing to kiss, then descended to the limousine. The driver was waiting, his cigarette quickly stamped out. For a second he turned and I saw he was young and dark and impossibly handsome. He waited by the open door as the bride threw her bouquet to the fuchsia-clad gaggle of bridesmaids.

"You're looking rested and fresh this morning." I turned to

find Jack Hardwick at my shoulder. The pastor was looking me up and down. His hand went out to grasp and hold mine.

"Thank you." I pulled my hand away and pointed at the wedding scene across the street. "I thought that midshipmen had to graduate before they married," I said.

"Oh, they do. This fellow must have graduated last year. Or before that." We watched together as the bland bridegroom entered the limo after his bride. Then the pastor turned back to smile at me. He was younger than I had realized, probably not more than thirty. I wondered if the vapid smile ever left his face. His light brown hair was thinning and trimmed neatly over his tan knit sport shirt and jacket.

"It gets rather busy at the chapel this time of year," he said. "One wedding right after another. In fact, I'm here to meet with the couple I'm marrying tomorrow. The groom grew up in the Pines and his parents still go to church there." He lowered his voice, confidentially. "I have to confess it'll be my first time and I'm a little nervous." I decided Lillian had her hands full with this pastor. He glanced back at the scene that was dissolving in front of us. "There will be another pair married in a few minutes. Sometimes, they tell me, the limos get backed up."

"This is how Hamm and Elizabeth got married, isn't it?"

"Yes, so I've heard," he said. Then a kind of remorse spread over his face. "Oh my, I'm sorry, here I'm talking about weddings." He grabbed my hand again. "I want to know how you really are this morning. Yesterday must have been such a shock." I nodded. He smiled encouragingly, waiting for me to elaborate. I didn't. "And Lillian and poor Elizabeth?" he asked.

"Surviving, I guess."

"I'll try to visit later. Or maybe I can get Elizabeth to help me at the church." He sighed deeply, the smile flickering for a moment. "I'm way behind getting our Spring fund-raiser organized. I'm not very good about raising money, but without it we'd have to cancel our programs." He seemed largely to be talking to himself. "And Howard's van is on its last legs, and if it goes, our feeding program in Baltimore City goes. Then there's our summer camp. The kids will be out of school and..." He sighed again, this time with the air of a man deeply worried. He'd also apparently forgotten he was still grasping my hand. I tugged free and the movement brought him back to the moment. "Maybe if Elizabeth's occupied, she won't think so much about what happened yesterday."

"Pastor...uh?"

"Jack," he said, touching my shoulder with his other hand. I shivered. Geez, he did a lot of touching. It was beginning to make me squirrely.

"Okay. Jack. Does Elizabeth do a lot of work for the church?"

"Oh, yes. Well, not as much as she used to, but yes, a lot, considering she's been job hunting." He shifted onto a different foot. "Both Hamm and Elizabeth do."

"She does the newsletter, I know. What else?"

"Oh, just about everything, I suppose, at one time or another. I don't have a secretary and the Church's outreach programs demand a lot of attention. She has a key, so she just comes in and does what needs to be done. Whether or not I'm there." He stopped suddenly, moving his hand finally, but still smiling slightly. "Why do you ask?"

"When Detective Clarke questioned Elizabeth last night, you said she was at the church with you the whole time on Thursday. From ten-thirty in the morning until she left for the mall at four. Is that really true?"

His mouth tightened a little, which with the persistent little smile gave him a kind of wolfish look. "Well, ah..." He stopped, his hands not knowing what to do with themselves. I could still feel his touch. "Elizabeth was with me the whole time that I was there. Yes."

Something buzzed inside my head. "But you weren't there all afternoon?" His odd smile stayed put, but his pupils constricted a little. "That detective didn't ask the question right, did he?" After a moment, he shook his head. "You weren't there all day, were you?"

He sighed deeply. "No, I wasn't...only until about noon, but what...?"

"So you don't really know if Elizabeth was there all afternoon or not?"

He shook his head again. I thought of the hidden parking lot behind the church, the unseen back entrance to the basement office. How long had Elizabeth really worked at the church that day? And more interesting, why was the pastor trying to protect her?

"Now, Eve...I may call you Eve?" I nodded. "Eve. You can't think Elizabeth...?" He stopped, either at a loss for words or not willing to take the thought further. I wondered which. He had unconsciously put his hand back on my shoulder.

"No, I don't think anything. I was just asking."

"She had enough on her plate. I didn't want the police making things more difficult for her," he said. We stood in front of the chapel, each pondering the implications of what had just been said. The wedding party was gone, as was the crowd of onlookers. The pastor stirred slightly. "I guess it was a mistake. Not to tell the police the whole truth." He sighed. "So if she wasn't at the church, where was she?"

"I didn't say she wasn't there. You will have to ask her that." My words hung in the air between us.

"Will you tell the police?"

"If you or Elizabeth don't."

"Okay, I'll call Detective Clarke." Then he brightened, as if the subject were closed and no harm done. I wasn't so sure Simmons would feel that way. "Lillian said you are living in Ray Tilghman's house," he said. "Are you with us in the Pines permanently?"

I started. If I could answer that my life would be a lot easier. "Maybe, I don't know," I said.

"Well, I hope you decide to stay. Your aunt is a rock. But I know she likes having you nearby." He had turned to face me. "Well, I'm sure you know that," he said. "Say, why don't you join us some Sunday. Tomorrow morning maybe. We'd welcome a little new blood. And...and we could use another pair of hands." He grasped my hand in his again, almost as if he were afraid I'd leave if he didn't hang on. I tried to relax.

Church, I thought. How long had it been since I had been to

church? Or even thought about it? Jack Hardwick, I realized, was waiting for some response. Smiling and waiting and holding my hand.

"Thank you. Perhaps. Tell me about the church's programs. Your feeding program, as you call it. And the tutoring." Hamm, Lillian had said, tutored students who needed help. I shifted my weight, wondering what I had gotten myself in for. I watched as something came into the pastor's eyes, something faraway. His abiding smile increased in strength.

"It's the church's work. And very dear to my heart, I confess," he said. "There's just so much to be done. So many people who need help." He stopped, pretending to be embarrassed at going on like this. "Sorry. You asked me about our programs."

"How come you didn't go into missionary work?" I asked.

He was silent a moment, his smile dimming as he pondered some long-buried disappointment. Then he noticed I was still standing in front of him and shrugged. "The tutoring program is run by an ecumenical group of churches in the county. We match volunteers from the workplace with kids, many from disadvantaged or one-parent homes, who need individual help in school." He seemed suddenly tired. "Employers support it. This is my year as chairman. It's a little overwhelming, particularly since the Church in the Pines also runs the nutritional program."

The sun streamed through the trees, seeping under my shirt, warming my shoulders. Behind us, in the distance and across from the chapel, on a series of low plazas between two large buildings overlooking the Severn River, a strange scene was taking place. A young woman in a brilliant turquoise ball gown and a stiff midshipman in full regalia were having a formal picture taken. Their faces were a blur from this range. On either side of them were some sort of large round sculptures. A midshipman nearby shooed a couple of curious tourists from the scene. Jack Hardwick turned, following my glance.

"It's for the Ring Dance. The Academy's Junior Prom. The juniors become seniors and get their class rings. Each ring is blessed by waters from the seven seas." The pastor glanced at his watch, then turned his flat smile to me, lightly patting my shoulder.

"I'm afraid I'm going to be late. Maybe tomorrow morning then?"

I shivered again, feeling very crowded. "Maybe." I watched as he hurried off, thinking about the Ring Dance and the wedding we had just witnessed. Suddenly the Naval Academy, with its incomprehensible traditions, was stifling. I longed for New York with its familiar dirty streets and strangers I would never meet. For Joe Lister and the cynical, funny world of advertising. No weird rites of passage and no good works. No light brown smiling pastors who gave me the creeps. Expectations of a different kind: the kind I understood.

Walking quickly to the gate, I stopped to shake a stone from my shoe. When I looked up, I saw Hamm Hammett standing under a green awning in front of the entrance to the Officer's Club. He was deep in conversation with a familiar man dressed in a business suit. I'd seen the man on television, but I couldn't remember his name. But I knew who he was: a member of Maryland's Congressional delegation. He and Hamm made a little island, surrounded by a sea of aging military men, their summer uniforms heavy with decorations and their little paunches tightly controlled.

FIFTEEN

OBLIVIOUS TO THE MOBS of tourists roaming Annapolis' historic streets, I retraced my steps to the car. Jack Hardwick had lied to the police to give Elizabeth an alibi. Because, he said, he didn't want the police to make things more difficult for her. Whatever that meant. Was he trying to protect her from something more than a repeat visit from the police? If so, what? Was it actually possible he suspected that Elizabeth was somehow involved in Leslie's murder?

Preposterous, I thought. Impatiently, I unlocked the car, my mind spewing questions. Why would Elizabeth be involved? And what on earth did she have to do with Rose Macklin? Or the obscene phone calls? Fastening my seat belt, a more thorny question occurred to me. Was I under any obligation to inform Simmons of what Jack Hardwick had revealed? Did I become an accessory if I didn't? I knew the answer. But for now, I pushed the thought away.

It took a little time, but after years of practice in New York, I extricated myself easily from the small parking space. Relaxing into the BMW's leather, I rechecked my map and found a route that took me around some of the traffic and confusion of historic Annapolis. I had promised Lillian I'd drop off my photo at the production studio. The new ads were scheduled to begin this evening.

Ahead of me, a sign said Route 2. Called Ritchie Highway by anybody who had lived in Maryland for more than a week, it ran north from Annapolis to Baltimore. True, it was long and slow, with too many traffic lights. Its endless commercial stretches—with their omnipresent strip malls and car dealerships—were occasionally broken by a couple of miles of woods or a few clusters of older houses. It was only a matter of time, I thought, before they'd be paved over, too.

I turned on the radio. "The police in Anne Arundel County," said a bass voice, "have no leads and no suspects in the second killing of a real estate agent in the county within a week. In separate incidents, the victims were found dead near the properties they were showing. Police believe that an unknown assailant may be posing as a home buyer."

A shiver ran down my spine. "In a related story," said the announcer, "the police are also looking for someone making obscene phone calls to local real estate agents." There was a moment's silence, then some static. "Officer Linda Rice of the Anne Arundel County Police Department is here to bring us up to date about their investigations. Good afternoon, Officer Rice." A no-nonsense female voice melted the airwaves. "Officer, do we have a serial killer on our hands?"

"The Anne Arundel County Police Department isn't prepared to characterize these crimes as serial murders," she said. "And we would like to emphasize that the public should not panic or jump to conclusions. We are investigating other explanations."

"Such as?"

"Possible robbery."

"What about a copycat killer? A second killer, who, for reasons of his own, is mimicking the first murderer?"

"It's possible." She didn't sound convinced.

"And the obscene calls?" The policewoman launched into an explanation indistinguishable from what Simmons had said at the self-defense workshop. Which meant, I thought, that the police have exactly the same number of leads that they had two days ago: none.

"Officer," said the announcer, "it's hard to ignore the fact that first a number of female real estate agents receive these obscene calls, then a few weeks later, two of them are dead. Are the crimes related?"

"We have no hard evidence of that," she said. "We are asking, however, that all women in the county, not just those in the real estate industry, take extreme precautions. They should not go out

alone at night or walk in isolated areas. If you must return late
from work, have a friend meet you.''

"But, Officer, both murders were committed during daylight?
Were they not?''

There was a short silence, then an uncomfortable laugh. "That's
true, and women *should* take precautions at all times," she said,
"but cover of darkness is traditionally what criminals use." She
gave canned answers to a few more questions, saying nothing we
didn't already know, then recited a hot-line number for tips, anonymous and otherwise.

"You have been listening to Officer Linda Rice of the Anne
Arundel County Police," said the announcer. "To recap, they are
not yet characterizing the murders of two real estate agents as
serial killings, but they are suggesting using extreme caution until
the crimes are solved." The announcer repeated the phone number, gave the dollar amount of the reward being offered, and then
did the news. The lead story was about an elderly woman found
barely alive in her home in Montgomery County, north of Washington, beaten almost to death by her grandson. I took a deep
breath and flipped the dial to WBJC in Baltimore. Mozart streamed
from the car speakers.

The clock on the dash said after four. This stretch of Ritchie
Highway ran mostly to superstores, what the business community
had labeled category killers: huge square boxes selling pet food,
computers and office products, and everything you could possibly
need to renovate your house and garden. I hated them. They were
big and impersonal and here to stay.

Ahead of me on the right, past the parking lots and monstrous
stores, I now noticed a small frame house set back in a heavy
clump of trees. I checked the address Lillian had given me, turned
off the highway, and parked. There was an old van parked nearby.
The first floor housed a mom-and-pop video store. In fact, it
looked like mom and pop might just live upstairs.

The front windows were filled with movie posters exploding
with Technicolor carnage. On the door, in uneven paste-on letters,
a small sign said Pinkston Productions. Opening the door, I found
I was just in time to see something blown out of the water on the

largest television screen I'd ever seen. Comandos, armed with assault weapons and sweating heroically, poured from the screen. The noise was deafening.

"Hello? Anyone here?" Behind the desk, almost hidden in an big armchair, her back to the door, sat an old woman. She cringed as the commandos rushed out from the screen. It took me a few minutes to make her realize that the real world was also trying to invade her life. "Hello, I just want to leave this for..."

"Pinky? That you?" She turned. "Oh, thought you were Pinky."

"Can you turn that down?"

She had a sweet, rubbery face. Her yellowish hair was permed tightly, and she wore a housedress violently patterned with peonies. Wordlessly, she handed me the remote. I muted the film. We both breathed a sigh of relief.

"God, oh, my, that's better. I couldn't see those tiny little buttons and I didn't want to mess Pinky's movie up." Her voice was way too loud, as if she could no longer adjust it. Behind her the commandos were advancing. "Thought you were Pinky," she said again. "He's my grandson. I'm just mindin' the store for him. He said he'll be right back."

I held out a manila envelope. "Can I leave this for him?"

"Guess so. Though I don't know nuthin' about it." She took the envelope from me, then examined the Weber Realty logo in great detail.

"You a real estate agent?" I nodded. "You heard about that pervert making calls to real estate agents?"

I nodded. She motioned me closer. I leaned over the counter. "There's one of them perverts in there now," she whispered. She flicked her head to the back of the store, in the direction of two swinging, louvered doors. Nearby, a large, hand-lettered sign read: No Admission Under 18. I could see pant legs and shoes moving beneath the door. I wondered if the customer were waiting for Pinky to return to check out his stuff.

The woman motioned me closer again. "Filthy sex stuff. I'm eighty-six years old and I never seen nuthin' like it. Every sick, damn thing you can think of. People makin' people do awful,

awful disgusting things. Turns my stomach.'' She was growing more and more agitated. She glanced again with disgust at the pant legs under the double doors. I began to wonder if I should leave her alone with whomever they belonged to.

''When's Pinky coming back?'' I asked.

''Dunno.'' She shrugged. ''Police wanna find a pervert, they don't have to look far.'' She pointed to the back again. ''You look like a nice girl,'' she said suddenly. ''You gotten any a those dirty calls?'' I shook my head. The murder of two real estate agents apparently hadn't made even a blip on her screen, I thought, but the obscene calls loomed large. Maybe because of what was in the back room. ''You know what Pinky says?''

''No.''

''Pinky says that it's some lonely loser who's doing it. Some guy...'' She leaned closer, but her voice was unnaturally loud. ''...who couldn't get it up with a crane. That's what Pinky says.''

I tried unsuccessfully to suppress the mental picture of Dan Lloyd that flashed across my brain. Pinky's grandmother was still talking. After a few more minutes of telling me in excruciating detail how the world was going to hell in a handbasket, she grew quiet, exhausted with the effort. Sinking back into her chair, she waved me off, and prepared to wait for Pinky to return. As I left, she was watching in eerie silence as the commandos stormed a skyscraper.

Settling behind the wheel, I wondered again if I should leave. I also wondered just what sort of videos Pinky rented. His grandmother had certainly described an over-the-edge, visual catalog of sexual sickness. Videos that had more to do with power and humiliation than with sex. I shivered.

A new Ford Escort pulled up beside the BMW, and a stocky young man, probably not even thirty, got out and walked to the house without glancing in my direction. The side of the car said Pinkston Productions. Pinky himself, I thought. I headed for home.

THE PINES' MAIN DRAG, Lido Beach Road, was empty. An old green Chevy, long in the tail and rusty, turned out of the Lido Beach Inn's parking lot in front of me. It had climbed Mount

Washington, according to a bumper sticker. The radio announcer's deep voice came back to me. The police had no leads or suspects. The Chevy turned left into a side street. Its Mount Washington climbing days were clearly over. I speeded up.

Will's truck was parked in front of his cabin. I knocked on his door, then waited. How far away last night was. And how sunlight changed the way the world looked. All traces of standing water and the heady ozone were gone. The door opened.

"Hi," Will said. Piano, this time the precise work of Bill Evans, oozed out around him, filling the clearing.

"Hi."

We stood looking at one another for a few seconds, both of us acutely aware of the silence. Last night's drama was also gone. What was left, I thought, were two people who had grown apart and didn't understand why. Two people getting ready to let go but not quite there yet. So instead we were going through the silent, miserable motions of pretending things were more or less okay. Knowing full well that they weren't.

"Do you want to come in?"

"No. I just wanted to tell you that when I left here last night I found an Anne Arundel County detective waiting for me at Ray's house." I took a deep breath. "He may have been wandering around while he waited for me to go home. I don't know."

There was silence. Somewhere high in the trees a thrush began its distinctive song. Will looked at the ground, at the pine needles slick and brown beneath my feet. "I'll get rid of the grass," he said quietly. "I'm using it to put off what I don't want to deal with. And putting both of us in jeopardy. I don't want to do that."

I nodded. My heart expanded with sadness at his tone. I forced my mind to hold steady. He looked at me now, his eyes dark navy in the late afternoon light. Then a luminous smile overtook his face. "Too bad really," he said. "It was really good stuff. And you thought so, too. You can't tell me otherwise."

We stood for another minute without moving. From the direction of Weller's Creek came the hiccup of a motorboat. Then Will took my arm and pulled me gently into the house. I shivered a little, not resisting. He led me to the bathroom, let go of my arm, and opened the medicine cabinet.

"We might as well have a little ceremony, I guess. Now watch." He opened a dark brown plastic pill bottle, dumped its contents unceremoniously into the toilet, and flushed. Then looked back at me. "So that's that."

I laughed, an empty effort, suddenly pained to find that I wasn't sure I wanted him to move on. "Where did you get the grass?" I asked, trying to keep my voice noncommittal.

"I found some plants in a garden I was doing. I took a few leaves and flowers."

"And left the plants?"

"Yes."

"Whose garden was it?"

"No. That I won't tell you."

We were back in his small plant-filled kitchen. The piano seeped into my consciousness again, expanding beneath my skin. Jazz piano. It was one of Will's loves. Odd, I had always thought, for someone twenty-five. It didn't have the same attraction for me. The riffs went on too long, turning in on themselves, widening and then growing narrow again. It created a tightness in my chest as I waited for resolution. Finish, I thought as I listened, just finish.

I contemplated the tiny seedlings in their peat moss containers and thought about last night. I needed to get out of here, to go home where I belonged to myself. And to the dogs and to old Ray Tilghman's ghost. Where the music had some resolution.

"I'm going," I said. Will breathed quietly, his arms at his sides, blue eyes flat now and unreadable.

A wave of gloom hit me hard as soon as I got into the car. Like a wall of heat when you go outside from an air-conditioned room on a July day. July 23. The thought was overpowering for a minute, resonant, grim. July 23 would come and go and what would I have? Ben's BMW and best wishes. A career I was lousy at, and if I wasn't careful, no dogs and no cottage snuggled in the pine grove on Weller's Creek. I turned on the ignition. Who the hell was trying to buy it right out from under me anyway? Trying to take the dogs? And who was killing real estate agents?

SIXTEEN

AN HOUR LATER, I pulled into the parking lot of a local Greek diner. Everything was oversized, from the menu to the food to the lines of people waiting for tables. Everything but the host, who could not have been thinner. "Smoking or non?" he asked. I pointed to the counter. Elderly couples waiting in line for their Saturday dinner watched with envy as I was led away. He handed me a menu and I sat down on a low padded stool next to the oversized desserts revolving under glass. They made my teeth ache. I was definitely ready for more than pastry. Or even a sandwich or a bowl of cereal. Elizabeth's eggs and toast seemed days ago.

I hadn't bothered to bring a book. I'd tried reading already, and found myself going over and over the same paragraph. Instead, I'd found myself mousing about the house, absentmindedly picking things up and putting them down. My mind whirred with questions and possibilities. Should I buy Ray Tilghman's property? Or go back to New York and Lawrence Schoenfeld? But then, where did that leave Lillian? I couldn't very well just up and desert her. Will's face surfaced from time to time, making me depressed all over again. I decided to think about him later. Same for Lawrence Schoenfeld and his damn job. But Weller and the anonymous buyer? I couldn't put that off much longer.

After tossing the book aside, I had tried to watch television. A lot of golf, complete with whispery announcer, and reruns of some ditsy sitcom were about it. I clicked it off and sat staring at the dogs. The radio announcer's voice came back to me: "The police in Anne Arundel County have no leads and no suspects in the second killing of a real estate agent in the county within a week.... And in a related story..." Unable to stand the noise in my head any longer, I had changed my clothes and driven to the diner.

"Hello." Scott Lisle sat down on the next stool. The young cop looked freshly showered, his blond crew cut bristly and getting a little long. His radio was pinned to the shoulder of a clean, short-sleeved white shirt. It made me feel dingy. I kicked myself for forgetting to ask Will when he planned to finish my bathroom.

A counterman put coffee and a red plastic tumbler of water in front of him without being asked. He took a gulp of the coffee, jumping a little when it scalded his mouth. I gave the waiter my order for spinach pie and Greek salad while Scott composed himself.

"Whoa, burned myself." He gingerly felt his upper lip. "You eating dinner by yourself?"

"Yes. Sometimes I do."

"Oh. Don't like to cook, huh?" A woman enjoying her dinner alone clearly wasn't within his range of experience. "How are you holding up after Thursday?" he asked.

"Okay, I guess. Well, not completely."

"Yeah. It's terrible to see stuff like that. Gives people post-traumatic stress disorder. And then there are the questions and all." He tried again with the coffee, sipping more cautiously. "Simmons is a tough cookie."

"Have you worked with him before?"

"Nope. He's pretty new to the county. Worked homicide in New York. The Bronx, I think. I heard he had a heart attack and wanted a less stressful job, so he moved down here to the safe suburbs." Scott Lisle peered sideways at me to make sure I appreciated his irony. "He's looking to make his mark in the department, I guess. Not making too many friends doing it." He turned to look at me directly. "I know you live alone," he said. "You need to be real careful until this thing is solved. Maybe you could stay with your aunt for a while?"

Instead of being grateful for his concern, I felt a flash of irritation. Why was it, I wondered, that every man I came in contact with felt an obligation—no, make that a right—to comment on my living arrangements?

"I'll be fine." He shrugged. About Will's age, he was fiddling with the cop junk around his waist. It didn't fit all that well when he was sitting down. Maybe, I thought, I could weasel some information out of him. Something more than the party line that Officer Rice had offered. After his comment about living alone, I wasn't even going to feel guilty about it.

"Scott," I began, then realized that I'd called him by his first name. Maybe I'd insulted him. "Sorry," I said. "I didn't mean to call you by your first name. I know you're on duty. It just sort of came out of my mouth."

That made him laugh. "It's okay. Just don't try it with Simmons. He'd probably take you in for insulting a police officer."

Whoa. Simmons really had made his list. I wasn't all that surprised, given the detective's fondness for sarcasm. "Scott," I began again, "do the police really believe two real estate agents were killed because someone wanted to rob them of their money and credit cards?" I pretended to think for a second. "I mean, it just seems like there have to be easier ways." When it came to fishing expeditions, I thought, Joyce Nichols and Marian Beall had nothing on me.

"I know what you mean." He sipped coffee carefully. "We're watching the ATMs, of course, but..." He shook his head when the counterman held out a menu.

"I just keep thinking about finding Leslie Ballard," I said, trying to sound innocent. "She wasn't struck in the head by something the way Rose Macklin was. I mean, I saw her face with its bruises and marks on one side, but..." The scene at the Hammett pool flew to the front of my mind, but under the diner's bright lights it didn't have the emotional impact it had when I was alone. "I think she must have died from hitting her head. And I know that she wasn't raped."

My sentence hung in the air. The cop looked straight ahead. "No, not raped," he said, finally.

"But there must have been something else." I tried to appear to be thinking out loud. "Something else that the medical examiner found when he did the autopsy." I, too, stared ahead, mesmerized as a waitress made a fresh pot of coffee.

"They found fresh semen," he said, his voice low.

"Semen. They found fresh semen?"

"You didn't hear that from me," he said. Out of the corner of my eye, I could see him still sipping his coffee.

"Scott, was Leslie Ballard married?"

He swallowed the last of his coffee, putting his hand over his cup when the waiter offered more, then swiveled around to look at me.

"Divorced. She has a kid who is fifteen or sixteen. Basically a good kid, I think, but he got in some trouble a year ago. Though he seems to have straightened out. He's doing better in school and all. But now who knows."

"Isn't there any family?" I asked.

"The husband ran out on her years ago," he said, "before the kid was born. She apparently had no contact with him. There are no grandparents, no aunts, or uncles. The kid's staying with another family from their church." The cop pulled his flashlight out of the way of an elderly couple hurrying to their seats. "Which is a whole lot better than what the social services people could probably do for him. Still, it's not great," he said. "I feel sorry for him."

He seemed genuinely concerned. "There's nothing you can do," I said, wondering if it sounded as hollow to him as to me.

He spun the empty red plastic tumbler between his fingers. "You know what the kid told me?" I shook my head. "He's planning to go to the Naval Academy." Scott Lisle looked at me and shook his head sadly. "Good luck, with his academic record and all. My brother graduated from the Academy, so I know something about it. I'd say his chances are slim to none. Particularly after all the problems the Academy's had lately."

"What kind of trouble was he in?"

"Joyriding with a friend."

"In a stolen car?"

"Of course, and now with his mother dead..."

The unfinished thought appeared to depress him. He got up, eyeing the sign labeled Rest Rooms. An arrow pointed down. He threw some money down on the counter and leaned over to me. "Somebody wanted those real estate agents out of the way," he said under his breath. "Someone that they knew. That's my opinion." Then pretending he hadn't said it, he headed downstairs.

The waiter settled two enormous plates down in front of me, one hot and one cold, more food than I would need for two days. I dug into the salad first, waiting for the spanakopita to cool.

My mind was reeling. Scott Lisle believed that the killer knew his victims. I thought about what I knew. Neither woman had been raped, but Leslie Ballard had made love the morning of her death. Had her lover killed her? So what was the connection between the two murders? I mentally checked off similarities: both victims had worked for Gaylin Realty, both were killed showing houses, both were killed in the daytime, both were attractive, if in quite different ways. That made me shudder as I remembered Dan Lloyd's theory.

Finishing my salad, I attacked the spanakopita. Rose and Leslie had died in different ways—Rose from something that hit her, Leslie from hitting her head when she fell or was pushed into the empty pool. Rose was successful. Leslie had told me she was struggling. Rose was unmarried. Leslie was divorced with a teenage son. Fresh semen had been found in Leslie's body. And Rose? I didn't know. Joyce Nichols' description of Rose's activities returned to me.

But if the obscene caller was somehow involved...? I tried to think about that and found my brain exploding. There were just too many possibilities. Too many unknowns. No wonder Simmons was stumped. I finished about half of the spinach pie, then pushed it away. If Scott Lisle were to be believed, the police were largely waiting, hoping someone would call in a tip.

"You didn't enjoy it?" asked the counterman, pointing to the spanakopita.

"No, no, I liked it a lot. It was just too much."

He gave me an understanding smile and a nod. "Doggie bag," he said. I smiled back.

Under the bright diner lights, the Saturday-night noise of people relaxing and eating had risen to a deafening level. It was comforting here, safe. I could push away the mental pictures. There was no nightmare specter, its mouth red and wailing, face bruised and shredded by black marks, savage teeth gleaming in the dark.

I shuddered. Leslie's murder felt personal somehow. I had to find a way to put it to rest. And maybe the way to do that was to see what I could find out. Like whom had she made love with that morning.

I thanked the counterman for the Styrofoam carton he handed me, left a generous tip, paid the cashier, and said good-bye to the harassed host. Although the line at the front door had grown longer and more impatient, he touched my shoulder and smiled, told me to be sure to come again soon. I told him I would.

Several cars were waiting for my parking space. It was all of seven o'clock. I headed up Ritchie Highway to Marley Station Mall.

SEVENTEEN

THE MALL made me feel strange, a woman alone with nowhere to be on a Saturday night. It was a new feeling. I had come only with the vague thought of picking up a few household items to make Ray Tilghman's cottage a little less spartan. Or maybe as a way to avoid going home just yet.

I wove my way up and down the wide corridors between the stores, dodging teenagers and baby strollers, window shopping mostly, occasionally going inside to examine something that caught my eye. Nothing pleased me enough to make an effort to buy it.

Some large department store was directly in front of me. Any other spring in New York, I would have already made a few trips to my favorite shops. Madison Avenue expected nothing less of its women executives than they look ready to anchor the evening news. Things had certainly changed, I thought. Working at Weber Realty, I could wear the same thing two weeks in a row, for all the clients cared. Or knew. Of course, Lillian noticed, but she had the good sense to keep her opinions to herself.

I walked into the store and found myself shuffling between over-crowded racks, trying to get my bearings. Like all department stores, this one arranged its clothes by age and size and economic status. Lost in a department filled with jeans and cropped tops, deafening teen music struck me between the eyes. You could, I thought, be blind and still know you were in the wrong department.

I trolled up and down the rows of merchandise. I decided it was another identity crisis. I no longer knew what to wear. Taking a deep breath, I plunged in between the tight racks. A short green jacket, slapped impatiently back on a rack by an uninterested buyer, fell off as I brushed by.

"May I help you?" I turned to find an excruciatingly thin woman dressed in a pink suit. The skirt was far too long and narrow for her weight. The requisite assistant manager name tag graced her lapel. "You seemed to be kind of lost, so I thought I'd ask. Anything I can help you find?"

I picked up the green jacket and handed it to her. "Oh, yes. I'm looking for something to wear this summer, uh, linen maybe." This wasn't working, I thought. I didn't have a clue what I wanted to wear. "I'm sorry I can't be more specific. It's one of those I'll-know-it-when-I-see-it things!"

She looked me up and down, then pointed. "Try the Better Department. Just around the corner from those silk dresses, the ones with the bow ties and pleated skirts over there."

I left her holding the jacket, trying to figure out where it had come from. The Better Department. Better than what? Rack after rack of silk dresses engulfed me, the kind of dresses which attract the fat and forty crowd. A bored salesgirl, her gold-colored hoop earrings dragging along her shoulders, was standing motionless behind a cash register, ignoring the heap of crumpled skirts and dresses on the counter, her ear plastered to a phone.

"Excuse me. Where is the Better Department?" She turned and pointed.

"Well, surprise. I didn't expect to find you here." I turned to find Elizabeth standing beside me. In her arms was a silky blue dress, patterned with small pictures of musical instruments: trumpets and French horns and violins. "Not in this department, I shouldn't think." She glanced down at my pants-clad legs.

The salesgirl hung up and Elizabeth wordlessly handed her the dress and a credit card, then turned back to me.

"I was just sort of looking..." I stopped. "Elizabeth, I learned something...can we talk somewhere?" She nodded. "When you get done here. I'll wait over there." I pointed to two armchairs at the outer edges of the Career Department. Miraculously, neither one was occupied by an exhausted man. I sat down. Five minutes later Elizabeth collapsed next to me, pulling her plastic dress bag onto her lap.

I couldn't think of any way to be diplomatic about what I had to say, so I took a deep breath and plunged ahead. "Elizabeth, I ran into Jack Hardwick earlier today at the Naval Academy. He admitted that he actually left the church about noon Thursday. Why did you agree with him when he told the detective that you were together for the rest of the afternoon?"

She pushed the long dress bag onto the table between the chairs, shoving aside a blouse displayed on a padded torso. It fell to the floor with a clatter. Then she began to cry. I searched my handbag for a package of tissues, thrusting it in her direction. She extracted a couple, her face congested and growing blotchy.

"Oh God, Eve," she said. "What a mess. You're right. I didn't tell the police the complete truth. It just sort of...sort of happened. I was in shock over Leslie Ballard's murder. And then Jack sort of jumped in and said I was with him. It was just easier." She blew her nose, then used the sodden tissues to pat dry her inflamed eyes. "Oh, I forgot you were there. You saw how it happened. And the detective appeared to believe it. And it was easier than...than..."

The assistant manager appeared out of nowhere behind us, smiling brightly until she saw Elizabeth's face. I handed her the blouse from the floor. It was still on its padded display hanger. She grabbed it and ran.

I turned back to Elizabeth. "Than what?" The woman in front of me was now crying quietly and steadily. "Where were you that afternoon, Elizabeth? If you weren't at the church?"

She began to cry harder now, great whooping sobs. I waited. A couple of shoppers tried to stare without being obvious. They moved on when I stared back.

"I'm sorry, Eve. Every time I turn around, I'm crying like a baby. It's all such a mess. And I'm so afraid."

"Afraid? Of what?"

"Change, I guess. My marriage is over." Her sobbing, which had been subsiding a little, renewed itself. "Hamm and I have been fighting for the last year. All the time. The more I became my own person, the more he hated it. We also fought about feminism, about gays and women in the military... You name it, we fought about it." She blew her nose. "And it's not just his fault.

As long as I stayed with him, I was sort of agreeing to be treated like a dishrag.''

I squelched my urge to ask why she had stayed with him as long as she had. I already knew why. My own marriage had taken a while to come unglued while friends stood by wondering why I didn't just kill off this thing that was causing me so much pain. I had a flash of the night I first knew for sure that Ben was having an affair. I had accidentally opened his American Express bill, thinking it was mine. On it had been a history of his love life for the last month: expensive gifts, dinners for two, a weekend at a country inn when I was away on business. Oddly, the knowledge had made me not enraged but helpless. There had been denial, then a desire to patch things up. Only later had fury taken over. So much fury I'd thought I'd burst.

I looked over at Elizabeth. The wadded tissues in her hand were a tight, wet, useless ball. Unlike me, she'd been the one to leave, moving in with Lillian. She cleared her throat, then looked at me.

"Eve, Hamm has been having an affair. One of many over the years. Only he's gotten more brazen about it recently." The quaver in her voice made me sorry for her. "This one's been going on for the last few months." She finally noticed the soaked tissues in her hand and discarded them on the table. "I asked him to go for counseling with me, but he refused and forbade me to go. Said he didn't want our dirty laundry made public. That was the last straw. So to answer your question about where I was, I went to see a divorce lawyer." She leaned back, exhausted from her confession.

"Oh."

"Hamm isn't going to change," she said. "Partly it's the military influence. That's always been there, as long as I've known him. I used to buy into it. But I began to change when my kids left for college. And now I'm finishing my undergraduate degree and starting a new job in a couple of weeks. And I'm going to grad school." She straightened her shoulders a little.

"Elizabeth, when *did* you leave the church Thursday?"

"Just after Jack left, around noon. I drove to Greenbelt. That's east of Washington, a little less than an hour from here. I had a one o'clock appointment with an attorney named William Card.

On the way home I stopped at a fast food place for a late lunch and then came here to the mall, just as I said.''

"Where did Jack go?"

"The parsonage, next door, I guess. He told me he planned to work at home."

"Did he know you weren't at the church?"

"He would have if he had looked out the window. You can see the parking lot from his house."

"But it's possible that he didn't know if you were there or not? It's possible that he didn't go home?"

"It's possible. If he went somewhere..." Elizabeth glanced at me suspiciously. "You don't think Jack had something to do...? I mean he's kind of annoying sometimes but..."

"I don't think anything. I just keep wondering why he said that."

Elizabeth shrugged, then opened her purse, took out pressed powder and a mirror, and tried to fix her appearance. Her face, especially around her eyes and nose, was still swollen, but her spirits seemed to be recovering.

"Elizabeth, how did you find out that Hamm was having an affair?" I asked. "No, wait, that's none of my business. Forget I asked."

"It sort of helps me to talk about it," she said. "There were just the usual signs. Like his working late and credit card slips. Mostly it was intuition." She blew her nose noisily. "Last winter I began to feel a sort of excitement from him. Nothing I can explain if you don't know," she said. "It always happened when he was seeing someone new."

"And then?"

"Friends of mine saw him with a woman. He was supposed to be at some sort of professional retreat on the Eastern Shore for the weekend. Instead he was in Annapolis that Friday evening, listening to Charlie Byrd at the Maryland Inn. My friends overheard him introduce her to another couple they ran into. That's how I know who it is. Then they saw the two of them head upstairs." She put the mirror away. I was beginning to notice a new resolve, a kind of toughness coming from her. "Amazing, isn't it," she said, "that he can flaunt his affairs like this and still think that I'll return home. Just to keep up appearances."

The other shoppers were ignoring us now, pawing with enthusiasm through the crowded racks, yanking out possibilities, holding them up and studying them, then stuffing the rejects back wherever they could be stuffed. Many landed on the floor between racks. The skinny assistant manager was going to have some straightening to do before she left tonight.

"Elizabeth, you said something earlier." She was completely calm now, listening with interest. "You said you were afraid. Those are odd words. Are you afraid of something more than the changes in your life?" I asked.

She took a deep breath before she answered. "I'm afraid that Hamm knows more than he is telling about the...about Leslie Ballard's death."

"You do? Why?"

"Because." She stopped momentarily, fiddled with the plastic garment bag beside her. "Because...because the woman he was with in Annapolis was...It was...her."

Leslie Ballard and Hamm Hammett.

Neither of us said anything for long minutes, nor looked at each other. We sat in Career Dresses in our matching overstuffed floral chairs. It was comfortable, facing outward into the store. To my right the escalators made their round-trip journeys, up and down. There came a horsey laugh from the direction of the Better Department.

"Eve?" I tried to focus. Elizabeth was leaning toward me. "Eve, can you help me find out what happened? I'm so afraid that Hamm is somehow involved with this whole mess." Her voice was composed now, even. "I'm furious with him, but I know he couldn't kill anyone. But if the cops find out he was sleeping with her, they will try somehow to connect her death with him. Please help me find out."

Yes, I thought, Simmons would certainly be interested. With fresh semen in Leslie's body, there was little chance he would overlook the obvious.

EIGHTEEN

THE WOODS near Weller's Creek were silent in the dark. But the honeysuckle seemed to grow more intense at night, filling the air like trashy perfume. I let the dogs out of the house, then sat down on the front steps to wait for them.

The surprise of finding out that Leslie and Hamm were lovers had worn off. What was left were a lot of questions. Why would Leslie, young and beautiful and smart, get involved with a married man with the sensibilities of the Joint Chiefs? And what did Hamm know about her death, if anything?

Zeke raced in my direction, planting his black head in my lap momentarily, grabbing the opportunity to drag a long pink tongue over my nose and mouth. Then he discovered the Styrofoam box holding the leftover spanakopita. "Not for you," I said. Sad brown eyes looked at me. Resigned, he snuffled the box one more time, then raced off. I wiped the dog kiss off my face.

Leslie and Hamm. There must have been nearly twenty years difference in age. So what? Besides, who was I to make judgments? Will was almost fifteen years... Oh, put a sock in it, I told myself. Weary, sick of questions I had no answers for, I whistled the dogs into the house.

Across the room, the infernal answering machine blinked red. Damn. Just one evening, I wanted to be outside the reach of telephones and voice mail and pagers. Pagers, in particular, took over your life. They followed you not just into meetings, but into the bathroom as well. Mitch Gaylin probably showered with his. Maybe, I thought, I wouldn't resent mine so much if someone other than Lillian needed me a little more often.

Pushing the button on the machine, I listened to a mortgage broker give me all the many reasons why he couldn't work with the client I'd referred. Call him back and he'd explain in more detail. I dutifully wrote down the number, wondering if I wanted more detail.

Then came a male voice, low and monotonous, a voice I didn't recognize. "I've been watching you. I know where you live," it said. A chill flowed over my shoulders. "I know what you do and who you do it with." I stood still, my heart clubbing the inside of my chest as an appalling blizzard of sexual pathology echoed across the empty room. Then the line went dead. Zeke whined. The machine clicked off. I stood quietly, pen useless in my hand, as the tape automatically rewound.

Shit. Someone *was* out there. Watching me and Will make love. Maybe watching even as I had sat on the front step. Simmons and Scott Lisle and Will had been right. Zeke rubbed against me. Lance stood nearby, on alert. Forcing myself to get up, I checked the doors and closed the downstairs windows. Then, my fear replaced by growing anger, I yanked the tape from the machine. The stupid creep had gone too far this time, leaving a message. Like he wanted to get caught. So I'd help him along, I thought. Maybe the cops could even do some sort of voiceprint. I reached over to pick up the receiver. The phone rang under my hand.

Then again. Then a third time. I picked up the receiver and slammed it down, then sat down at the desk, my heart hammering hard all over again. Simmons' card lay where he'd dropped it. I fiddled with it, forcing myself to think about what the tape had said. "I know where you live." Where was the nearest pay phone? Something scuttled across the roof, whipping up my pulse again. No. Don't give in to it. Stay calm. Don't panic. That's what he wants you to do. Think, I told myself again. The nearest pay phone had to be at least a half mile away, near an abandoned gas station at the outskirts of town. He wasn't outside, couldn't be. Zeke pushed his way into my lap. The phone rang. I pushed the dog away, and again I slammed the receiver into its cradle.

I dialed 911. A canned voice told me to hang up and try again. Damn, I'd misdialed. Putting down the receiver for a third time, I turned to see the lights of a car sweep across the darkened porch, illuminating first one side, then rounding the corner to the other. Lance and Zeke were barking hard, Zeke's front feet pummeling the front door. A car door slammed. Opening the desk drawer, my hands wrapped around a metal ruler.

"Eve?" I didn't recognize the voice. "Eve, it's Hamm. Hamm Hammett."

I could feel crazy, out-of-control rage filter through me, rage born of misplaced fear. I took a deep breath. Zeke growled, deep in his throat. My heart rate began to slow.

I went to the screen door, keeping the dogs behind me. Hamm was standing on my steps. He looked awful, I thought, the circles under his eyes deep and shadowy in the dim light. "I'm sorry if I scared you. I tried to call a few times from my car but something's wrong with your phone machine. It kept hanging up on me," he said. "I need to talk. May I come in?" I didn't answer, but he stood his ground, not moving.

Hamm and Leslie Ballard. It still didn't make sense. Could Elizabeth be wrong about them? But she had said that there were credit card slips, too.

"I won't take much of your time," he said. "It's about Elizabeth."

"Elizabeth?" I suddenly heard again that terrible low voice. He knew where I lived, he had said.

"Please, it's important."

I opened the door, the dogs behind me. I still had the ruler in my hand. Hamm saw them, too, and looked at me. Then, overcome with misery or exhaustion or both, he collapsed into a wicker chair. Light from the living room and the outside flood diffused into a glow on the porch. Lancelot dropped into a far corner, relaxed but vigilant. "Zeke, come." The dog wedged himself beneath my legs.

"I'm really sorry," he began again.

I nodded. Curiosity had replaced my rage. "Why are you here? What about Elizabeth?"

He relaxed a little. "I'm worried about her."

"Why?" I wedged my bare toes under Zeke's body, glad for the soft, heavy warmth. The dog looked up momentarily, but he didn't move.

Hamm fidgeted, his hands giving away his anxiety, then sat up

straight. "Look," he said. "You and I, we're not much alike..."
He stopped, looking down at his lap.

I continued to stare. His hair had been cut by someone who had
never worked for the military. His nails were buffed. His suit was
expensive. And he looked about as miserable as it is possible for
a person to look.

"Hamm, just tell me why you are here." We were back where
we had been when he first sat down. He sat up straighter.

"Elizabeth," he said. "She...how can I put this?" He thought
for a while, then gave up. "I know she wasn't at the church all
day on Thursday as she told the police."

"How do you know that?" I asked.

"Jack Hardwick told me. He's ashamed that he let the police
think that."

"Where was she then?" I had been asking questions I knew
the answer to all evening. "Do you know?"

"No."

I decided to face the issue directly. "Are you afraid that Elizabeth is somehow involved in Leslie Ballard's death?"

He looked over at me. "Yes."

If this didn't take the cake, I thought. Elizabeth was fearful that
Hamm had something to do with Leslie's death. And he had the
same fears about her. And even more surprising, not to say probably stupid, they had both come to me.

"Where were *you* Thursday?" I watched as he tried not to
bristle. When he spoke, his voice was even, controlled.

"Fair question. I was at a management conference in Baltimore.
National Association of Engineering Managers. All day." Then
his neutral tone dissolved and impatience filtered through. "Exactly as I told the police."

Did I believe him? And Elizabeth, did I believe her? She certainly had a motive to want Leslie out of the way. And Hamm
must have known it. But she also had an alibi I could check: an
appointment with the divorce attorney.

We sat in silence as thoughts flooded my mind. He put his head
in his hands. I almost felt sorry for him. But what could possibly
be Hamm's motive for wanting Leslie dead? Suddenly, a thought

surfaced and spun in my mind. Was it possible that Leslie's appointment with the Fawcetts had really been later? Had she and Hamm planned to meet for a quick lunch time tête-à-tête in his own house before her client got there? It would add juice to the proceedings, I thought, making love with your mistress in your own bed, across from your wedding picture on the bureau. With a client showing up any minute.

I looked at him. Hamm was studying a hole in the window screen at the far end of the sunporch, closed off in his own thoughts. Had Leslie wanted more from him than he was willing to give? Like money? Or marriage? Had she threatened to go to Elizabeth? Had things just gotten out of hand? Was it possible he had shoved Leslie into the pool during a fight? After they made love? And then feigned surprise at coming up from the cove to find me kneeling on the patio looking down at her body?

My mind dissolved back to Leslie's body dark against the peeling blue of the pool. I heard the rasping scream that came from me, then its echo as Hamm came up the steps and stood behind me on the patio. The sound had been raw, openly suffering. Had Leslie's death been an accident? One he couldn't admit without implicating himself?

Hamm looked up. His hands were busy again in his lap, this time forming into a child's church and steeple, turn them over and see all the people. They were the hands of someone who used his mind for a living. He was still wearing his wedding ring, I noticed. And he wanted Elizabeth to come home, had even come to the self-defense workshop to try to persuade her.

"Hamm, was anything taken from your house?"

"No."

"And the key that was in the lockbox? The one that Leslie Ballard used to open the door?"

"Not found," he said. "The cops searched the bushes. They think it may have been in her handbag. Which they haven't found."

I watched Hamm for a few seconds more, then decided to turn the screws a little, to see what happened.

"Did you know Leslie Ballard, Hamm?"

His eyes darkened, but his voice remained even. "Yes," he said. I tried to keep my surprise to myself. "I tutored her son through the church program. And before a tutor works with a child, he meets with the parent."

"Does Simmons know this?"

"I said that I'd met her twice. That I tutored the boy." Tiny lines of annoyance were spreading out near his mouth. Zeke stirred by my feet, half sitting up.

"And the kid? What was he like?"

Hamm relaxed. "Not such a kid. Almost sixteen years old. Nice boy at heart, but he needs discipline. The military would be good for him."

"Naval Academy?"

"It will be tough with his grades," he said, fiddling with his fingers.

"And with his police record?"

Hamm's eyebrows went up. "He doesn't have a police record. His friend was charged for that car theft, not Dennis." The annoyance lines had returned, I saw. "And his study habits have improved. If he can get through the next couple of years...maybe. If I..." His voice trailed off. It was apparently a big "if."

Exhaustion was setting in. I took a deep breath, hoping for a second wind. "Hamm, you still haven't told me why you are here."

"Can you find out where Elizabeth was Thursday afternoon?" he said.

"Why me?"

"Because I think Elizabeth will talk to you. And I don't know anyone else to ask. Certainly not that arrogant son-of-a-bitch detective." He sat forward, his head in his hands, then looked up. "I just want Elizabeth to come home." He looked down at his agitated hands. "She won't even talk with me."

I toyed momentarily with confronting him about the affair, then decided it was a bad idea. Maybe I should just call Simmons, I thought. Get him over here with his pad and pencil. Let him do what he got paid to do. Between the obscene call on tape and all I'd learned today, we could make an all-nighter of it. A picture of the detective—red hair and pale eyes and ashen eyebrows drove its way into my consciousness. No. Not tonight. I couldn't. I wanted to put my head down and sleep.

The dogs stirred. Hamm was standing. "You can reach me at work," he said. "I would also appreciate it if you didn't mention this visit to Elizabeth. Or anybody else." He handed me a business card, apologized again for frightening me, then with a bang of the screen door, strode to his car. He was very sure I wouldn't tell Elizabeth, I thought. Or Simmons. Would I? I didn't know. I was too tired to know anything.

I carefully locked the doors. Once inside, I sat down at the desk, dropping Hamm's card onto the green felt blotter next to the one Simmons had left. Beside it, the tape from the answering machine mocked me. I picked it up, put it down, then studied Simmons' phone number. I couldn't. Not tonight. Tomorrow, I'd call. The revolting monotone voice played in my mind's ear, sending fear like a spike through my body. The guy could show up. Maybe he was already outside. Was Hamm...? No, that was too ridiculous.

Taking a deep breath, I considered my choices. After another moment's hesitation, I decided not to be a dead hero, then called Will. What are, I asked myself, friends for?

NINETEEN

SURPRISINGLY, I found I had slept. Long and deeply and well.
Will and I hadn't talked much. He had listened to the tape, only
his eyes giving away any emotion, nodding when I told him I
planned to call Simmons in the morning. Then he had settled down
to read on the couch. Zeke and Lance had padded upstairs after
me.

Awakening at dawn I had been content to doze in bed with the
dogs. They were warm and redolent from slumber, still twitching
in their sleep, not yet ready for a new day. No yowling specter
had spent the night with me, poking at my psyche. Instead, there
was just the enveloping darkness and the unremembered dreams
that cleaned house and swept the sidewalks of my mind.

When I came downstairs around eight, Will was making coffee.
I called 911. Around 8:30, a young policeman came by to pick up
the tape. The three of us listened as the low, chilling voice burst
through the sun-dappled morning. The cop asked a few questions
and left a police flyer with tips about handling what he kept calling
unwanted calls. Unwanted, all right. The telephone company
would put a trap on my phone in case the guy called back. And I
should be extra-careful.

Will had nodded his agreement, mysteriously saying nothing
else. Something, I thought, was different between us. Some frayed
edges had softened. We took our coffee to the couch. I glanced
over at him lying at the other end as he clicked through channel
after channel, finding only the Sunday-morning talking heads. He
was way ahead of me, I thought. We hadn't talked about it, but I
knew he had somehow made peace with what could be between
us. I sighed, wondering when I would do the same. Would I even
stay here? Or would the lure of advertising and the streets of New

York prove stronger? Will pushed my legs aside and got to his feet. He had decided to finish renovating my bathroom.

"Turn that to the real estate channel for a second," I said. He clicked and the loop began. The faces of women agents I knew by sight alternated with the properties they were listing. As picture after picture slipped across the screen, I wondered if Dan Lloyd ever watched. A smooth voice described waterfront estates and more modest four-bedroom colonials. Pinky's voice? It seemed hard to believe. Maybe someone else did the voice-overs.

Suddenly my face slid across the screen, followed by pictures of several large tracts of undeveloped waterfront property Lillian had listed. Will's mouth tightened, but he said nothing. The loop continued, with Mitch showing two executive homes in a new subdivision he was developing. More agents, more properties. A chill ran down my back.

"Mute that, will you." Will looked over at me. "Something just occurred to me. Do you suppose that...that the guy making the calls is watching this? Getting his names from this?"

"What makes you think that?"

"Last night I got my first call. And last night our ad was on for the first time. And..."

"And?"

"And Rose Macklin and Leslie Ballard both advertised on cable. I could probably check the others."

Neither of us spoke. In the corner, Lancelot turned and turned until he was satisfied that it was okay to lie down. The silent cable loop was halfway through again. My throat constricted. Was this guy sitting in front of his set right now? Watching even as we watched? I stole a glance at Will, afraid to say it aloud. He began to say something, thought better of it, then shrugged. As he turned to leave, I saw his eyes, shadowy blue, sick with worry. He still didn't say anything.

I found I was a little worried myself. After he left, I located Simmons' card and called the number he had penciled in above the office number. The cop that answered the phone seemed surprised.

"He's not available. This is, uh, his private line. Can anyone else help you?"

"No. Just tell him I called." I left my name.

"Detective Clarke is here," said the cop, helpfully. "If this is an emergency."

"It's not an emergency. If you'll just tell Detective Simmons I called."

"Well, okay, but I don't know when he'll be..." His phone rang and the connection went dead.

I replaced the receiver. Well, I'd tried. Feeling vacant, at loose ends before the MacAfferty open house this afternoon, I took another cup of coffee to the porch, turned on the radio, and wished I had a Sunday paper. Instead, I tried to make do with yesterday's *Washington Post*. But the adventures of Congress and the White House, the whole sorry lot of them, were more unaffecting than usual. A faint green breeze filtered through the window screens.

I flipped off the radio and stood at the screen door, looking out toward Weller's Creek. The morning was still misty, the sun a mere promise. It didn't matter that Simmons wasn't available. I'd done what I could, giving them the tape. I went upstairs, changed my clothes, and headed for Pines on Magothy.

CHURCH WAS ANOTHER WORLD, one I had long forgotten. My Episcopalian-in-name-only parents had never been sufficiently interested to take me, preferring the *New York Times* on Sunday mornings. Instead I had gone with my small friends and their parents. And if my parents cared that Ben was Jewish, they had never commented. My in-laws, on the other hand, had had a few things to say on the subject of my indifferent Christian upbringing, things about raising the children. But children hadn't come. So everybody in both families conveniently forgot about religion.

I was wedged into a pew near the back of the Church in the Pines, still a little surprised that I had come. Something to do with feeling unhinged and at loose ends. The church was quiet except for low mutterings and laughter. Lillian and Elizabeth, sitting up front, hadn't seen me come in. Jack Hardwick wasn't in sight. Six maroon-draped singers sat in straight chairs facing the audience.

As they shuffled their music, a woman in a matching robe began work at an upright piano. A hymn, its name lodged deep somewhere in my memory, set off on its journey of many verses. I studied the mostly middle-aged and elderly crowd of fifty still willing to forgo a warm spring morning in search of something longer lasting.

The pianist jerked me back to the present. The congregation had opened their hymnals and was standing. Shaken by my daydream, I stumbled to my feet, my hands empty. A man I guessed to be in his early thirties, neatly dressed, his face vaguely familiar, offered a hymnal. I took it, thanking him. Instead of singing, I looked around, taking in the small plain church, its walls bare, its windows unstained. The altar was unadorned except for several pots of mums and a light-colored wooden podium unsullied by cloths of gold and silver. The familiar music stopped and the congregation sat.

The pastor made his way from a door somewhere behind the altar. He wore a plain black robe and placed a few sheets of paper on the lectern next to a large Bible.

"Good morning and welcome," he said. "We are here this fine spring day to celebrate the way God works, the mystery of His ways." He studied us. "We cannot begin to understand Him. Or the beauty and rightness of His ways. We can only have faith." The crowd sighed, aware of what was coming.

There was a momentary diversion, as Lillian's crutches slipped and fell into the aisle at one side with a slight crash. On crutches still, I thought. She was probably furious. I expected the doctor was taking no chances with her seventy-odd-year-old bones. Elizabeth got things settled and sat back.

Jack Hardwick's drone brought me back to the service. Taking my cues from those around me, I managed to sit and stand and bow my head at the right times. The prayers were familiar, the simple words at once powerful and meaningless. During the hymns, the pianist and choir attempted to energize the flagging congregation by playing and singing faster and louder. The result was a noisy round, a kind of ecclesiastical "Row-Row-Row Your

Boat," with the congregation unfailingly a phrase or so behind. We sat.

The pastor took his place again behind the podium. "We have had a tragedy in our community this week," he said. "A beautiful young woman, in her prime, was senselessly murdered. And before that, there was another. We are here this morning, not to make sense of these murders, for we can't, but to mourn the loss of two lovely women, taken in their prime. And to give praise to the Lord, who understands why He needed to gather them up."

The church was silent, the congregation uneasy. Next to me, the man who had offered the hymnal fidgeted, crossing and recrossing his legs, shaking his head.

"So we must accept that which we can't understand," the pastor was saying. "What we can do is cultivate our own garden. We can help our fellow man. In small ways and in big ways. With the sweat of our brows and the resources and health He has seen fit to give to each of us." What followed was a diatribe about good works and fund-raising, delivered with missionary zeal. Then he got specific, with a ringing call to action, to save our earthly souls through the Lord's work. He named committees and dates and times. The congregation perked up, energized to action.

I felt empty and useless. Empty, because I did not, could not, believe a fraction of what I heard. Useless, because the causes were good. Children needed to learn. The hungry needed to be fed. Just because I found the pastor's words hollow, it didn't make his good works any less good. The congregation stood for a last hymn. We ended with a prayer.

The man beside me shuffled his feet, released from the torture of sitting still, holding out his hand at the suggestion we greet our fellow worshippers.

"I'm Howard Lucas," he said shyly, not quite looking at me.

Lillian's friend. "Eve Elliott." I suddenly glanced at my watch. It was just twelve. The MacAfferty open house was scheduled for one. And I needed to go home first.

"Are you late for something?" he asked.

"Sorry, I'm not always that rude," I said, "but I have an open house soon."

"You're a real estate agent?" I nodded. "Oh, you're Lillian Weber's niece," he said. As always, Lillian's presence smoothed the way, proceeding me wherever I went, making conversation easier. "Your aunt's one great lady," he said.

"She's the best." I agreed.

"But you have to be careful at open houses," he said, suddenly. "That killer…"

"Yes, I will. I'm the one who found Leslie Ballard's body," I said.

Something in his eyes went a little off and he drew back a couple of inches. "Oh. Well, I'm sorry. I didn't know that."

"No."

"Your aunt is the best," he said again.

"Yes, she is, isn't she?"

Howard was nodding. "I was downsized a few months ago and she has helped keep my spirits up. I've found volunteering for the church programs has helped, too." He smiled for the first time. "Actually, we could use another person…so if you…I'm sorry," he said. "You probably don't want…"

"That's okay," I said.

Then to my surprise, Howard then leaned in my direction and lowered his voice. "I'm going to buy a house soon," he said. "My mother died and left me some money. I was going to talk with Lillian about it, but maybe I should work with you. Since she's still on crutches."

"We work together," I heard myself say. I fished in my handbag and handed him a business card, green and white with the Weber Realty logo. He took it in both hands, like a Japanese businessman. I half-expected him to bow.

"Christ threw all of the moneychangers out of the church," said a voice behind us. The pastor, smiling widely, draped his arms around our shoulders. I felt my usual pull away from him. "Just kidding. It's good to do business among friends." He turned to me. "I am very glad to see you came after all. I didn't know if you would."

"I didn't know either," I said.

"I hope you'll join us again soon." He was now grasping my

hand. "Maybe you could help with our tutoring program. We could really use help there."

I murmured something noncommittal. Where was Lillian when I needed her? In the distance Marian Beall waved. I withdrew my arm from the pastor's grip to wave back. He appeared not to notice, switching effortlessly to greet Howard. Then he excused himself and was off to talk with another member of the congregation.

"Eve Elliott," said Lillian, holding out a free hand to Howard, but looking at me. Elizabeth wasn't with her. "I never in a million years expected you here. In fact, it never occurred to me to even ask you to come. Your family didn't...I would have asked, you know. Why didn't you come and sit with us?"

"I got here late. Howard gave me a hymnal."

"Next time you can sing," he said. I rolled my eyes. "Well, you can't be worse than I am," he said. Lillian and I politely disagreed. Then Howard excused himself to go downstairs and get coffee ready for the social hour.

"God, Lillian, they mean business around here. Everybody's trying to recruit me as a tutor or to distribute sandwiches. I mean, they're very nice about it, but I don't think your friend Howard is going to take no for an answer."

Lillian laughed, then grew serious. "Frankly, I think the volunteering has kept him sane after he lost his job. Of course, now he at least has a part-time clerk job at one of those big office supply stores over on Ritchie Highway." My aunt waved at someone across the church. "And of course, everyone here was supportive after Irene's death."

As they had been of her after my Uncle Max's death, I thought. The generosity of friends. I looked around at neighbors catching up. And if the party line was soothing, even redeeming, well, who was I to judge?

"Where does Howard live?"

"Way on the other side of Charles Cove, in the woods. It's just a small, tacky cottage and kind of isolated. Why?"

"He told me he wants to buy a house."

Lillian's carefully penciled eyebrows registered surprise. "He's got his inheritance, I guess. Irene had some money. Well, we'll find him a nice little house." She hopped slightly with the help of the crutches.

"I ran into Elizabeth at the mall last night. Did she tell you?" I didn't mention Hamm's late-night visit. Nor the revolting phone message.

"She did. I don't know what you said, but I think it calmed her down. She slept some last night." Lillian maneuvered out of the way of someone coming through. "That's a start. And if we can sell their house soon...I'm going to call the agent whose buyer made that low-ball offer last week. See what I can do."

Howard Lucas had rejoined us, offering Lillian his arm. She took it, not wanting, I could see, to offend him. Knowing Lillian, she'd have preferred to stumble down the stairs by herself.

I suddenly remembered the time. "Gotta go."

"Your open house?" asked Howard. I nodded. "Where is it?" I told him. "Can I see it? If I can get done all the stuff Jack's got for me to do, I can maybe get there before you leave."

"Sure. But we can always go back another time, if you don't make it before four."

"Thanks." He looked grateful.

"Be careful," said Lillian. "And phone me later." We had already discussed safety. I planned, I told her, to rely on dog security. She wasn't completely happy, so I had also promised to buy us both foghorns tomorrow. What she had in mind, I knew, was more like a nice Lady Smith.

I kissed her good-bye. It was 12:15. The pastor, to my relief, was tied up, smiling and clutching at someone else in another part of the church.

TWENTY

THE SUN WAS HIGH IN THE SKY when I turned into the clearing, the morning's mist burned off. I wanted to throw on jeans and go for a long walk with the dogs in the fragrant woods along Weller's Creek. Instead I changed into flat shoes, gathered up flyers about the MacAfferty house, and snapped a leash on Lancelot. At my signal, the Chesapeake Bay retriever jumped into the back seat of the car, pleased with this turn of events. I could hear Zeke—his hopes crushed, his eyes heartbroken—barking as I drove away. It couldn't be helped. I needed protection but I also needed buyers in one piece.

A few minutes before one I sat at the MacAfferty dining room table, Lance snoozing underneath, my business cards, listings, pictures, and sign-in sheet laid out neatly on top. I had planted a few Open House signs along the way at strategic intersections. I had also scouted the house and yard, watered a few plants, and picked up a couple of small branches off the deck. I had even dusted the sideboard with a damp paper towel. To my surprise, the phone rang. MacAfferty's daughter had apparently forgotten to have it disconnected. I made a note to take care of it.

"Eve," said Lillian, "the newspaper ad got the times wrong. They put in two to five, not one to four. Thought you should know. You've got the dog?"

"Right here. Thanks. 'Bye."

I put the phone down and looked at the dog. He was standing at my side, his head resting on the table. "Now what do we do? We have an hour to kill."

I turned on the TV. Like the phone, the cable service was still connected. Like a sore that needed to be picked, I tuned in the real estate channel and watched the pictures slide by, not knowing what I was looking for. "I know where you live," the voice on the tape had said. I shuddered. Did he also know where I went and what I did? Should I tell Simmons about my theory? When he finally got around to calling me back. Ambivalence crowded me. Was I also ready to tell him about Leslie and Hamm? About the pastor's exact meaning? About Elizabeth's visit to Greenbelt? The pager at my waist buzzed. I picked up the phone.

"Hi." Mitch had answered on my first ring. Probably in his car, I thought, on his way to sell a few more properties.

"Thought I'd offer that dinner again," he was saying. "And a sail. About six-thirty or so? At your dock?"

Leslie Ballard's lilting voice came back to me: "Try night sailing on someone else's boat."

"Eve, you still there?"

"Uh, yes." What the hell. I needed a break. Away from the phone and the pager and most of all, away from that revolting monotone voice. "Okay, sure."

"Bring a sweater," he said. "Sometimes the wind kicks up."

I hung up. Motioning to Lance, I locked the house, then walked across the wide lawn that led down to the cove. The long, pale clumps of grass were still in the midday sun. A worn path led past an overturned and rusting dory, through the grass to the dock. I jumped over a wet patch of brown muck. The dog was waiting for me, tail wagging.

On my left were acres of protected wetlands, the swampy shoreline giving way to dense woods and steep inclines. Hidden away were more than a few houses, waterfront in name only. I scanned the opposite bank and within seconds was rewarded with a back view of the Hammett place. The edge of the pool was just visible through the trees, the patio not at all. The house rose up behind it, on a different and higher plane from George MacAfferty's dock.

A picture of Leslie Ballard's broken body swept through my mind. Had she cried out that day? In surprise or fear or anger? Had she put up an arm to protect herself from the dark, shadowy figure I could imagine but not see? At the moment I was finding it was hard to think of death, in general or in particular. It didn't seem to go with the midday sun and rustling grasses or with the powerful red-brown dog at my side.

I looked up and down the cove. Even if no one on this edge of Charles Cove could see the Hammetts' patio, had someone heard something? A sharp word? A scream? Sound carries across water. Surely Simmons had talked to the neighbors. But had he talked with anyone across the cove? At my feet Lance stirred, eyes anxious, pleading for a swim.

"No swim. Too muddy. A walk instead." I realized I was hungry. "Come on, let's walk to the 7-Eleven and get me some lunch."

I started up the road, the dog at my side. Houses were set back behind dense shrubbery. There were no sidewalks. I wished I were wearing sneakers, not thin-soled flats. Maybe I should have driven. Reaching a T in the road, I headed right around the cove, coming quickly to another intersection. My Weber Realty Open House sign had slipped and fallen. I righted it, then wound my way left as the road twisted. To the right, Charles Cove Road branched off. The Hammett property must have been four or five houses in that direction. Across the street a runner yelled a greeting. And a woman walking a cocker spaniel waved hello.

Not a single car passed me until I reached Pines on Magothy's main drag, Lido Beach Road. Crossing it to the convenience store, I commanded Lance to stay as I ran in to get a sandwich. It was almost a quarter of two when I came out, stuffing wads of pre-packaged tuna hero into my mouth. When the dog saw I wasn't likely to part with any, he trotted over to a tan Mercedes parked nearby, and defiantly lifted his leg. As I watched, my mouth full, a yellow stream of dog pee ran down a bumper sticker that demanded that I Eat Bertha's Mussles. Whoever Bertha might be.

My sandwich swallowed, I glanced at my watch. First I was early, now I was going to be late. Lance sprinted in front of me, then waited until I caught up, then sprinted again. It took fifteen minutes to reach the Charles Cove Road intersection, then another ten to the MacAfferty house. A late-model Buick was parked out front. And a lumpy couple in matching white sweatshirts was standing in the flower beds, peering into the side windows of the dining room.

"Sorry I'm late," I said.

The woman turned, her sweatshirt drizzled with what I took to be artistically placed paint daubs. I wondered if she did it herself.

The husband, his face kinder, smiled weakly at me. "We just got here," he said, with a nervous glance at his wife.

"Actually, we've been waiting for a while," the wife said. In her hand was the real estate section of the *Baltimore Sun.* Five or six open houses had been circled in red. "Your friend there thought you probably walked to the store."

I followed her glance. Will waved from halfway down the lawn. For the first time, I noticed his truck parked by the BMW. Lance raced down to greet him.

I let the couple in, offered a brochure, and pushed the sign-in sheet in their direction. While the husband wrote, the wife took off like a shot, opening doors, inspecting closets, cupboards, and appliances like a pro. I heard her take to the stairs.

"Have you been looking long?" I asked the husband.

"A few months. We're not in any hurry. We own a town house, but we're interested in moving up to waterfront," he said. He glanced at the house price. "Well-priced waterfront." No buyer here, I thought, as he lumbered after his wife.

"Hi." Will entered the dining room, Lance at his heels.

"Just keeping me company, I suppose?" I asked. It was hard not to smile at him.

"Sure. Can you think of a better way to spend a beautiful spring Sunday afternoon?"

"I wondered this morning why you didn't make a big deal about this." He shrugged. "Well, thanks, but stay out of the way." He threw up his hands, then faded outside, onto the deck.

"Hello," called a voice. "Anybody home?"

An elderly couple was standing inside the front door. They both had bushy white hair and thin bodies. "We're the Robinsons," she said. "We live in the neighborhood."

"Come in."

Mr. Robinson looked around at the formal living room, its furniture and Oriental rug a little worn but still good. "Never liked the son of a bitch," he said. "Didn't return things he borrowed.

I loaned him a wrench seven years ago and I want it back. Part of a set.''

He looked meaningfully at me, as if it might be in my pocket. I said I'd look for it, that I was sure Mr. MacAfferty's daughter would want him to have it. Mrs. Robinson had the good manners to look mortified during this exchange.

"Thank you, dear," she said. "Since we saw your sign, we'd also thought we'd try to find out what our property was worth. We're thinking about retiring to Florida."

I handed her my business card. Open houses for the public are usually more about finding clients for agents than selling houses. And if you are very lucky, you might even come away with a house listing from neighbors like the Robinsons. And open houses put you in the path of buyers who are actively looking and haven't chosen an agent. They also serve to placate sellers like the daughter MacAfferty who are anxious and don't think you are doing enough to sell their house.

Lance was lying in the front vestibule by the stairs, out of the way, quiet but alert. He sat up each time a car stopped. Through the narrow windows around the front door, I saw a young couple get out of a sports car. Both were dressed in casual clothes and both were wearing sunglasses. I hated talking to people when I couldn't see their eyes. But if they weren't serious buyers, I knew they'd probably leave them on. Behind them, a thirty-something woman with a teenage girl parked an old Volvo and set off around the yard to see the waterfront my sign boasted. Other cars were arriving.

It had suddenly begun to look like a party. I forgot the Robinson's wrench, ran to greet people and hand out brochures. People were everywhere, signing their names, asking questions, running up and down the stairs, opening and closing doors. I heard the upstairs toilet flush, the deck door slide open and shut. Voices came from the basement. The woman in the splattered white sweatshirt told me the shower head in the upstairs bath needed fixing. Also, she said, a window in the garage was cracked. I thanked her. A young couple, without a prayer of qualifying for a mortgage, wanted to discuss financing anyway. Maybe the house was priced too low. Or maybe, and more likely, I thought, people just wanted to check out the Hammett house. Everybody had certainly made a beeline to the MacAfferty dock. I could see a bunch of them down there now.

Hearing a sound in the living room, I went back in to greet a tall, slender man with a wide smile. Just looking, he said. I nodded. George MacAfferty's daughter and I had already removed all valuables in the house. There was stealing during open houses, a dirty little secret irresponsible agents didn't tell their clients. It was just too easy for someone to drop something into a pocket.

Lance stayed close to me, watching and wagging his tail when spoken to. I talked and smiled until my teeth ached. I passed out information, ran up the stairs, then down to the basement, out to the deck, even once halfway down the lawn to examine an exotic rosebush. A plump woman who raised roses wanted to know if it conveyed, as she put it. Looked like any other rosebush to me. I glanced at Will, quietly reading on the deck, and said I'd find out. She said never mind, she didn't like the house that much anyway.

Finally they were gone, the house empty. Even the Robinsons had disappeared. I wondered if they had found the wrench on their own. I locked the front door. My sign-in sheet listed forty-three names, some sort of open house record. At least for me. There were no takers, of course, not even a nibble. And most people had left only addresses, not phone numbers. And I was sure at least a couple of them had not signed in at all. All perfectly normal. Open houses attract the curious who have no intention of buying. For some it's a kind of hobby. Others are looking for decorating ideas. Nosy neighbors sometimes wait years for a chance to get inside.

"That it?" Will sat down at the dining room table.

"That's it." I waved the forty-three names in his direction. Suddenly, a chill passed over me. Was it possible that among them was the...? Maybe the tall, thin man who'd come late. I shoved the thought away and smiled at him. "I'm about done. I think it's safe for Lance to take over the guard duties."

Will nodded. I suddenly wondered if he had plans for us this evening, then remembered that things had changed. He said nothing, merely patted the dog, then my shoulder, and, without a word, left. I ran to the door. He was down the road, getting in his truck.

"Hey, Will, thanks." If he heard, he gave no sign.

Lancelot stood at my side, eyes locked on me, trying to explain he was desperate to go out. I opened the kitchen door to the deck. No swimming, I told him. George MacAfferty's kitchen stove clock said a quarter after five. I was supposed to meet Mitch in just over an hour. And I still had to go home, feed the dogs, call Lillian, and change my clothes.

Hurrying now, I locked the kitchen door, checked the basement, then ran upstairs. Everything appeared to be in order. The shower even ran fine when I tried it, but someone had left a huge muddy footprint on the light-colored bathroom rug. I stooped to brush it out. The phone rang. Dashing into the master bedroom, I grabbed an extension. A vile stream of sexual recommendations poured from the receiver. Slamming it down, I went to the window. Lancelot, his reddish mahogany curls gleaming in the late afternoon sun, was chasing a squirrel across the lawn.

TWENTY-ONE

I TOOK A DEEP BREATH, forcing myself to think. If the call had come from the pay phone at the 7-Eleven, the guy was only about two minutes away by car. I raced downstairs, scooped up my handbag and folders, and ran out the front door, locking it behind me. Whistling for Lance, I held open the car door until he was safely in the back seat. He was panting hard. Simmons, I suddenly realized, had still not called me back.

Throwing the car in reverse, I backed out of the MacAfferty driveway and onto the pavement. My heart surged as an old nondescript brownish van turned the corner and lumbered slowly down the road in my direction. It could be him. The monotone voice, with its loathsome words, played in my head. The van drew closer, slowing. From the driver's seat, Howard Lucas waved wildly at me. I took a deep breath. Lance barked once.

Howard was motioning me back to the MacAfferty house. I pulled the BMW back into the driveway. He pulled in beside me and came running over. He was sweating and out of breath.

"I'm too late to see the house? I am, aren't I? I was afraid of that." In the back seat, Lance stood up, slipping and sliding on the tan leather. "I rushed around to get done at the church, but..." He stopped, studying me closer. "Something wrong?"

My God, the fear must be written all over my face. I was letting this phone creep frighten me enough so that even a complete stranger like Howard could tell something was wrong. As I forced my shaking to stop, the anger set in. It was, I noticed, becoming a pattern: first panicky fear, then rage.

"You know what just happened? Not five minutes ago?" Howard shook his head and jumped back as I got furiously out of the car. "I just got an obscene call. Here. Upstairs. My second in twenty-four hours. The bloody creep's watching me. Otherwise, how in the hell would he know to call me here? How?'' Howard's eyes opened wide. Something like amazement edged into them. He appeared to be more in shock than I was. Something occurred to me. ''Oh, God, Howard. Please don't tell Lillian about this. I don't want to upset her. Promise.''

He was nodding and shaking his head all at once. ''No. No. Of course not. She won't hear about it from me.'' He shook his head a final time, then shuffled his feet and his hands, apparently at a loss at how to comfort someone who has just been the victim of an obscene call. ''Did you...did you call the police?''

''No, not yet. Not for this call. I did for the other one.'' I could feel the exhaustion that came after fear and anger, when the adrenaline backed off, leaving my body limp. And I was suddenly embarrassed for my outburst. I glanced at my watch. Late again. ''Howard, I know you rushed here to see the house, but could we do it another time?''

He looked disappointed, but nodded. ''Sure. It's okay. And after what you've just been through, I don't blame you for not wanting to go back in there.'' By now he was trying awkwardly to pat my shoulder. ''Another time. Don't worry. It's okay.''

''It's not so much that I don't want to go in there, as that I have to be somewhere. Tomorrow would be fine. If you want to see the house.'' I reached into my car and pulled out a brochure, complete with listing and picture, and handed it to him.

''Thanks,'' he said. ''I live pretty close, so it's easy enough for me to come back.'' He hesitated, looking first at the listing, then at the house behind us. ''You know I don't think I can afford this.''

George MacAfferty's house was listed at nearly $310,000, largely because of its tract of land, all waterfront. It also had four bedrooms, three baths, a double garage, the downstairs office, and an amazing garden.

''How much money do you have?'' Had I really said that to a client? God, was I ever tired. If he noticed my rudeness, he didn't let on. ''Sorry. I mean how big a house are you looking for?''

''Two hundred fifty thousand dollars,'' he said. ''I don't need a mortgage.''

Surprised, I turned to look at him. "A quarter million? In cash?" I wondered what Lillian would say to that. Probably that Howard's mother Irene had more money than anyone expected.

"My mother had some money," he said, echoing my thoughts. "But I think I'm looking for something smaller, since there's only me, but maybe on the water and with a nice yard. I like to work in the yard."

"So this is too big anyway?" He nodded. "Are you looking for any neighborhood in particular?"

"No. Just somewhere in Anne Arundel County. Waterfront. Just show me whatever you've got," he said. "I'm open-minded."

"I'll check the computer tomorrow morning," I said. "Can I reach you somewhere?"

He nodded, futilely searching his pants pockets. I handed him my pen and pulled out one of my own business cards, flipping it over. He carefully printed his name and phone number and handed it back.

"Is this your home number?" He nodded. I dropped it into my pocket. "Okay, Howard, I'll call you tomorrow."

"Sure." He looked more pleased than I could have thought possible. "Oh, I forgot," he said, "you can also get me at the Office Giant on Ritchie Highway. Let me give you that number." He motioned for the card back, then wrote while I got back in my car. He handed it to me through the window. I mumbled something about the time and then, with a wave, again backed out of the drive. He was still standing outside his van. He waved once.

I had never heard of someone paying a quarter of a million dollars in cash for a house. But people were funny about money. I knew people who had survived the Depression often distrusted credit. Maybe that was what had happened to Irene Lucas. And maybe her habits had rubbed off on Howard. Or maybe it was just that most pedestrian of real estate problems: an interested buyer with lousy credit.

MITCH GAYLIN was waiting for me at the dock on Weller's Creek, listening to classical music on a small boombox and reading the business section of the Sunday *Washington Post.* I arrived breathless and sweaty, the dogs at my side.

"Sorry, I'm late. I had a zoo of an open house. Forty-three people." He held out his hand as I picked out a foothold on the boat, then jumped. I pointed to the dogs waiting hopefully on the dock. "I hope they can come. You allow dogs on this thing?" The sailboat, I noticed, was named the *Laura.* I didn't ask why.

"Sure." Mitch leaned over to scratch ears and chests. They both looked properly pleased and Zeke's pink tongue reached out to lick his hand. Lancelot vaulted into the sailboat like an old hand, making it sway and tilt from his hundred-plus pounds. Mitch laughed. The Labrador followed, and was soon sniffing and poking at a picnic hamper in the surprisingly large cabin. I settled myself on a bench, leaning back against the cushions.

"There's no wind, so we'll power out. You all set?"

"Sure." I watched as he untied the sailboat, leapt back on deck, and maneuvered away from the shore with the same sureness with which he did everything else.

The evening was calm, quiet, with the ever-present bouquet of honeysuckle drifting out over the water. The boat's engine broke the silence with a slight chugging sound. There were a couple of clouds on the horizon. We didn't talk. Instead I breathed deeply, glad to be away, with no responsibilities, no problems, no fears. And no loathsome voice. For the moment, anyway.

"Let me know if you'd like me to do something," I said.

"You don't really mean that," he said.

"No." I laughed. "I don't. I want to sit here and do nothing. I want to be waited on hand and foot."

"At least you're not shy about it."

Lancelot was happily sitting beside me on the bench, nose in the air, sniffing whatever there was to sniff. Zeke had had more problems finding his sea legs and decided the cabin was better. He had settled in the doorway, guarding the food, making slight adjustments in his balance as the boat rocked.

As we moved out into the center of Weller's Creek, Mitch cut the engine, raised a sail, and sat back down, one hand on the tiller, a foot propped on the opposite bench. He was dressed in worn jeans and deck shoes with no socks. A gray sweatshirt which said Johns Hopkins University was tied around his waist. We sat for a few minutes as he observed the wind and sky. The sun dribbled away near the horizon.

"There's a bottle of wine in the cooler," he said. "I'll get it. If you will just hold this." He handed me the tiller. Although the boat seemed not to be moving, the scenery on shore was changing slightly. Mitch disappeared past Zeke into the cabin, returning to hand me a wineglass of something cool and clear, something delicious and wonderful, almost too good to drink.

"Cheers," he said.

TWENTY-TWO

I COULD FEEL the last few days sliding away. No one said anything for a long time. The boat shifted slightly and Mitch readjusted the course. Bach and Mozart had been replaced by a classic rock station, tuned low. Petula Clark sang about not sleeping in the subway. Zeke ventured from the safety of the doorway to lean against my legs.

The horror of finding Leslie Ballard's body had receded. It had been replaced by sadness. You hardly knew her, I reminded myself. Suddenly, I could feel my throat clutch, my eyes ping. Some dangerous emotion had strayed close to the surface, making light-hearted conversation out of the question. Zeke's cold nose poked into my hand. I looked down into liquid eyes, golden brown, flecked and tender, and wanted to cry. This was awful, I thought. I took a sip of wine, swallowed, and tried to smile. Mitch said nothing, watched, waited, and then looked away.

"Sorry," I said. "I'm a little edgy." He nodded, watching still, waiting. "The last few days..."

Suddenly I wanted to tell him everything. About how that awful low voice had rubbed me raw, making me afraid to go home. About Leslie Ballard's wild hair and glad laugh, about Elizabeth and Hamm Hammett's fears about each other, about Lawrence Schoenfeld's damn job, about how someone was going to buy Ray Tilghman's house if I didn't. I wanted to tell him about Will. And about July 23.

"You okay?" he asked after a while. I shook my head, then laughed, embarrassed. "You want to talk about it?"

I swallowed. "I've gotten two obscene calls, one on the machine last night and one this afternoon just before I left the MacAfferty house. He said he knows where I live."

All pretense at lightness, at a holiday mood, was gone. "You call the cops?" Mitch asked.

"About the first one. This morning. They picked up the tape. I guess the phone company is putting a trap on my line." He topped up our glasses, then sized up the wind and the water. He was right. I needed to tell someone. "Mitch, there are other things, too. I don't know what they mean. Maybe they mean nothing, but..."

"What things?"

"Hamm Hammett was sleeping with Leslie Ballard. And the police found fresh semen in her body."

"God," he said. There was another moment's silence. "How do you know this?"

"Elizabeth Hammett." I retold her story, feeling relieved and guilty at the same time. But it was too late to stop. I told him about Hamm's late-night visit to the cottage and his fears about Elizabeth. I told him how Jack Hardwick had not told the police the complete truth about where he was on Thursday from noon on.

I drank off my wine and held up my glass for more. The sun was making progress on its crimson journey toward the horizon line draped gracefully beyond the trees.

Mitch had been listening without moving much. Now he sat up. "It sounds as if you believe Elizabeth," he said.

"Yes, I think I do. She was very open about where she was." William Card, I thought. I could probably check it with a phone call.

"And Hammett?" he asked, refilling my glass with the remainder of the bottle.

"He's not my favorite person, certainly. And Simmons sure didn't cut him any slack the night that he found Leslie's body. I don't know what his motive would be. Unless Leslie wanted more from him, like marriage or something. Though I can't imagine that she..." I drank, letting the wine roll around in my mouth before swallowing. "...that she would put up with the kind of life that Elizabeth described."

We let that thought hover between us for a second. "And he

has an alibi anyway," said Mitch. "Right?" I nodded. "And Jack Hardwick?"

I shrugged. It was beginning to occur to me that maybe the pastor had not been completely honest with the cops, not because he was protecting Elizabeth, but because he was protecting himself. "What about him?" I asked. "You know anything about him?"

"Only what I read in the newspapers. Seems like he does a lot of good work for the community."

I was silent, thinking of his annoying and creepy habit of touching you as he talked, as if he feared you might leave if he didn't hold you there.

Mitch let the boat drift to the middle of the creek. I had no idea how far we were from Ray Tilghman's secluded cove. And I didn't care. Weller's Creek was hushed, with the feathery breeze skimming my face in small aromatic bursts, the air laden with spring. I felt safe, like an island.

"Mitch, what did Rose and Leslie have in common? I mean other than the obvious?"

"And the obvious is?"

"Both worked for you. They were about the same age. Both were attractive, if in a different way. Both were killed between twelve and two in the afternoon while showing houses." I tried to think of more similarities and couldn't. "From what I know, which isn't much, that's where it stops. Rose was wildly successful. Leslie was having trouble making a living, though she told me she'd done okay in the past. Rose, at least according to Joyce, slept with her clients. Who knows about Leslie?"

"There's Hamm."

I thought about that. "You're right. There's Hamm," I said. "Maybe she slept with someone else and he found out about it." I looked over the skeptical expression on his face. "Okay, so that's conjecture. We don't know if she slept around. Another difference: Rose wasn't married and had no kids. Leslie was divorced with a teenage son."

Mitch sat mute, breathing in the night air, surveying the water. His presence was comfortable, restful. I'd buy a house from him,

I thought, if not from some male agents. Success in this business required empathy, the kind women often found easier to communicate. Lillian had it. So had Leslie Ballard. She had, I remembered, been quick to commiserate when my client had not shown up at Wildwood Bay. Rose Macklin had been another story. My few dealings with her had been oddly strained, polite on the surface, wary underneath.

I forced myself back to the moment. ''What other differences can you think of?''

''Different styles,'' said Mitch. ''Leslie was more given to hand holding. And she seemed to deal well with everyone, though...'' I waited, as he apparently thought something through.

''Though what?''

''Oh, sorry, I was just thinking about something else. Office stuff. I'm usually better at putting it out of my mind. But talking about Leslie's way with people made me think about it.''

When he didn't volunteer anything, I said, ''When business was slow, I hear there was a lot of rivalry between agents.''

''And you know this how?''

''Leslie told me.'' He looked surprised. I could hear Simmons' admonition not to talk, but it suddenly didn't matter. ''Look, I ran into Leslie the morning she was killed. I was probably the last person to see her alive.'' I told him about Wildwood Bay. He was silent when I finished. Together we watched as Lancelot stumbled to his feet, found a more comfortable position six inches away. ''Mitch?'' He looked up. ''What about Rose? What was she like?''

''More aggressive, less likely to cut you a little slack,'' he said. ''She did a lot of business with people from Washington. Lawyers and political types.''

''Like Richard Canin?''

''Yes, like Richard Canin,'' he said. ''Actually, I must confess I never had a problem with Rose personally. She was always very professional with me.''

That made me laugh. ''Of course she was professional. You're the boss. My take on Rose was that she was the kind of woman who treated men and women differently, the kind of woman who manipulates men. Men never seem able to see through these women. For whatever reason." He was almost motionless, one hand gently patting the sleeping red dog. "Women, on the other hand, know intuitively that such women are insincere. Sometimes it amuses us. And sometimes it makes us angry. Maybe she made someone angry."

"Angry enough to kill her?" he asked.

"Well, I don't know about that. But it's hard to ignore. Think about it. Rose was attractive, smart, successful, and manipulative. A lot of men would fall for that. I'd say that a lot of women, on the other hand, would see right through her, maybe even dislike her openly."

"Meaning?"

"My guess is that most women clients would steer clear of someone like Rose. Find another agent. Like Leslie, for example..." I stopped. Where was I going with this?

"And?"

"Huh?" I wasn't aware I'd stopped talking. "Oh. Well, I suppose you could look at this two ways. If...I'm just thinking out loud. You sure you want to hear this?"

"I'm sure."

"Well, maybe Rose made some female client so envious or angry that she killed her. Slept with the woman's husband or something."

"And?"

"Or maybe she manipulated some man and he fell for her. Then she dropped him when he was no longer useful to her—perhaps after he bought a house."

"Simmons has a list of previous clients." He said nothing more for a second. "Besides, then why was Leslie killed? And how are the phone calls related? If they are." I shook my head. He shifted the course of the boat a little. "Maybe the motive was robbery," he said. "Someone who wants money and credit cards makes an appointment under a fake name. With a plan to ransack the house, grab stuff, then run off. Maybe it just turned ugly and desperate. Rose's death certainly doesn't seem premeditated."

"Maybe that's the way Rose's death happened, but Leslie knew her clients." I stopped, thinking about what the young cop, Scott

Lisle, had said. "In fact, maybe Leslie and Rose were chosen by the killer. Maybe they *are* connected. We just don't know how."

"Unless this was a copycat crime," Mitch said, "which, I gather, is a popular theory at the Lido Beach Inn."

"Or maybe someone who wanted Leslie dead is using Rose's death as a sort of cover." I tried to organize the possibilities in my mind. A mental picture of Simmons with his pouchy face and his albino eyebrows came to me. What did he really think about these murders? Did he just ask questions until someone said something that rang a bell in his head? Or was he a kind of scientist proposing a hypothesis, then trying to prove or refute it? And why the hell hadn't he called me back?

I looked over at Mitch, off in his own world of wind and water. "And the obscene phone calls?" he asked. "Where do they fit in?"

Again I could feel my mind laboring, trying out different combinations of facts to see if anything fit together. "I don't know about fitting in, but I have a theory about them."

"Why am I not surprised?"

I ignored that. "I think the caller is choosing his victims from the real estate channel on cable. Both Leslie and Rose got calls. And I..."

There was a moment of silence as we both considered the obvious. "Look, others have gotten calls, too," I said. "And they haven't been killed. Maybe it's not the same person making the calls. That's what the cops keep saying. That there is no evidence that the murders and calls are related."

Mitch fiddled with the sails, sending us in a slightly different direction. When he spoke, his voice was low, evenly modulated. "Did you stay by yourself last night?" I shook my head. He nodded, his mouth a straight line, then looked beyond me, deep into the woods. "Okay," he said.

"Mitch, we need the names of the other agents who got calls to see if they advertised on cable." I thought of something else. "And if they had their pictures taken by Dan Lloyd." I told him what the photographer had told me.

Mitch listened, then shook his head, emphatically this time.

"Not *we*," he said. "Simmons." He turned around to face me directly. "You have to talk to him. Otherwise, you could conceivably be considered an accessory. To say nothing of the risk."

"I called Simmons this morning. He hasn't returned my call."

Mitch was looking off into the distance, his eyes squinting slightly, the crow's-feet etched deep in tanned skin. I realized how little I knew about him. He must have been in his mid-forties. Had he ever been married? Did he have children? I'd known him for the better part of a year now. But some part of him didn't invite questions. He stared into the darkening water, watching it lap gently against the side of the boat. The radio played in the background, the song familiar. I couldn't remember its name.

"One thing," he said. I turned to look at him directly. "You have to promise that you won't stay alone tonight. That you'll call your friend again. Or take the dogs and go camp with Lillian." I didn't say anything. "Promise?"

I shrugged. I guessed that was a promise.

"Let's eat. Inside," he said. "It's more comfortable at the table. Besides, I actually brought a tablecloth in honor of the occasion. Since it only took me the better part of a year to get you out here."

He anchored the boat near the center of the creek. I stepped over Zeke and looked around the cabin. Again I was surprised at how spacious it was.

"Want a tour?" he asked. In a couple of minutes I had seen it all, the tiny bathroom with shower, the modern kitchen, the comfortable sleeping quarters with a large-size bed fitted neatly into the triangular space. It must, I thought, be pleasant to sleep here, rocking gently all night.

I glanced at Mitch. He was looking intensely at me, his eyes dark in the dim light. I shivered. He put his hands on my shoulders and rubbed the outside of my arms to warm them. A jolt of electricity ran down my legs. I jumped back a little, self-conscious. He unwound his sweatshirt from his waist and handed it to me.

Around nine, after dinner and some conversation awkward enough for two teenagers, I pleaded exhaustion. Mitch expertly took us in, tied up at Ray Tilghman's dock, then insisted on walking me to the cottage. There were no lights in the house. I promised him I'd call tomorrow morning and hurried in, before he changed his mind about leaving and found an excuse to join me.

Locking the doors, I dialed Lillian, then put the receiver down before she could answer. Calling Lillian meant giving in to fear. Worse, it meant telling her about the obscene calls. A pine bough scraped along a window near the desk, sending me first into shock, then rage. Tomorrow, I was going to saw the damn thing off. Getting up, I looked out into the night. Was someone watching me? Even now? Ridiculous. Not with the dogs nearby. But a shiver passed through my body. I considered my choices: Lillian, Will, Weller, Motel 6. The phone was silent. In the distance, an engine died. The dogs barked.

"Eve?" Will stood on the steps. Suddenly, I was furious. How long was I going to go on letting myself be rescued? Tomorrow, I vowed to the dogs, things would change.

TWENTY-THREE

MY CLOCK said 7:15. The day had dawned drippy, gray, with the soaking all-day rain that plants love. Too many glasses of good wine had disturbed my sleep, giving me a bruising headache. I finally dragged myself out of bed and stumbled downstairs to find a glass of water and aspirin. No sign of Will. A jar of instant coffee and an empty cup sat on the counter. I put water on to boil, fed the dogs, and collapsed at the kitchen table, thinking about last night.

Though Mitch hadn't mentioned it, I suddenly realized I'd turned him into an accessory. Getting up, I shuffled around the desk until I found Simmons' card, then hesitating briefly, picked up the phone. I had enough problems. Enough decisions to make the next few days. Let Simmons handle this. He was getting paid for it. A different cop took my call this morning. Simmons was still unavailable, he said. Out of town for a day or two. He would let him know I'd called a second time. I again left my home, office, and pager numbers. I was back to waiting.

The teakettle screeched, breaking into my thoughts. I returned to the kitchen to make coffee. Zeke and Lance padded back after me, slumping under the table. Swallowing the hot liquid, I could feel my energy returning. And it wasn't just the caffeine, I knew, it was the thought of actually doing something other than waiting.

I threw on a pair of favorite slouchy gray slacks, with a clean white shirt, and a summery jacket, then headed for the office. "The police," said the radio announcer, "have no new leads in two separate cases of murdered real estate agents. Women in Anne Arundel County are still being encouraged not to walk alone at night and to take exceptional precautions at all times." The announcer then turned to news of the Orioles and their seven-game losing streak.

Thankfully, the office was empty when I arrived. Half an hour later, I put the phone down. I had an appointment with attorney William Card. One that I didn't need. A gushy-voiced secretary had asked how I'd gotten his name. "Oh, yes," she said, when I told her. "I remember Mrs. Hammett. Came in just last week. Friday, I believe. Lovely woman." So Elizabeth was in the clear. We chatted a little more. I felt only moderately guilty at the deception. And, with luck, I'd remember to cancel my appointment.

I spent the next hour in a mood of bleak expectation, waiting for Simmons to call. He didn't. Maybe I should talk to Detective Clarke. My head drummed. I took some more aspirin, then remembered I'd promised Howard Lucas I'd check for waterfront houses in his price range. At least it was something to do.

The computer in front of me hummed and flickered as I searched: waterfront, in the quarter-million-dollar range, in Anne Arundel County. There were three finally, including the little house on Sassafras Lane at Wildwood Cove. It *was* cute, I thought, studying the listing the printer spat out. Great view and the boat lift. I wondered if Howard sailed. It didn't seem likely, but people kept surprising me.

I called the listing agent, Marsha Rowen, about showing Wildwood Bay. No problem, she said. The sellers hadn't been there for a couple of weekends. I then left a message on Howard's answering machine and checked my watch. Barely nine o'clock. Shirley, her umbrella streaming, mouthed "Good morning" through the glass partition and got busy making coffee. Soon the office felt like an office, with the copy machine humming, and the phone ringing. I hoped no one would call.

"Eve," said Shirley, "Howard Lucas on line three." I poked the flashing button. Five minutes later, we had agreed to meet at 5:00 p.m. at Wildwood Bay. I put down the phone. My head was still pounding. Maybe the rain would stop. Unable to think of anything else to do, I called Mitch at his Annapolis office. I'd already gotten him in this up to his ears, I thought, so I might as well use him as a sounding board.

"Not here," said Joyce, "hold on, will ya." Her voice was even more irritable and edgy than I remembered. These unsolved murders, compounded by the calls, were getting to all of us. There had been, Shirley had told me earlier, a slowdown of house showings and open houses all over the county. And here it was May, prime house-hunting season. But agents were worried, waiting for the other shoe to drop.

"I'm back. So, what's up? You hear if the police got off their butts and started finding us a killer?"

Hmm. Well, that's one way to put it, I thought. "The radio said they have no new leads."

"Makes you wonder how hard they're looking, doesn't it?" I could hear some papers shuffling in the background. "So you got any good guesses?"

"Me? Guesses? Uh. No. No guesses."

"I heard Leslie wasn't disfigured," she said. "Like Rose."

More fishing. But the thought of Rose made me shudder. What kind of person threw something so heavy and so well-aimed that it tore through someone's face and left gaping mush? Someone strong, I thought. Someone in the heat of passion. Someone who is so outraged that he thinks there are no other choices. "Hey, you still there?" asked Joyce. "Your pal just came in." The phone clicked as she put me on hold. After a minute or so, Mitch's voice came on the line.

"Hi, you okay?" he asked.

"Of course. No more calls," I said. "And, yes, I phoned Simmons again. And, no, I haven't spoken to him yet. He's out of town."

"Maybe you should talk to someone else."

"Yes. Maybe. I'll think about it." I lowered my voice. "Elizabeth was at her attorney's office on Friday afternoon."

"I won't ask how you know that." I also noticed he wasn't asking where I spent the night. I was about to hang up when something occurred to me.

"Would you put Joyce back on the line?" I could hear a strange little noise on the other end, something between resignation and alarm. "I want to ask her which other agents have received obscene calls. She knows these people."

I could hear him suck in his breath. "Bad idea," he said. "You

don't want to get Joyce in on this. Really. Or if you do, I don't.
No.''

"Okay. Okay. But it all seems harmless enough.''

"Planting ideas in Joyce's head is never harmless. Who the hell
knows who she'll tell.'' He coughed slightly. "Forget playing amateur detective. Wait for Simmons. Or talk to someone else.'' He
hung up to take another call, then phoned back to apologize and
plead with me to have lunch with him.

I agreed, mostly to get rid of him. I'd meet him at his Severna
Park office between 12:30 and 1:00. I hung up. Then, checking
my calendar, I made an appointment with Weller Church in his
Annapolis office for tomorrow morning. Finally, I collected my
jacket and umbrella and headed for Baltimore.

GEOGRAPHICALLY, Maryland's largest city still made very little
sense to me. I was about to pull off into a side street to get my
bearings when Oriole Park at Camden Yards suddenly loomed on
my right, large in its redbrick glory. At the next red light, I
checked my map, and then found my way to the hotel where
Hamm's management conference had been held. Beyond it was
Baltimore's pride, joy, and economic lifeline: the Inner Harbor. A
parking space was directly in front of me, so rather than looking
for the entrance to the garage, I slipped a pile of quarters into the
meter. After a couple of rain-soaked seconds studying the gray
harbor, with its double pyramid-shaped Aquarium, I went inside
to talk with the hotel employees. I wished I had a plan. But since
I didn't, I'd have to wing it.

A bespectacled young woman behind the front desk, her face
gloomy with the Monday-morning blues, stepped up to help me.

"Good morning,'' I said. "I work for Thomas Hammett, who
was at the Engineering conference last Thursday. He thinks he left
a manila envelope.''

The woman wordlessly ducked down to look under the counter,
then in a couple of bins behind her. "Nothing's been turned in.''

"It's important,'' I said. "Could I speak with your conference
organizer, please.''

"It won't do you any good,'' she said. But she picked up the phone and said, "Meetings, please." She stared steadily at me, without rudeness, without consciousness maybe, handing the phone over the counter to me when someone answered. I told my story to a second woman, who agreed to meet me in the lobby in a couple of minutes. I thanked the woman behind the desk. She suppressed a yawn, then told me to have a nice day.

Jeannie Curtis was about five feet tall in heels, wearing a little black suit, suitable, I thought, for all business occasions. I didn't see her coming, having collapsed on a pink and green overstuffed couch to enjoy my headache. Aspirin hadn't worked so far.

"Hello," she said, sitting down beside me, careful not to touch my dripping umbrella. "Nothing has been turned in. I think I would remember since I spoke with Mr. Hammett first thing Thursday morning when he registered. Very nice man," she purred. "Must be great to work for."

"Sure is," I lied. Idly, I wondered why women were susceptible to his charms. "Have you got any idea who might have picked up the envelope? He's sure he left it here. It had some personal records in it."

"Not really." She handed me a large white booklet. "The only thing I can think to tell you is to contact the others on the panel with Mr. Hammett. Perhaps his envelope got mixed up with someone else's papers on the table. Their phone numbers are in the program."

The program. Yes. I thanked her. "One other thing," I said. "Where do conference participants usually park?"

"Downstairs. There's an entrance on the other side of the building." She pointed to a map of an enlarged section of downtown Baltimore on the back of the program, then gave me directions through the hotel. "You think that maybe the parking attendant found Mr. Hammett's envelope?"

"Could be. Unlikely, maybe, but since I'm here..."

"Good luck." She rose from the couch. "And give Mr. Hammett my best."

She was gone in a swish of pantyhose. I studied the booklet. My spirits rose when I found a small picture of Hamm beside a description of the afternoon panel he had chaired. Something about personnel policies during times of downsizing. There was a brief paragraph about his qualifications. They were impressive, as was his haircut and tailoring. I also studied the events of the day, from the keynote speaker at 9:00 a.m. through the cocktail party at 4:30 p.m. It had been a full day, complete with informal box lunch.

I walked to the hotel elevator and took it down to the garage. It opened near a small glass booth. The attendant was busy annihilating his hearing. Heavy-metal music blared through his headset. I motioned wildly. He removed it, the music still screeching.

"Did you work last Friday?" I yelled.

"Who are you?" he yelled back.

"I want to know if my husband was at the conference the whole day?" He was pimply and maybe eighteen. His eyebrows raised, then he smiled smugly. The wife checking up on the cheating husband. It wasn't all that far off, I thought. I showed him Hamm's picture and described his Ford Taurus. The kid must have taken pity on me, because he turned down his music, took the program, and studied it carefully.

"Nope, I was here the whole day. And I never saw that guy."

"You're sure?" He nodded. "Thanks." I left him adjusting his earphones. Now what? Hamm had to have parked somewhere. I looked at the map on the program again. There were three other garages or lots listed. Reluctantly I walked out into the rain.

An hour later I was no further along. I was also soaked. No one recognized Hamm. Where did this leave things? Hamm had been seen at the conference in the morning and at his panel in the afternoon. So where had he parked?

I tried to get my bearings, using the harbor itself as my guide. I headed back to my car in what seemed the most direct route. Ahead of me road construction crews blocked the sidewalk. Unable to cross, I walked for two extra blocks, my temper rising at the inconvenience. I was hungry and I was wet. And it was still morning of what promised to be a long day of waiting for Simmons to call. I stopped and looked around, the umbrella dripping onto my shoulders. Where in hell was I?

A narrow parking lot stuck between two abandoned buildings was on my left. A middle-aged and overweight black woman was sitting in a lean-to, watching the world walk by, the world which was trying to cross the street but couldn't because of the construction.

"Morning." She nodded. "I'm trying to find out...did you see this man last Friday? Did he park his car here?"

She took the program booklet and peered at Hamm's picture, then back at me. "Not coming to me jus' yet. Need somethin' to maybe remind me." She smiled radiantly. I took a twenty out of my handbag and handed it to her. "Now," she said, "now, it's comin' back to me."

"Well?"

She plopped off her stool and fished around on the damp cement floor, coming up with a grimy shoebox of tickets. Pulling out a wad labeled Friday and rubber-banded together, she looked up. "Car make and color?"

"Gray Taurus station wagon."

Within a few seconds she had pulled out two tickets. "Got here at 7:34 a.m., left at 9:05 a.m." She fumbled some more. "Came back at 1:33 p.m., left at 4:49 p.m." She looked up. "You the wife?"

"Uh, uh, yes."

"Jus' a guess. Happens all the time. Jerks know better than to park at the hotels if they wanna go out for a quickie for lunch." She pulled a cigarette out of a pack lying nearby and lit up, not offering me one. She inhaled deeply. "Ain't no question some guys get away with murder. Still, gives me a livin', don't it?" I thanked her. She grinned at me, then took another good, long appreciative drag on the cigarette. "You shine his shoes good, Hon. You take him right to the cleaners."

Was I good, I thought, or was I good? Maybe, if the real estate business was a bust, I could go into the private eye business. Then the meaning of what I had just found out hit me. I had confirmed what I really didn't want to know: Hamm hadn't been at the conference all day. That meant he could have been with Leslie Ballard. Opportunity. Even if Hamm had no known motive for killing her. But how did Rose Macklin come into it?

Deflated, I rounded the street corner near the hotel and set off to my car. I had learned something, yes, but maybe it wasn't all that much. In the distance, the wide promenade along the Inner Harbor was still totally uninhabited. A parking ticket was neatly wedged under my windshield wiper.

TWENTY-FOUR

A HALF HOUR LATER I was sitting in Lillian's kitchen, my feet encased in a borrowed pair of dry socks. She was eating a fried egg sandwich and listening to the news on a tiny TV on the kitchen table.

The phone rang. Lillian grabbed it, then hobbled around the corner into the living room to talk. I dug in my bag for another aspirin and swallowed it with a glass of grapefruit juice.

Lillian stuck her head around the doorway, her hand over the mouthpiece of the phone. "This is Marianne Pinot. She wants to list her house with us. Can you meet with her between two or two-thirty this afternoon? Hawk's Bay?" I nodded, then reluctantly hauled myself out of one of Lillian's comfortable kitchen chairs to fetch a map.

Lillian made arrangements and hung up. Marianne Pinot was, she explained, Elizabeth's advisor at the University of Maryland. She had just been appointed an Associate Professor of Psychology at New York University, a step up, maybe two, from her current status at Maryland. She needed to sell her house quickly.

Within a few minutes, I had used Lillian's computer to search for house listings in the vicinity of Hawk's Bay. My aunt collected forms for me to take, dozens of legal pages that all looked alike. We had taken to using a list in order to keep track of them. Lillian had, I noticed, given up on the crutches, and was cheerfully hopping around the house on one leg, hanging onto whatever was available: furniture, walls, me. A few minutes later, a pound of paper in my briefcase, I was on my way to meet Mitch for lunch.

Severna Park, the community named for the Magothy's sister estuary, the Severn, lay just north of Annapolis. Mostly upper-middle-class families lived privileged lives on quiet streets. On warm evenings, people donned helmets and mounted new mountain bikes to join the hordes of inline skaters, runners, walkers, and the occasional Golden Retriever exercising on the county's narrow bike path. Remnants of an old railroad track were visible here and there. I turned off Ritchie Highway and drove along Old Baltimore Annapolis Road, which ran parallel to the path. Mitch's Severna Park office was on my right, but his Jeep wasn't in the parking lot. My car phone rang.

"Miss Elliott, Detective Simmons. What can I do for you?"

Finally. "I've had two obscene calls, one on a tape, which I turned over to the police this morning. But, more important, I've found out a few things. To begin..."

"Miss Elliott, where are you?" I told him. "I'll see you there in ten minutes." The phone went dead.

The Severna Park office was a clone of the Annapolis office. Same colors, same furniture. And, to my surprise, Joyce Nichols.

"I thought you were at the..."

"Annapolis Office. Mitch needed me here today." So, I thought, this was Mitch's solution to the Joyce problem. Of course, he was going to run out of offices to move her to, but I expected he already knew that. "Sit," she commanded. "He's on his way."

"Thanks." I began to busy myself with organizing the contracts Lillian had shoved in my hand. To my surprise, I discovered Joyce had sat down next to me, put up her feet on a coffee table, pulled out an emery board, and gone to work on her nails. With no prologue, she picked up the conversation where we'd left it earlier.

"So, you hear anything from your pal, Mr. Big Shot, Detective Patrick X. Simmons, sir?" I shook my head. "Two murders and all those calls and the guy hasn't got a clue."

"So you think that they're related? The murders and calls?"

"You don't?" She looked at me like I was more stupid than glue. "Of course, they're related."

"I'm not so sure." I had another flash of Leslie's body lying against the peeling blue of the pool. Her face bruised and marked. She must have fought back, I thought again. What was I missing? What wasn't I remembering right? I looked up to find Joyce watching me. Something was crowding the back of my mind, something slouching around waiting for words to make it whole.

"I keep thinking that if I just leave it alone, maybe I'll actually remember something useful for Simmons."

Joyce wagged her head furiously, apparently speechless for once. It was hard to know if the cause was my mention of Simmons or her disbelief in the powers of the unconscious mind. There was silence, with only the sound of a computer clicking somewhere in the depths of the office.

"By the way, Simmons is on his...," I began. Movement outside the window grabbed my attention. Mitch had pulled into the parking lot. We both watched as he sat in the Jeep for a moment, looking down at something and writing. Then he walked in the direction of the office, his muscles loose and confident, his face noncommittal. Joyce, I noticed, had taken her feet off the coffee table. I stood up.

"Hi, sorry I'm late." He seemed about to kiss me, Hollywood-style, then thought the better of it with Joyce staring placidly in our direction.

"It's okay. I just got here," I said.

He looked in Joyce's direction. "That Lindstrom contract arrive?" She shook her head. "Call me when it does. Please." He turned back to me. "There's a diner over on Ritchie Highway. That okay?"

I nodded. "But I can't go just yet. Simmons is supposed to meet me here any minute." I glanced at Joyce, who was still sitting on the couch. Abruptly, she rolled her eyes, groaned, and flounced off to the reception desk.

"You can use my office," Mitch said. Through the window I could see Simmons pull up and get out of his car. He looked like hell, I thought, his pale eyes more washed out than I remembered, his skin almost white. I wondered when he had last slept for an entire night.

"Miss Elliott. Mr. Gaylin."

There was a loud thunk from behind the counter. Joyce stood up, and with a glance of contempt at the detective, swept into the back office, sending her chair crashing into the reception desk.

"Joyce?" I said. "Are you okay?"

"You can use my office," Mitch said for the second time. His voice was calm, but I saw his eyes. Joyce had, I thought, just used up his supply of patience.

"This will be fine," said Simmons. He pointed to the couch. I sat back down. Mitch disappeared into the back. "So, what do you have to tell me?"

I explained about Jack Hardwick's half lie to protect Elizabeth from more hassles, about her appointment with the divorce lawyer, and about Hamm's absence from the Baltimore conference. After five minutes, I caught my breath.

"So, Miss Elliott," he said, leaning back, "you've been very busy."

I grated my teeth. No wonder Joyce was slamming things. I felt like it myself. "There's more. I know that Hamm told you that he knew Leslie Ballard through the tutoring program, but what he didn't tell you was that he was having an affair with her."

There, I'd said it, feeling more relieved to be dumping the whole mess on Simmons' tired shoulders than I had expected. For the first time, he was at full attention, his pale blue eyes concentrated with a new energy. He sat forward on the couch. "How do you know this?" I told him about Elizabeth's friends running into Hamm and Leslie at the Maryland Inn in Annapolis, about the credit card slips. He made a couple of notes. I felt vaguely guilty at not telling Elizabeth first what I had found out about Hamm. But how would that have helped?

"For what it's worth, I also have a theory about the obscene phone calls. You want to hear it?"

"I expect you're going to tell me even if I don't." But he listened without interruption as I told him about the cable channel. When I was done, there was a little silence. "That it?"

"Well, almost." This time there was no sarcasm. He instead looked at me with disbelief. Before he could say anything, I told him about Dan Lloyd and his theory about only certain women needing to be careful.

He made another note, then looked up. "And really that's it, right?"

"Yes," I said.

"Well, on behalf of the Anne Arundel County Police Department, let me begin by thanking you for all your work." Damn. And here I thought we had achieved a kind of detente. "By the way, have you talked with either of the Hammetts?" he asked. "Told them what you found?" I shook my head. "Good. Keep it that way."

Loud voices came from the back of the office. Simmons and I listened. Joyce was arguing, her tone shrill and piercing, but the words were incomprehensible. Mitch's voice was low and controlled. Then there was silence. In a couple of minutes, Joyce burst into the reception area, carrying a jacket and handbag. Not looking at either of us, she stormed out the front door and headed for the parking lot.

Mitch walked back into the reception area. "I apologize for that."

"What happened?" I asked. But I knew. "You fired her?"

He nodded. The phone rang. Someone in the back office picked it up. There was an awkward silence. Simmons, I saw, just for a moment, looked sympathetically at Mitch. Then he stood up, turning to me before he left.

"Miss Elliott, do me a favor." I waited. "Stay out of things. We've got a trap on your phone and we're analyzing the tape. The calls may not be related to the homicides, but if they are..." Leslie Ballard's face flashed in my mind's eye. "I want you to call me if you think of anything else." He pulled out another card and wrote in numbers. "My pager number. Call me. Anytime." With a meaningful lift of the nearly nonexistent eyebrows, he headed for his car.

I looked at Mitch. "I'll be with you in a minute," he said.

I gathered up my paperwork and went outside. Joyce was sitting in an old beige-brown car that had been round the block a time or two. She got out and came over to me.

Her face was inflamed from emotion. "Mitch fired me, but you know that, don't you? I thought he was different, but he's just like the rest of them. I expect you are, too." Before I had time to ask what that meant and how I had mysteriously made her hit list, Mitch came out. Joyce threw first him, then me, a look of anger mixed with despair. She got back into her car and backed out of the lot as we watched. The car's bumper stickers winked at us.

"She's completely out of control," Mitch said. "This rudeness, no, downright animosity, toward Simmons...I don't get it. I give her a job so she can survive. I continue to let her sell part-time. I cut her lots of slack." He looked at me directly. No smiling eyes. "Do you get it?"

"Nope." I sneaked a glance at him. "Nor do I know what I've done to make her angry at me."

"Maybe associate with me." I watched as he took a deep breath, then smiled, as if the associating was okay with him. He was like Lillian, I thought, always able to move on. The crinkles at the corner of his eyes fanned out to his graying hairline. "How'd Simmons react?" he asked.

"Wrote down what I said, then told me to mind my own business."

"That's probably not a bad idea."

"Easy for you to say. You don't have a picture of Leslie in your head. Or a low voice that plays over and over."

His smile flickered out. "No, no I don't."

I checked the time. Late again. I had to be in Hawk's Bay in thirty minutes. Taking a rain check on lunch, I got into my car. In my rearview mirror, I watched Mitch return to his office, realizing I was hungrier than I had thought. Steering onto the highway with one hand, I groped under the seat until my fingers found a box of peanut butter cheese crackers I'd stashed there for days like today.

TWENTY-FIVE

HAWK'S BAY nestled in an elbow of the South River. South of what I didn't know, Annapolis maybe. A community of small cottages huddled on the hilly knob of land above the water. Most were wood, painted green, with screened porches. The narrow lanes were a car width apart, provided you didn't own a Buick Riviera. A century ago these must have been the summer homes of Baltimore's laboring class, families driven out of the city by heat and nasty warm-weather diseases inspired by the open sewers.

Fortunately, the weather had improved, with blue sky and a hesitant sun peeking through the clouds. I stumbled down the steep stone steps leading to Marianne's cottage. They were in sorry condition, requiring my full attention and the help of some pipes welded together to form a railing. A minor landslide washed gravel from beneath my shoes. Mud caked over my heels.

"Eve? Down here."

I shook Marianne's offered hand, taking in her abundant gray hair and the large gold hoops in her ears. She was about fifty, an aging flower child. "Lovely." I pointed to the open water behind her.

Marianne nodded. "Hawk's Bay. I'm not happy to leave it, but..." She shrugged. I could feel my stomach clench. I, too, would have to make this decision soon. A gray cat with a fat head, a Russian Blue, I think, buzzed around our legs.

The house could have been designed by Matisse early in his career. Each room sat on a slightly different angle and plane from the next, the textures rich and busy, the colors deeply saturated. Marianne explained that it hadn't been built all at once, that the original two rooms had been constructed during the twenties, the rest added in the forties and fifties. An enclosed sunporch cantilevered out over a lawn and garden. Beyond that was a sturdy seawall and water. Sailboats were anchored at nearby docks. A few headed toward the mouth of the South River in the swelling breeze, sails billowing white and triangular against the clearing sky.

After a tour of the small house, I sat down on a slipcovered couch and looked around. This was the home of someone who enjoyed and nurtured the small, important things in life. Unlike some shrinks' offices I'd been in, there were no framed diplomas from universities or rented plastic couches. Only brilliant yellow flowers in a blue vase and the souvenirs from what looked to be a lifetime of travel.

"Oh, good," said Marianne. "I see you've got a tape measure. I couldn't find mine. Now, what do we do?"

"First, you'll need to read and sign these," I said, handing her a stack of papers. I began to hand them to her one by one, but she held out her hand for the whole bunch and went to work signing her name. "You don't want me to try to explain them? Or at least read them?"

"Nope," she said, handing them back.

I stuffed them into my briefcase. I handed her the next stack. "These are listings of other, similar homes that have sold or were listed in this area in the last six months. They'll give us an idea of the market value of your house."

Marianne went back to work, reading and nodding and underlining, while I made notes about the property, then took rough measurements of each room.

"How much do you think I should ask?"

"Probably somewhere between two hundred and fifty and two hundred and seventy thousand," I said. "The view and landscaping are wonderful, but the house is small, with only one bathroom, and it doesn't have central air and a new kitchen. And it needs new steps or at least a new railing."

She nodded. "And I'm certainly off the beaten track," she said. "Okay, let's start at two hundred and seventy thousand," I wrote that down, asked a few more questions, and then went to take pictures of the outside of the house and the view of Hawk's Bay. In a couple of minutes I was done.

"Coffee?" she asked. "I've got a couple of minutes." I agreed and soon we were chatting about New York. Then she sat back in her chair, looking out. "Elizabeth told me you found the real estate agent who was dead in the swimming pool. How are you handling it?" Once a shrink, I thought, always a shrink.

"The image is hard to shake. It's half on my mind all of the time. I go back and forth between horror and questions: kind of what's-wrong-with-this-picture-type questions," I said. "It's almost as though if I think hard enough or long enough, I'll come up with something."

"Give it to your unconscious mind," she said.

I stared at her as she casually sipped coffee. Joe Lister, my old advertising mentor, would have agreed. Oh, not in those words, but the same thing, really. "You mean sleep on it?"

"Well, yes, sleep on it. You could also try hypnosis."

"Hypnosis?"

"Well, self-hypnosis. More like a kind of directed meditation really. I'm not an expert, but I know people who find it very helpful for getting in touch with things out of reach of the conscious mind." She smiled broadly. "Too flaky?"

"Well, yes and no. I gather what you have in mind is some sort of thing where I count backwards from one hundred and imagine myself on an escalator going down?"

"Some people do that. Others use other methods. Only a thought."

"Be nice to be able to focus my unconscious mind, instead of sitting around waiting for it to tell me what I want to know. Still..." I watched her serenely looking out the window. Something else occurred to me. "Marianne, you've heard or read about these two murders. What do you think?"

"You mean like a psychological profile?" I nodded. "Well, anything's possible, but if it's a serial killer, there's a standard profile."

I thought for a bit. "Rigid personality, intelligent, a history of childhood abuse. That sort of thing?"

She nodded. I wondered if Simmons were thinking in these

terms. "And if this is not a serial killer," I asked, "say, someone with a grudge or vendetta or something?"

"Then, it seems to me, the field is wide open." She stroked the gray cat when it rubbed against her legs. "But I'm not an expert."

I stood up, thanking her. She walked me to the door. I left with barely a glance at Hawk's Bay. The pager on my belt went off. I phoned from the car. Lillian wanted me to pick up a contract on my way to Wildwood Bay. I noticed that my headache had lifted. Must have been the peanut butter crackers.

THE PILCHER AGENCY in Crownsville was smaller even than Weber Realty, so small, in fact, that Vera Pilcher didn't even have to leave her house. A grandmotherly woman in a brightly flowered housedress answered the door on my first ring.

"Hey, Ma, who's there?" An identical younger woman, maybe thirty-five, poked her head around the corner.

"Hi, you must be Lillian's niece." Her eyes nearly disappeared when she grinned at me. Then a sturdy, well-worn hand shot out as I introduced myself. I recognized her from Mitch's workshop the other morning. "I'm Vera. You met Ma. Come into my office, why don't you."

We spent a fair amount of time on pleasantries—the weather, how did I like Maryland, was Lillian recovering. I accepted a cup of coffee from her mother as Vera put on a pair of magnifying half-glasses from the drugstore and glanced over the contract. Her buyer was making an offer on a property in Pines on Magothy that Lillian had listed a couple of weeks ago. Mrs. Pilcher had plunked down on a small straight chair near the door, her hands in her lap. We waited.

"Okay," Vera said, looking up, then waving the long legal sheets in my direction. "Your seller better love it. The buyer certainly made things easy. Not even a home inspection." She leaned back in her chair. "So...so I'm so glad Lillian's better," she said, reopening a topic of conversation I thought we'd finished. "And I'm so glad you're here to help her."

I made what I thought was an appropriate noise, wondering how fast I could get out of here. I finished my coffee. Mrs. Pilcher was at my side refilling my cup before I could refuse. Vera had settled back to chat. They didn't get many visitors, I gathered.

"I hear you found Leslie's body," she said. If there was any chance of forgetting it, I thought, it wasn't going to be today. "I worked with her a few years ago. Rose Macklin, too."

Although it seemed my turn to say something, I didn't know what. Vera came to my rescue.

"We all worked for Ed Templeton in Arnold after getting our licenses," she said, "before the horny old coot retired and sold his brokerage to Century 21. Then Rose went to Coldwell Banker and Leslie to...to...I forget where. Anyway, eventually both she and Leslie later moved to Gaylin. Smart cookie that I am, I got my broker's license instead and opened this thriving establishment." Vera looked at the silent phone and laughed. Before long, Ma and I joined her.

Vera recovered first. "They both were smart going with Mitch. Not surprising, of course, since for a growing brokerage he's got the best reputation around. No slightly irregular business practices, if you know what I mean."

I shook my head. "No, I don't. What practices?"

Vera looked surprised but didn't comment. "Well," she said, leaning back in her chair, "for example, old Ed used to own a termite inspection company. Nobody much knew since it wasn't called Templeton Extermination or anything. Anyway, he required that we all use his company for termite inspections. And guess what?" I shook my head. "We always found termites. And the sellers always had to pay to have these nonexistent termites exterminated."

"Oh."

"Ed had friends. Anyway, he's deader than his termites. Fell over a week after he retired to enjoy his ill-gotten and buggy wealth."

"Vera, how well did you know Leslie Ballard?"

"Not as well as Rose, but she struck me as smart and good at what she did. And gorgeous."

"And Rose?"

Her plain face darkened. "Better than I wanted to, I guess. She was ambitious, that one. Always working. Have to give her that. She worked hard." I wondered what that meant. "Now, don't get me wrong. I don't think she deserved to die for her ambition."

I opened my mouth with another question, but Vera was staring out the window, lost in her thoughts. "Business," she said, "ain't what it used to be, I'll tell you that. No more handshakes; everybody's covering their butts with contracts, keeping an eye out over their shoulders, just in case you have a lawsuit in your pocket. And too many people involved. Too much money and too few ethics." She had forgotten me and Ma. "That's why I guess I went out on my own. I'll never be rich, but who cares? To be successful today, even in a good agency like Gaylin, you need to be young, beautiful, and socially connected." She laughed. "As you can see, I'm a little lacking."

I fidgeted in my chair, not knowing what to say. I wondered how to get away. I needn't have worried. Vera smiled and stood up, her hand out. I thanked Ma for the coffee, then walked to the car, thinking about her words. And how similar they were to those of Leslie Ballard that spring morning at Wildwood Bay.

TWENTY-SIX

WILDWOOD BAY was as lovely as I remembered, more draped in green than last week. The day had grown tranquil, warm, and fragrant. Across the protected bay came the sounds of ducks, their squawks echoing over blue water. "If your clients don't love sailing, maybe they will love ducks," Leslie Ballard had said last Thursday morning. I looked at my watch. Almost five o'clock. Returning inside, I closed the windows I'd opened earlier to air out the house. I called Howard's home and the number at the Office Giant. No luck.

For something to do, I found paper towels under the kitchen sink and tried to wash the Hawk's Bay mud from my shoes. There was no hot water. Damn. I glanced down again at the old-fashioned *H* and *C* taps over the sink. Then, standing at the sink, my hands muddy from the caked shoe, some logjam broke loose in my mind.

My shoe still in my hand, I hopped into the bathroom. The sink top was the same jumbled mess as it had been Friday morning: an assortment of makeup, little brushes and tubes and pots and jewelry filling every inch. With mounting excitement, I picked through the tangle of earrings and chains. There it was. A signet ring. A Naval Academy signet ring. Turning it over, I saw the owner's name. So that, I thought, was the real reason Hamm had made that nervous late-night visit to my cottage. He wasn't just worried about Elizabeth, he was worried about *himself.*

I tried to get a grip on my careening thoughts. Leslie and Hamm had used the Wildwood Bay house as a rendezvous. I could half imagine the scene. After sex, Hamm would have fastidiously washed his hands. Had Leslie then surprised him as he stood at the sink, lured him back to bed a second time? Whatever happened, he had taken his ring off, then forgotten it. Maybe in the heat of the moment or the rush to leave. Then I'd interrupted Leslie as she put things in order, before she could have made a last check of the house. She probably stood where I stood now, looking in the mirror. She would have freshened up, reapplied her lipstick, whipped her dark curls into their frenzied halo, and buttoned and smoothed her dress. A couple of minutes more and she would have found Hamm's ring.

I looked in the mirror over the sink. And suddenly thought again of the bruises and little cuts on Leslie's face. If there had been a fight on the Hammetts' patio, why were the marks deep and short, not long and shallow like regular scratches? And why on only one side of her face? Had Hamm...?

Taking the heavy ring with me, I sat down on the sofa in the living room and stared out at the small cove, trying to order my thoughts. Just because Hamm was sleeping with Leslie in other people's houses didn't mean he was a killer. Leslie's presence swirled around me in the little house. It was likely no one had been here since Friday.

Shaking off my theories, I forced myself back to the facts and thought about the timing last Friday. I had arrived at Wildwood Bay about a quarter of twelve. A few minutes after noon Leslie had gone to meet her client and her death at the Hammett house sometime before two. Or so the medical examiner thought. Hamm, I knew, had returned to Baltimore at about one-thirty, according to the parking attendant.

I sat thinking and staring at the sailboats rocking in the sunlight. A drip came from the kitchen tap where I hadn't quite turned off the water. Where had Hamm gone? Suddenly, I was again standing on the patio of his house that late afternoon. I could hear my own scream as it rose in my throat as I knelt on the stones. I listened hard now, hearing my scream, and then his wail. Had Hamm gone back to his Charles Cove house and killed Leslie for some reason I couldn't know? Had he then returned to pretend to find her? Where had he gone after he'd left Wildwood Bay?

I looked at my watch again. Five-thirty. I'd been waiting here for over half an hour. Howard wasn't going to show. Odd, since he had seemed sincere, someone who would have at least called.

Echoing my thoughts, the phone rang in the next room. I hesitated. What if it wasn't Howard? What if it was a replay of yesterday? Would the same stream of filthy obscenities gush from the receiver? The phone rang again.

I could feel the creeping fear already being replaced by anger. It would, I knew, soon be followed by an all-consuming exhaustion. The three stages—fear, anger, fatigue—were becoming routine, even predictable. I ran into the small front bedroom and, picking up the phone after the fourth ring, slammed it down hard. It felt good. I picked it and slammed it a second time, then sat down on the bed to think. What the hell was I doing? Already, the beginnings of exhaustion were nibbling at the edges of my body.

The pager at my waist buzzed, making my already tattered nerves clang. I looked down at the number. Lillian. A kind of internal shaking gripped me again. I forced myself to keep calm, then picked up the black phone and dialed.

"Hi," said my aunt, answering on the first ring. "That was fast. Howard just called to tell me he's had some car trouble and he's going to be late. He's at some garage near Ritchie Highway. I tried to call you at the Wildwood Bay house, but there's something wrong with the phone there."

I could feel my rage returning. Fear was making me act irrationally. The phone creep had me just where he wanted me, I thought. The realization made me boil over. "Lillian, do you suppose that just once a client could actually get to an appointment? Even be on time?" My aunt clucked. "It's a disease with these people." Lillian's other phone rang and she apologized and left me holding. Maybe it was this house, I thought. I found that Hamm's ring was still in my hand.

"Eve, you still there?" I grunted. "That was Howard again. I've got him on hold. He wants to meet you there in an hour and a half. It'll still be light. I said I'd ask. Okay or not?" I didn't say anything. I just wanted to go home, to sleep off the exhaustion that was peddling fast toward me. "Eve?"

"Yeah, it's okay. Seven p.m. And tell him to be on time."

"I'll tell him." She coughed briefly. I could almost see her fiddling with the pencil stuck in her blond hair, the layers of shellac strong enough to hold half a dozen pencils. "Eve?"

"I'm here." I took a deep breath.

"You're all set then? You don't want to reschedule?"

"No, it's okay." We hung up and I went back to the living room, my fingers turning Hamm's ring over and over. The rapid-fire emotions had left me feeling spacey. I needed to get out of here.

I put the Naval Academy ring back on the sink. No one would take it since no one knew it was there. Except Hamm. I suddenly had a picture of him sitting on my porch a few nights ago, his hands forming themselves into a child's church and steeple, open it up and see all the people. He'd no doubt been missing it for days. And if he hadn't found a way to get it back by now, he probably wasn't going to try.

The dying sun was warm on my face as I locked the front door. I'd think about what this all meant later. Right now I wanted food. Comfort food.

ANN'S DARI-CREME, home of her Famous Footlongs, stood in solitary glory at the southern entrance of Marley Station Mall, just off Ritchie Highway. The parking lot was jammed with people leaning against cars, licking their melting cones. I squeezed into a parking space. Ann's, Lillian had told me, had survived progress in the form of the gazillion-square-foot mall behind the tiny drive-in. It was a little bit of the 1950s, marching head held high toward the millennium.

Inside, the counter, with its eight red stools, was four deep with customers, some ordering ice cream, some the famous footlongs with fries. I could feel my hair awash in suspended grease. Not that it mattered, I thought. With an Ann's ice-cream cone in your hand, I'd discovered what generations of locals already knew: during the few moments it took to eat, nothing much mattered. An efficient young woman took my order and made change from a ten. I carried my prize back to the car. In two minutes, slurping away, driving with one hand, I'd parked in a lot in back of the mall. Behind me, on the old railroad bed, wove the upper reaches of the Baltimore Annapolis bike path. With some fast licking, I managed to climb up a short incline without dripping ice cream on myself. I sat down on a bench.

My mind tried to shuffle and deal theories. But for a few moments, with the ice cream sweet and cold, I could turn them off. Then the cone was gone, and I found myself sitting on the bench, watching the ballet of cars in the parking lot and trying to catch any elusive musings my mind was attempting to offer. What had Marianne suggested? Self-hypnosis. I closed my eyes and started counting backwards from one hundred, willing myself into a state of deeper consciousness. Still counting, a noise jarred me. I opened my eyes to find a loose-limbed kid with baggy pants nearly running over my feet with his skateboard. He was followed by a helmeted young matron on a bike pulling a toddler in some sort of yellow plastic rickshaw. So much for self-hypnosis, I thought. If I was going to figure things out, I was going to do it with my eyes open.

It felt safe and comfortable sitting on the bench. I made myself think about the evening. I'd show Howard the house, then go home. And then what? I wasn't calling Will again, I thought. Glancing at my watch, I got back in the car and found a parking spot near an entrance to the mall, next to an empty slot with a sign that said Reserved For Police. Somewhere in the mall, I remembered seeing some sort of store that sold security devices. Time to arm myself—if not with a gun, at least with whatever else was available in the way of home protection.

Marley Station Mall was bustling, mostly with teenagers trolling for love. I moved around them, the girls with big hair and bare bellies trying to attract boys with bad attitudes and worse skin. A fragrance cart spewed a cloying cloud of sweet scent into the air. Honeysuckle. Like there wasn't enough of it outside. I walked past a toy store with a small door for kids to go through, past a store selling fake antiquey-looking furniture that let you pretend the stuff had been in your family for years. There was a store selling men's shirts and ties. Across the corridor an accessory store stood next to a beauty parlor. Inside a buxom teen-woman sat at the front counter contemplating some weighty question. Then I spotted what I'd come for, a small shop called Safe and Sound.

A young man, but not that young, his hair sticking straight up with some sort of goo, welcomed me with a wave and a smile filled with pepperoni pizza. Seated in the back, he suddenly disappeared behind the counter to fiddle with his dinner. Despite the ice cream, it smelled good.

"Sorry," he said. I could hear him but not see him. When he popped up, his face was freshly wiped. "Dinner. Can I show you something."

"Maybe. I'd like to just look around first." He nodded, then glanced longingly under the counter. "Go ahead and finish your dinner," I said.

"Thanks." He disappeared for a second time.

I began to browse. Most of the cheaper stuff was lined up along the walls, with the electronic surveillance equipment safely under glass. Who was using this stuff? On the open shelves, I spotted canisters of pepper spray and alarms of every variety imaginable: car alarms and house alarms and personal alarms; police locks that wedged in the floor sat next to packages of the Club, and triangular metal plates that fitted over trunk locks. The Club now came in multicolors, I noticed. Did that help sales? There were listening devices and tiny cameras that could fit in overhead light fixtures or outlets. Next there'd be the sticky goo that shot out of a gun and glued your opponent in his tracks. I'd seen it demonstrated on TV. I looked around. No goo gun. It looked like I wasn't going to have the opportunity to engulf anyone in glop.

I contemplated the sets of security lights for the outside of the bungalow, but figured I could get them at half the price at the local hardware superstore. Finally, I browsed along the counter where the clerk was finishing his dinner, balling up greasy paper and tossing it at a wastebasket behind him. He missed and was sheepishly forced to get up and try again.

"Find anything?" he asked.

"I don't know. I was thinking of getting an alarm system for my house."

Within a minute, he had shown me a nearly incomprehensible

array of choices, from the cheap and easy to install to complicated systems that needed to be installed and monitored by professionals. This was going to be more involved than I had thought. "I guess I have to think about this a little. How about a smaller alarm to carry with me. For tonight." Trying to mask his disappointment, he pulled out a tray of objects all designed to be carried or worn. I chose a personal alarm which hooked onto a belt or handbag, then fiddled with a pepper spray on a key chain. The policewoman's words of warning came back to me. As did the memory of the quick cloud of choking spray. I put it down.

"There are other key-chain items," said the clerk, pulling out another tray. "Like this. Nasty, no?" He was holding out a kind of brass knuckles object, but with double points on the other end to discourage your attacker. God, I thought, it was like the scissors thing Christine McGrath had shown us. I shivered and nodded my head. Why not? This was war.

Paying for my purchases, I glanced at my watch. I had barely twenty minutes to make it back to Wildwood Bay. I was going to be late. But Howard wouldn't dare leave. If he did, I told myself, I'd immediately call Lawrence Schoenfeld in New York and take his damn job.

TWENTY-SEVEN

To MY SUPREME annoyance, Howard wasn't waiting for me at Wildwood Bay, but I didn't call New York. Instead, I tried to keep my anger under control by examining my new purchases. In about two minutes, the alarm was back in my bag. And the pointy thing was hanging menacingly on my own key chain. Now what? The view from the deck was lovely, but I wanted sleep and real food, not sunsets. I went back inside and phoned Lillian.

"Lillian, Howard's still not here. I'm not waiting much longer." I felt defeated. Then I thought of something else. "Did he ever talk to you about financing?"

"He told me he has an inheritance, yes. Nothing else." I told her about his insistence on paying cash. She listened without comment. "Well, it's unusual and probably financially stupid, but it's his money," she said. There was a moment's silence. "You need to find out the details of the settlement of Irene's estate. When and how much."

Great. Being a real estate agent had to be the world's nosiest profession. I hated this part of the job. It was no wonder an undercurrent of gossip raged in many offices. It was just too tempting for some agents to talk about their clients' personal lives: how much money they made and whether they were getting along with their spouses. Lillian coughed, bringing me out of my reverie. "Okay," I said, "just exactly how do I go about doing that?"

"If Howard finds a place he likes and plans to pay cash, we'll need some sort of letter from the executor of Irene's will or a banker before the seller will take the house off the market," she said. "He's a friend, but you still have to know exactly how good a buyer he is."

"Lillian, are there other children or family?"

"No. His father died in a car accident when he was little. A couple of years later his mother sold a number of acres of waterfront in South County. I know because I handled the sale for the buyer.''

''Much money involved?''

''I can't remember. But even then waterfront was quite valuable.'' Lillian was silent, probably racking her brain to remember the details of one sale out of thousands over a forty-year career. ''You know,'' she said, suddenly, ''I've always wondered what Irene did with the money.''

''Why?''

''Well, she continued to rent that shabby old bungalow. But some people are just eccentric about money. I remember the neighborhood kids used to tell stories about her and Howard, the kid stuff that is usually fiction.''

''Like what?''

''Like they were crazy millionaires,'' said Lillian. ''I don't know about that, but Irene was very protective of Howard, not letting him play with the others or wait for the school bus by himself. They generally just kept to themselves, particularly as Howard got older. And I don't think he's ever dated. It's too bad. I think that's probably what has made him so shy.''

''Lillian, why did Irene move to Florida?''

''She had a stroke and was left partially paralyzed. Her sister-in-law Greta in Fort Myers is a retired nurse.''

''Did Howard ever talk to you about what the kids said?''

''Not really. But it wasn't until Irene moved that he started coming to church. A couple of us got to know him, little by little, because he volunteered his time. We were just so grateful for the help.''

''Well, it must have been good for him. He hardly seems shy around you.''

''It's a little easier for him, I think, not being under Irene's thumb. Probably it's the first time he's had a chance for a real life, without jumping every time Irene said jump. Then, the poor man lost his job.''

''So what did he tell you about his inheritance?''

''A while back he said that there was some money, but that

there were a few legal hurdles." Lillian was suddenly very quiet. "You know, Eve, to tell you the truth, for some reason talking about all this makes me worry a little."

I, too, was getting a bad feeling. Howard was going to run into some obstacles buying a house. I heard my aunt's other phone ring. "Call me later," she said.

I hung up. Where was Howard? Five more minutes.

I sat for a couple of seconds, then shrugged to myself. Without really understanding why, I picked up the phone again and dialed Florida information. In about two minutes, I had the numbers for two G. Lucases in Fort Myers. I picked one and dialed, half-wondering what I was doing. I imagined Simmons would have had a word for it. The phone rang four times. A halting female voice answered.

"Greta Lucas?"

"Na, not here. I'm her sister-in-law." My skin tingled. Unless ghosts had begun answering phones, something was mighty wrong. Trying to squelch the quake in my voice, I introduced myself.

"Mrs. Lucas, did you used to live in Maryland?"

"Yes?"

"Mrs. Lucas, I'd like to talk to you about your son."

"Who are you?"

"My name is Eve Elliott. I'm a real estate agent. Your son, Howard, has asked me to show him some houses."

There was silence. "I ain't got no son. I got a dirty little ingrate who wouldn't take care of me when I got sick," she said. "After all the years I did for him. You wanna 'ssociate with him, waste your time, that's your business. But don't call me to talk 'bout it." I could hear the TV in the background. When she spoke again, her speech had deteriorated. "Bastard wants my money," she gasped, "the son a bitch." A long pause. "I ain't got no son. You hear?"

I put the phone down. My heart was crowding my chest. I looked around the small bedroom. I had to get out of here. And now. I grabbed my handbag and keys just as Howard's brown van pulled into the front yard. He jumped out, his face red and perspiring. I took a deep breath and ran toward the door. Too late. He was already planted in the doorway of the small kitchen. Blocking my way out. Standing far too close.

"I'm sorry I made you come here twice. Car trouble," he said pleasantly. "Second time in a week. I'll trash that thing as soon as my mother's money comes through." He turned and looked out the window in disgust at the van. "I hope this was okay? Lillian said it was. Do you have time to show me the house?"

"Not really." I could see something change in his face.

"Oh, like the other time. You have to be somewhere else. But I'm sure you can make time." He seemed bigger than I remembered, and everywhere at once. His voice was low, menacing, unrelated to the innocent church voice. It was as if I were seeing and hearing someone else. He grabbed my arm, loosely at first.

"What's the hurry, anyway? What's there to go home to?" he asked. "Oh, I know. Your boyfriend next door. You could go home to him. But, no, not tonight. Tonight, you'll stay right here with me. What could possibly happen? I'm just a lonely loser. A pervert who couldn't get it up with a crane."

Some knot in my mind unraveled and I could picture the video store. The sweaty commandos, their bodies stoked with testosterone, lunging at Pinky's grandmother and me in living color. In the next room, beneath the swinging half door, the silent voyeur, visible only by pantlegs and shoes, was choosing his fix for the evening, listening. Maybe watching.

Herding me in front of him, his grip tightening on my arm, Howard walked us into the living room with its secondhand furniture. He glanced around the room, then out to the water. Sailboats stirred in the slight breeze. The sun was setting, red on the horizon.

"It's pleasant, isn't it?" he asked. "And everyone wants waterfront. It keeps its value because there is only so much of it." I nodded, reaching for the alarm canister in my handbag. My fingers closed around the device. "Did you know that there are eight thousand miles of Chesapeake Bay waterfront?" he asked.

His eyes trailed to my side, to the open handbag. He suddenly lunged forth, grabbing and upending it. The contents spewed over the wide-planked floor, with lipsticks and pencils darting everywhere. I watched him smile. I tried to pull the pin on the alarm, but he was suddenly on top of me, grabbing my wrist. The alarm fell at his feet. He kicked it away, picking up my key chain.

"How nice," he said. "Get up," he said. "There's an attic, I believe." He pointed to the trapdoor in the ceiling that pulled down to reveal the rough set of stairs. "I think I'd like you to show me the attic."

With one hand he yanked the stairs down, then pushed me up the unsteady rungs. The keychain was in his other hand, the steely prongs visible. I could feel him close on my heels. His breathing was oppressive, his breath itself feverish. The heat rose as I climbed.

"It needs insulation up here," he said, almost conversationally. "But no matter. We don't mind, do we?"

As it had the day Leslie Ballard died, soft light came from dormer windows, bathing the unfinished room in a tender pink glow. The two single beds and the chest of drawers lay untouched. I stepped into the room, with Howard just behind me, grunting. Leaning down, he pulled the trapdoor shut.

Suddenly he came at me from behind, spinning me around. His grip was tight, his embrace suffocating. His mouth covered mine, opening my lips, his tongue searching the far corners with sticky insistence. His body pushed violently. A sweaty insistent hand found its way over my breasts. A thump told me the keychain had fallen.

I could feel his penis thrusting into my crotch. He was pulling at it with the other hand. Shit, shit, shit. The stupid, cretinous little bastard. Sex was his weapon. Fear once again gave way to fury and I shoved him back with all my strength. "What the hell was that about? You goddamned, fucking little weasel." I wiped my mouth, trying not to spit the taste of him onto the floor. Revulsion sent shivers through me. I felt out of control and I didn't care. "You miserable, lying little prick." With the palm of my hand, I shoved him against the sloping wall. He fell onto the nearest bed instead. Then he was on his feet.

"I wouldn't do that," he said. Something in his quiet tone

warned me. Anger backpedaled again to fear, then disgust. He was near me again, his wet breath spewing saliva over my face and throat. Find a way out, my mind said. He is a killer. He has already killed twice. Where was the keychain? Find a way out.

I lunged toward the trapdoor, then felt his hand grab my arm. I struggled free, pulling away, but he grabbed me again, this time with both hands. "Get away, you slimy rat-faced little shit." I found I was shouting. Maybe someone in a neighboring house would hear me. His left hand fiddled with his crotch. I could see the swelling grow. Think, I told myself. Pay attention. Get his trust. Talk to him.

"Howard," I said, "why don't we talk. You can tell me what happened with Leslie. And Rose."

"No. No." He shook his head violently. I could smell the wet, sour odor coming off him. Prickles of rage and impotence swirled through me. I suddenly stamped on his feet, reaching for his crotch, but he had moved back. I stumbled for the trapdoor a second time. Then he was behind me, his hands fiercely clawing their way around my neck. I felt my chest tighten and my breath come harder. The scene in front of me blurred. But Christine McGrath's level voice came to me: "If someone grabs you from behind, you grab their two pinkies and you snap down. Hard." It would never work. Choking, I willed myself to try. In a motion born of desperation and adrenaline, I threw my body backward and upward into his, seizing his little fingers. With all my strength, I jerked downward. There was a light snapping sound. I let go.

The unearthly shriek that filled the room was unlike any I'd ever heard. Even the creature of my nightmare hadn't made a sound like this. I fell forward onto the floor, then turned to watch him dance around the narrow attic room, yowling in agony. Late-evening light was draining over the twin beds. He kicked over furniture, shoving and throwing odds and ends from the bureau into the middle of the floor. I clawed at the trapdoor, tugging at the contraption that let the stairs back down. They stuck. I pulled again, barely daring to turn to see what was happening. The stairs suddenly gave way and fell down with a thud.

It couldn't have taken more than a few seconds. The howl continued. If anything, the pain had him made him even crazier. Eyes on fire, he suddenly seemed to remember I was there. With a roar, he came toward me just as my feet felt the first rung. The last thing I saw was his crippled right hand, his little finger hanging useless.

Then I was downstairs, not thinking, just running. Out the back door, through the last dim rays of sunlight, around the bushes at the side of the house, into the front yard and past the car and van. From the house, the yowl still came. From rage or pain or both, I didn't know. Running into the street, I flagged a car coming in my direction by standing in the middle of the road waving my arms. It didn't slow. By God, they would have to hit me, I thought. The brakes squealed and an elderly woman with a frightened face peered over the steering wheel.

I ran around and spoke to her through the passenger's window. "I need help," I gasped. "I need to call 911." My breath was coming in spurts. Turning, I spat into the nearby grass to get rid of the taste in my mouth. Goddamn it, I thought, she was paralyzed. "Have to call 911," I said again. "Find a phone. Now." Looking down, I saw my sleeve was dirty from something, my skirt still hiked halfway up. Shoving it down, I opened the door and got in the car. Her eyes filled with terror, she began to drive away slowly, her fingers gripping the wheel, staring directly ahead.

TWENTY-EIGHT

AN HOUR LATER I was sitting on the couch in a small cottage, its homey old-folks smell welcome and comforting. My mind skipped around, sorting through a jumble of impressions. From the tidy cottage to the blue police lights swirling in the spring night to Howard's deranged yowl of pain and rage, the time and sequence of events hopscotched back and forth. I noticed that the precise details of what happened at the house at Wildwood Bay began to melt together in a fog of exhaustion. Sitting up straighter, I tried to think.

Once inside the car, sitting beside the terrified elderly woman whose car I'd half hijacked, my breath coming fast and hard, I had tried to explain to her what had happened. "Real estate agent killer" had been the magic words. Remarkably, she had gathered her wits and taken me home to her bungalow three blocks away. Her husband had proved to be resourceful and kindly once the initial surprise of finding a half-demented stranger demanding to use his phone had worn off.

Mr. Winters had watched as I called the police. In a couple of minutes both Mrs. Winters and I were sitting side by side on the couch. Ten minutes later a patrol car showed up, lights flashing. The officer, an efficient and unruffled man with an unexpected Elvis-like pompadour of graying hair, had listened to an abbreviated version of my story, then offered to take me to the hospital. I shook my head. Instead, I described Howard's nondescript brown van. The engine trouble had been a hoax, I thought. There had been no garage. He had, instead, just been waiting for dark.

"Miss Elliott," the cop said, breaking into my thoughts, "I also need a description of this Howard Lucas."

I did the best I could, then listened as the cop put the wheels of authority into motion. Talking into the radio pinned to his

white-shirted shoulder, he passed along my description of Howard
and the van.

I suddenly wanted to spit, to wash my mouth out with soap, to
brush my teeth until my gums poured blood. How must rape be,
I wondered, if this is what a forced grope felt like? I shivered,
thinking about my description of Howard. They'd find him, I
thought, but not based on my generic portrait of everyman: medium brown hair and medium height and weight. Thinking about
my words, I also found they had no emotional weight. I should
have described, I thought, how his penis felt pressed against me,
his blistering breath on my neck, saliva at the edges of his mouth,
his eyes queer with the need to gain control over me. The experts
were indeed right. Sexual assault was only marginally about sex.
It was about getting power over someone. It was about taking
power when you felt you didn't have any. Not even power over
your own actions.

I took a deep breath, trying to be calm. I had done what could
be done right now. Oddly, I kind of missed Simmons' bunchy and
sorrowful face with its pale eyebrows. My left wrist was sore when
I pressed it. But that was all, I thought. I was alive. Which is more
than Leslie and Rose were. Vaguely, I wondered what they'd done
to outrage him so badly he'd completely lost control and killed
them. Then, overtaken by the memory of the suffocating attic with
its warm light and narrow beds, I could only think about the ob-
session in his eyes. I forced myself not to think about what might
have been.

"Officer, there's one other thing I forgot to tell you." The cop
looked over at me. "I broke his little finger, maybe both little
fingers. He screamed in pain." Mrs. Winters gasped. And the cop
looked at me curiously, with admiration or surprise, I couldn't tell.

"How did that happen?" he asked.

I explained about the self-defense workshop, about Christine
McGrath's suggestions and admonitions. I wondered what kind of
grade she would give me for what had happened tonight: probably
an A for using what I'd learned to get out of a mess and an F for
finding myself alone in a deserted house with a killer in the first
place. What had I missed, I wondered. Surely there were clues

that Howard was... It occurred to me that I should call Lillian. Howard was a killer and sexual psychopath, but he was the same Howard who had ferried her on errands after she broke her ankle. The same Howard who volunteered his time at the church. Would he go to her? Was she in danger?

Suddenly, a picture drove its way into my mind. Howard had been at the church last Thursday morning at the workshop, filling coffee urns and later cleaning up. I could see Leslie Ballard's Styrofoam cup, half filled with cold coffee with its coagulating milk, its rim bloodied by her lipstick. It had been sitting on the kitchen counter as he bagged garbage. Had Howard been looking us over? Choosing his victims? Even as we tried to learn how to defend ourselves against him? Was it possible that the police would find that smeared coffee cup at his home? I looked across the room at the cop and wondered if I should tell him. No, it would be easier to wait for Simmons.

"Miss Elliott, why don't you drink this?" Mr. Winters held out a steaming mug of something. "Bouillon," he said. "Warm you up." I started to refuse, but something stopped me. Chicken soup. I downed it gratefully. My host, I noticed, was treating his wife exactly as if she'd been assaulted, too. But, then, I supposed she had been. By me. After all, how often does a shrieking and disheveled woman run into the road at nightfall, nearly hijack your car, and demand that you call the police?

I took another sip, letting the warm liquid fill the gaps in my body and soul. "Here. Wrap up in this." Mr. Winter offered a homemade crocheted comforter, the kind whose bright squares can be found on half the couches in America. I took it, glad to be warm and cared for. Despite the warm evening, laden with the ever-present honeysuckle, I was still shivering.

"Officer, I need to go back and close up the house." I also noticed again that my keys were missing. He nodded. Somewhat reluctantly, I unwrapped myself, deposited my empty soup cup on a nearby table, then rifled through my pockets for a business card. Mr. Winters, I noticed, was carefully printing his name and address and phone number on a piece of paper torn from a corner of the phone book.

"Please call us," he said. "Let us know you are okay."

Thanking them profusely, I left, getting into the front seat of the police cruiser. In five minutes, we were back at Wildwood Bay. Two police cars were already there, lights flashing against the tall trees, illuminating nearby yards. Neighbors were standing at the edges of the property, making up theories to fill the gaps in their information. Police radios echoed and buzzed in the darkness. It was, I thought, only a matter of time before the TV trucks pulled up.

The cop led me inside. A couple of others were poking around. And someone was upstairs, apparently picking through the attic. The contents of my handbag lay scattered across the living room. Through the windows looking out to the water, I could see a narrow crescent moon, fuzzy in the warm night, sending weak light over the quiet cove. It looked peaceful, calm. And to my surprise, the house did, too. Despite the violence of an hour ago, very little had been disturbed downstairs. And there was no blood. Only the memory of that unearthly howl hung in the air.

"I'd like to go up." The cop nodded, admonished me to be careful.

Climbing the unsteady rungs, I could feel my heart beating a little faster. But except for a few books and odd knickknacks out of place, it, too, seemed strangely innocent. There hadn't been all that much to mess up. I could see the jumbled bedclothes where Howard had fallen onto one of the single beds during our struggle. I found my keys, with the pointy self-defense weapon still attached. For all the good it did, I thought. I went downstairs to wait.

Simmons hadn't come. Maybe he had been called out of town again. Or had gone home to bed. Instead, another plainclothes detective arrived to ask me the same questions I had answered earlier in the safety of the Winterses' modest living room. I sat quietly on the couch. Someone got me a glass of water. In the bathroom Hamm's ring lay innocently tangled with the other jewelry. Excusing myself, I went to make sure.

Closing the door, I pawed through the tray, my fingers closing on the ring. So, it finally meant nothing more than Hamm and

Leslie had grabbed an opportunity to be together. And if that opportunity was on a Friday morning in some stranger's bed, well so it was. Why Leslie had chosen Hamm, I'd never know. I guess she had had her reasons.

Returning to the living room, I also suddenly realized that I still had no real idea of what had actually motivated Howard. Outside, a media truck pulled up. The small house felt claustrophobic. And the police cruisers were too much of a replay of last Friday. I wanted to go home, to feed and hug the dogs. And to talk to Lillian before she heard about this on the 11:00 p.m. news. To warn her that Howard was still out there.

A roar went up outside. I could hear excited voices, see dark figures milling about half a dozen cars. Grabbing my handbag, I met the cop with the gray pompadour by the door.

"We've got him," he said. "He went to the Magothy General emergency room. Shrieking in pain, I might add, thanks to you."

So that, I thought, was that. I checked to make sure I wasn't needed any longer, then waited as two cruisers were moved in order for me to be able to back out of the yard. Tomorrow, Weller Church would handle the police, I thought, walking me safely through all the statements and paperwork. I unlocked the BMW just as a TV crew spotted me and ran into the yard. Their lights struck me full in the face. I saw the business end of the camera. A reporter yelled something I didn't understand before the cops were able to pull the cameraman away. I got into the car and backed out with difficulty, my hands trembling all over again. Once more, the television lights hit me through the windshield as I turned into the street and pulled away. With luck, I thought, I'd never see Wildwood Bay again.

TWENTY-NINE

RAY TILGHMAN'S COTTAGE looked especially dear in the scant moonlight, the sliver of Weller's Creek shimmery black from this distance. After jolting down dark rutted roads, trying to remember the way home, I was grateful to be there. I sat in the car for a couple of minutes, clearing my mind of what had happened. It was over.

Howard's arrest, I thought, meant closure for Leslie's and Rose's deaths. We'd find out the reasons later. And it meant freedom for the rest of us caught up in escalating fear. I could again hang out down by the water, throwing sticks for the dogs to fetch, watching the waves lap gently on shore. Spring would turn to summer, with cicadas shrieking in the overheated pine woods. The thought brought me up short. Weller was going to make me make a decision about Ray Tilghman's house very soon. And if I didn't, that decision would be made for me.

Inside the house, I could hear the dogs barking, hungry and anxious to go out. I thought I also heard the phone ringing. Lights suddenly swirled up behind me as Will's truck growled to a stop beside the BMW. He was out before I even had time to gather my stuff and open the door.

"I heard what happened," he said, helping me out, like a celebrity alighting on Oscar night. "You okay?"

"Sort of. If anyone is okay after they are assaulted by a psychopath." He closed the door and folded me a familiar hug, then pushed me away to make sure I really was okay. "But they got him. Guy named Howard Lucas from Lillian's church."

"I heard."

I glanced at my watch. It was almost ten. "There were media crews at the scene when I left. I'll probably make the late news."

We walked in silence to the cottage, Will's arm draped com-

fortably and a little unexpectedly over my shoulder. He unlocked
the door and the dogs poured out, running in figure-eights in the
yard and nearby woods. In two minutes, Zeke was back to check
me out, uncanny in his ability to sense trouble, past or present.
Lancelot followed, his intuition not so finely tuned, but his interest
in companionship and food keen.

The phone rang. This had to be Lillian. I picked up the receiver.
Where had I been, she asked. She'd called earlier. Twice. Hadn't
I gotten her messages? She was worried sick about me. And sick
about what had happened. I thought I heard a note of something
I hadn't heard before in her voice. Maybe people were not to be
trusted, after all, her voice said. They cheated and lied and har-
bored terrible sickness. I couldn't blame her for thinking that. First
the Canins' decampment, and now, worse, much worse, Howard's
unexpectedly awful crimes.

I told her what had happened, from my conversation with Irene
Lucas to an abbreviated version of Howard's attack. There was no
response on her end, unusual for Lillian, who usually clicked and
clucked to let you know she was still there and absorbed with
what you were saying. I described briefly the scene afterward at
Wildwood Bay, first with Mr. and Mrs. Winters, then back at the
Sassafras Lane house. She'd know soon enough, I supposed, all
the really sickening details. As she would also probably hear,
sooner or later, about Hamm's affair with Leslie. And, once again,
feel betrayed by someone she thought she knew.

"Lillian?"

"Yes, I'm here. Just weary, I guess. I miss Max, Eve." I let
the silence ride. Then she cleared her throat with a little cough.
When she spoke again, I could hear the strength returning to her
voice. I could only imagine what it cost her. "But," she was
saying, "I'm just grateful that you're okay." The unspoken end
of the sentence was, I knew, that I was also here, in Maryland. I
pleaded exhaustion and told her I'd phone tomorrow.

I was grateful to find my shower in working order. Ignoring the
red flashing lights on the answering machine, I brushed my teeth,
then I let the hot water wash away the feel of Howard's hands on
my body. I could hear Will moving around the kitchen, feeding

the dogs and putting a pot of water on to boil. Sliding into jeans and a sweatshirt, I realized I was already feeling better. I stood in the doorway to the kitchen, watching Will pull out a package of spaghetti from the overhead cupboard. There were no wasted movements, no self-consciousness. Unlike Ben, I thought, who had not only been incompetent in the kitchen but also downright dangerous. Twice, I'd rushed him to the emergency room at Lenox Hill Hospital, his hand wrapped in a bloody dish towel. Bagel injuries, both times. The second time the doctor had half-seriously told me to remove all the knives from our apartment. Or give up bagels.

In fifteen minutes, I was sitting at the table with a plate of pasta with butter and grated Parmesan in front of me. Will was drinking beer. Between forkfuls, I told him about what I'd discovered earlier in the day. Elizabeth's visit to the divorce lawyer. My morning trip to Baltimore. Finding Hamm's ring at the little cottage on Wildwood Bay. It seemed very long ago. And if Will was miffed that I hadn't confided in him earlier, he kept it to himself. Finally, I put my fork down. Odd, I thought, food had never tasted this good.

The phone rang. Probably Lillian again. I picked up the phone to hear Simmons' unmistakable voice.

"Now?" I asked. "You want to come over now? I told that other detective everything. You know everything I know. Oh, except one thing." As he listened, I explained about Hamm's Naval Academy ring still resting on the bathroom sink. "So that's what Hamm was doing," I said. "That's it. Can't we talk tomorrow? Unlike you, I need to sleep."

"Tonight, Miss Elliott, just for a few minutes. It's important." I groaned, then relented.

Will was in the kitchen doing dishes at the old sink. I sat down at the desk, thinking about the last few days and my misplaced suspicions. I'd managed to make murder suspects of both the Hammetts, Jack Hardwick, and even Dan Lloyd. Staring at the red flashes, I silently promised myself to stay out of other people's business. Zeke licked my hand just once—dog love at its purest and most restrained—then pressed up against me.

I sat fiddling with my keys, the useless gouge thing still hanging from the chain. A shiver split my spine, and my mind resisted the image of what I now knew to be true: Howard had made the crescent-shaped marks underneath Leslie's eye. He had tried to kill her by gouging out her eyes, just the way Christine McGrath had described. Surprised, Leslie must have slipped and fallen into the pool before he could do much damage. It was, I thought, a kind of savage justice that I broke his fingers. After all, he had known all about that, too.

Resolutely trying to put all thoughts from my mind, I punched the flashing button on the machine and listened to my three messages. The two from Lillian and one from Mitch. Tomorrow, I'd call him. Not tonight. It was bad enough that Simmons was coming over.

"That's it," said Will, drying his hands. "You look all in. You need sleep." I nodded. "Will you be okay tonight? With the dogs? I thought I'd go home, if it's all the same to you."

"That's fine. Thanks for everything, Will." He nodded, slightly embarrassed. Sadness clogged my throat as he hugged me. I watched him pat Lance on the head, then head out. It was really over between us. There was no looking back now. We'd found each other at a crossroads in each of our lives. Although our friendship would survive, a kind of melancholy enveloped me. The lights on his truck swirled through the pine clearing and then disappeared. I got myself a glass of wine and collapsed on the couch, wondering what might have been. There was a rap on the door. The dogs barked as I let Simmons in.

He looked about the same as earlier today. But his shirt was white and clean and pressed, probably fresh off its dry cleaning board not more than a few hours ago: But above the starched collar was a face that looked like it had been pulled out of a laundry bin and slipped into place above his neck. His light eyes did whatever the opposite of sparkle is. Like black holes, I thought, they consumed energy, rather than emitted it. Someplace, well beneath the surface, something was wrong in his life. Something had hurt him and he was avoiding it with work. I wondered what he'd say if I told him I knew.

Instead, I pointed to the couch at the far end of the room. The dogs had accepted him, not happily in Zeke's case, but at least there was no growling, no circling, no evil-eyed dog glare. I sat down in Ray's overstuffed chair and thought how far we'd come from last Friday night. Lancelot's heavy body rested on my foot. Zeke was more spacey, unable to find the right spot to lie down. Every few minutes, he got up and tried again, as if he, too, was too addled by the events of the past few hours to get any rest.

"I know it's late, Miss Elliott," Simmons began.

"Since we are apparently in this for the duration," I said, "you might as well call me Eve." He nodded without smiling, then offered Pat in return. A little reluctantly. Patrick X. Simmons. I wondered again about the X. Xavier? Was he named for a saint or some New York parochial high school?

"You're right about the duration," he was saying. "I wanted you to know that Howard Lucas did indeed make obscene calls to real estate agents all over the county. And he admitted choosing some of his victims from that cable real estate TV channel. He's a nasty bit of pathology that some shrink will no doubt analyze to death." He hesitated. Something scuttled across the roof. "But he's not the killer. Not only has he denied killing Rose Macklin and Leslie Ballard, we know he's telling the truth." I opened my mouth, then closed it. "Miss Elliott...I mean, Eve. Half a dozen people at Office Giant have already alibied him for the time of both deaths."

We sat in silence, Zeke rustling slightly. Ray Tilghman's old-fashioned bell-jar clock chimed midnight.

"So you see...," he began, then stopped.

I saw. All too well. It wasn't over. A killer was still out there: someone capable of smashing open a head and poking out eyes, someone whose motives we didn't understand. I was suddenly overcome again by the need to sleep. The exhaustion part of the cycle was kicking in. I wanted nothing so much as to put the whole thing away for a while. Until I was rested and ready to take it on. Whenever that would be.

THIRTY

SIMMONS AND I sat contemplating each other for many minutes. The clock ticked. The dogs groaned with vivid dreams, their feet paddling the air. Simmons' pale blue eyes were bleak, sleepless.

"Is this going to be an all-nighter?" I asked.

"Maybe."

"Don't you have any other leads?" He shook his head. I sighed. This day had begun a century ago, in another life. Even the horrible scene with Howard seemed long ago, in a distant time and a faraway place. "I'll make us some coffee."

"Yeah, good idea. Thanks." He followed me into the kitchen. Lancelot stayed put, but Zeke padded along, just in case he was needed. "I'm sorry, you know, about asking this of you. I know you're exhausted. But the killer is still out there. Others are..."

I looked up from the coffee grinder. "Okay, okay. I'll drink coffee and talk, but I don't guarantee you more than an hour of consciousness." This whole thing felt, I thought, like nothing so much as one of my early years in advertising. The creative team would stay all night at the office dreaming up wonderful ad campaigns between catnaps and Chinese takeout. The ads were always too clever by half and the clients inevitably rejected them the next morning, but it had been fun. This wasn't. I poured coffee for both of us. Simmons laced his with several spoonsful of sugar, tasted it, added a few more, then poured in milk.

I collapsed in my chair again. My eyes felt scratchy, my body oversensitive with the nerve endings exposed.

"First," I said, "before you ask me your questions, I want to know about Howard Lucas."

"What about him?"

"Why did he make obscene calls?"

Simmons tried not to show his impatience, but it was clear he was not happy to be going backwards over what he considered finished business. "He wanted power and control, I guess. His weapon was sex."

"Yes, yes. But did he say anything to you?"

"Only that after his mother moved, he sort of lost control of himself. No longer anyone there to rein him in, as he put it." Simmons took a sip of his coffee, more relaxed now. "We searched his house."

"And?"

"God-awful mess. You should have seen the bathroom. No, better, you should have smelled it." For a second, I thought Simmons was going to spit in disgust. "And the kitchen. Rotting food. Crap all over the floor. The mess was about waist-deep in the other rooms." He leaned back into the couch and actually grinned at me. "Probably his mother made him take too many baths or something when he was a kid." The grin grew wider. "You know, I'd make a friggin' wonderful shrink. Pay's better, too. And the hours."

I suddenly had a bad thought. "There's no chance they'll let him go, is there?"

"No chance. Trust me on this one. He's sedated and in a guarded room at the hospital. You did far too good a job on him. The emergency room doctor said he was screaming bloody hell when he came in, absolutely nuts with pain. They don't even know how he drove." Simmons took a mouthful of coffee, swirled it around to cool, then swallowed and grinned at me a second time. "All that pain was very helpful to us, you know. We told him no serious medication until he confessed to assaulting you. So, did he talk. And fast. And loud enough for half the hospital to hear."

Despite Simmons' grin, or maybe because of it, I was half hearing Howard's blood-curdling yowl again. "He tell you his mother is alive?" I asked. "In Florida? How he lied about that to everybody?"

"Yeah."

"Why?"

"Didn't tell us."

I thought a bit. "Do you remember at the workshop when someone asked you about Peeping Toms?'' Simmons nodded. ''Was he doing that? Was he watching me? And the others?'' The cop fidgeted, getting Zeke's attention. I touched his sleek black head and the dog relaxed. ''Was he?''

''I didn't ask. We'll know tomorrow.''

I remembered the sensation of being watched, the twigs scraping along the roof and windows, of someone outside, beyond the windowpanes. My spine vibrated a little.

''And then what?'' I asked. ''When calling wasn't enough?''

''I guess he began looking for another way to control you. Look, the shrinks are probably already fighting over this guy.'' Simmons finished his coffee and set the cup on a table. ''Let's move on. You ready to talk?''

I thought that's what we'd been doing, but I kept my mouth shut. Although the coffee had awakened my body, my mind idled, then spun in circles. I felt wired and twangy.

''First,'' he said, ''about Leslie Ballard's death. Here's what we know: She was killed between noon and 2:00 p.m., when she fell into the swimming pool. The M.E. says the jolt of her brain against her skull killed her. The only other signs of trauma were bruises and crescent-shaped marks under one eye. She had had sex recently, which we now know was with Mr. Hammett, whom we will question again. She had not been raped. Her handbag was taken, but that may mean nothing. No one has used her credit cards.'' He recited the facts dispassionately, as if for a judge and jury. ''We don't know what made those marks under her eye.''

The clock ticked. I shivered, thinking back to the workshop, realizing that Simmons wouldn't have known about the scissors thing. So I described it and Christine McGrath's comment about killing someone by poking out their eyes with your fingers. ''There wasn't a person in that room,'' I said, ''who didn't flinch when she said that. In fact, I was sitting next to Leslie. We talked about it afterwards.''

''And?''

''We agreed that neither one of us could possibly put someone's eyes out. Even to defend ourselves.'' I thought for a bit. ''Her killer must have been in that room. If that's what the marks mean.

That someone tried to..." It wasn't a thought I wanted to expand upon. "Elizabeth and Hamm Hammett were there. A hundred or so real estate agents, mostly women, including my aunt, Lillian Weber. The pastor. Mitch Gaylin. And Howard." Simmons got up and paced. The dogs looked up but stayed down. The clock chimed one. He sat back down. "You don't still think this was some sort of random killing? For credit cards and money?"

"Nope."

"Look," I said. "This is ridiculous. I don't think we're getting anywhere. I'm half asleep. I think you better go back and shake Howard's cage again. Maybe the people at Office Giant were mistaken about him."

"And maybe you don't want to believe that the killer was in that room Thursday morning?"

That stopped me short. Maybe I didn't. A shudder, more from a kind of electric exhaustion than from fear, rolled through my body. Where had Hamm gone after he left Leslie at Wildwood Bay? Was Elizabeth justified in her fear for him? Was Leslie blackmailing him? It seemed out of character, but then I'd only met her twice. And where did Rose come into it? Same old questions, I thought. I looked over at Simmons. He'd slumped down the couch, one leg half on, half off the cushions. He looked whipped. I noticed he wasn't watching me any longer, just sort of lying there trying to make some sense of the pieces of the puzzle.

Marshaling what little energy I had left, I tried hard to think. The silence grew denser as minutes passed. Simmons didn't move, nor did I. Hamm Hammett had some explaining to do, I thought. And Jack Hardwick. Where did he come into it? But that was Simmons' job. My brain sputtered and skidded to a halt. My arm dropped toward the floor. I jerked awake, realizing that I'd been dozing. I wondered how long. I glanced over and found that Simmons, too, was asleep. He looked surprisingly peaceful.

I leaned down, touched both dogs, shushing them, then motioned them to follow me. I didn't bother to turn out the lights or brush my teeth. I hoped the door was locked, and if it wasn't, I thought, there was a police detective napping on my couch.

The dogs padded up the stairs ahead of me. Halfway up, I turned and looked down at Simmons. His mouth was slack, his head slumped among the couch cushions. Why had he really come over? To chew over my theories about the murders? Or had he really come over because he knew that Howard hadn't killed Leslie or Rose? But he could have called and told me that. It was an interesting thought. I plodded up the last few steps, then crashed into bed like a dead woman.

Sleep dropped down around me like the curtain of tall grasses that surrounded Charles Cove. Soon I lay quietly next to an overturned dory, hidden from view, listening, a red dog at my side. A cry went up, reverberating in the noonday sun. It gathered strength, a mounting cyclone of sound. Then I was no longer among tall grasses. Instead, a wide, sunlit patio overlooking a swimming pool was behind me. But still the cry did not stop. No, this was not a random act. I looked down, past the blue peeling paint of the pool, and I knew. Somewhere a door closed, an engine purred.

I sat straight up in bed, my heart pounding, my mind swirling, my sweatshirt soaked. All around me, pale morning light filtered in the windows. A steady rain tapped the roof overhead. The dogs came racing into the room, tongues lolling, anxious for me to get up. The clock said 5:45 a.m. I felt like I'd been mugged. Grabbing my sneakers, I sprinted downstairs. The living room was empty, I realized with regret that it wasn't the only thing. The dream so vivid only moments before had fled my mind, to be replaced by a dim, wordless dread.

THIRTY-ONE

AFTER LOOKING THROUGH the clutter on the counter, I sat down at the kitchen table. There was no note, just an empty coffee cup on the dish drainer and nothing left of the pot I'd made fresh last night. I wondered when Simmons had left and why the dogs hadn't awakened me. Or maybe they had, and then I'd gone right back to sleep, incorporating the closing door, the simmering car engine, into my dreams.

I put my head down on the table, trying to remember and forget all at the same time. The content of the dream had vanished, leaving only a hangover, but last night had been real. My sore wrist vividly brought back the stifling attic at Wildwood Bay. I could feel Howard's hot breath, his body pressed against mine. I could hear the snap of his fingers as I pulled hard and back. The sound in my head sickened me, set me shivering.

But Howard had not killed Leslie. And for one moment someplace between wakefulness and sleep I had known who did. Closing my eyes, I strained to imagine the scene by the pool. It was no use. And would Simmons have believed me anyway? Without any proof? A mere shower of brain waves after a traumatic evening?

I dragged myself into the living room. It was too early to be up. Too early to call Simmons, wherever the hell he had gone. I tried again to think and found I wasn't doing a very good job of it. Collapsing onto the couch, Zeke at the other end with his head planted on my legs, Lancelot slumped on the floor beside me, I let myself close my eyes. I would talk with Simmons. Later. Let him handle this, or not handle it, as he preferred. With that much settled, I drifted off again, this time in a spent and dreamless sleep.

When I woke a couple of hours later, the clock was approaching eight. My earlier brainstorm was far away, a mere sensation. After letting the dogs run outside a little, I showered again, washed my hair, and made another pot of coffee. Then I sat down at the rolltop desk and punched in the numbers for Simmons' pager, leaving him mine.

Plodding upstairs, I found a clean cotton shirt on a shelf. Tunneling deeper into the closet, I was rewarded with a favorite spring suit from what I now was beginning to think of as my previous life. I pulled it out of the dry cleaning bag and held it up. Nope. Fine for New York. Too much for Pines on Magothy. Stuffing it back into the closet, I slipped into a pair of all-purpose gabardine trousers. How, I wondered, was Simmons' shirt holding up after a night on my couch and the morning rain dripping through the trees.

Back downstairs, I found an orange and sat down in front of the TV to eat it. Katie Couric was chirping about something.

"We interrupt this show for late-breaking news," said an unseen announcer. A Baltimore anchorman, whose name I didn't know, appeared, his face serious. "As reported earlier, Anne Arundel County detectives have arrested a man who may well have killed two real estate agents. We take you live to..."

I put the section of orange down. Simmons peered out at me, his face bleached with exhaustion. A young reporter, her blond hair slicked back with hairspray and rain, had just stuck a microphone in front of his mouth. He reacted with anger, then realized that the camera was running.

"Detective, can you give us any information about the man you arrested last night at Wildwood Bay? Did he kill those two real estate agents?"

"No, he didn't." The reporter said nothing, waiting, trying not to act surprised. Simmons watched her, a game of cat and mouse, to see who would cave in first. Served her right, I thought, for asking a question that could be answered with three words. Simmons grimaced and fidgeted. Then, with grudging deference to the world of public relations, he added, "We will make information available to the public as it becomes available."

Ah, Simmons, I thought, too many "availables." His New York accent was more pronounced than I remembered. The blonde frowned, then tried again. "The man you arrested"—she glanced at her notes—"a man named Howard Lucas—that man, he didn't murder the real estate agents?"

"No, he didn't," said Simmons.

The blonde looked first disgusted, then, as his words sunk in, slightly confused. "The man you arrested at Wildwood Bay..."

"Has been charged with assault with an attempt to rape and making harassing phone calls."

There was a bad, long silence, as the reporter gathered her wits. "Then, who, in your opinion, Detective, is murdering real estate agents?"

"We are following up a tip given by a member of the real estate community," said Simmons. He began to say something else, thought the better of it and closed his mouth with a decisive snap. The real estate community? Why didn't he just give my name? To my horror, as if in response to my thoughts, I watched as the station cut to a video clip of me getting into the BMW at Wildwood Bay last night. There was a final and better picture through the windshield as I backed out of the fenced yard and onto Sassafras Lane.

The blonde was back on her game by now. "Detective, there is a rumor that the Anne Arundel County Police have brought in a psychological profiler to work on the real estate murders. Can you confirm that?"

A wave of contempt passed over his face. "No, I can't." Simmons looked furtively around him, probably for an escape. Even in the rainy early-morning light, I could see the reddening edges along his nostrils and lips as he controlled his temper. After another long standoff with the blonde, the camera went to a prerecorded clip of the regular police spokeswoman, her manner smooth and easy, her voice confident as she explained what the police knew about the murders of two real estate agents. I flipped off the set and called Simmons' pager again, leaving him Weller Church's number this time.

IN A COUPLE OF MINUTES, I was on my way to Annapolis, my mind a jumble of disconnected thoughts. Simmons had said the police were following up on a tip from a member of the real estate community, as he so carefully put it. It had to be me. They had the tape from last night. Unless someone else had phoned them with something. I felt like a worm at the end of a line. Had Simmons gotten an early-morning call? Did he know who had killed Leslie? And Rose?

The traffic in Annapolis the day before the Naval Academy graduation was worse than ever. Cars with out-of-town license plates—always a fact of life in Annapolis—were moving cautiously in the two narrow lanes rendered slippery from the light rain.

Weller Church's office was located in an old house on Duke of Gloucester Street, off Church Circle. Impatiently waiting at a light, I was finally able to take a right turn into a cramped off-street parking pad behind his building. Getting out, I found my way past dripping bushes, around the house to the street. The elderly lawyer was waiting for me on the front porch. A spike of lightning split the sky, followed by rolling thunder.

"Smells good, doesn't it? Ozone," he said, opening the door and pointing down a dark hall that led to his office. The room was surprisingly large, with a fireplace, built-in bookshelves, and a view of the garden and my BMW wedged in the visitor's parking space. So that's how he had known to greet me, I thought, watching him close the window.

He motioned me to a large couch, then sat down at the other end. I could smell his damp, fussy male smell. It was soothing, as was his voice.

"Almost need a fire today, don't we?" he said, settling in. "I heard what happened last night. I'm so sorry. We haven't treated you very well here in Maryland, have we?" He picked up his coffee cup, then realized that he hadn't offered me any. I declined before he could offer. "I know that Howard Lucas admitted to assaulting you and making those obscene phone calls but that he denies killing those two agents. And he has an ailibi, I heard."

I nodded.

"I don't recognize the lead detective in this case."

"He's new. From New York. Named Simmons. And he seems to be spreading a rumor that someone in the real estate community provided him with a tip," I said. "I feel like bait." I explained to Weller about Simmons' late-night visit and our discussion, leaving out the part about his nap on my couch. "Do you know what's going on? Or if the police have a real, honest-to-God tip?"

The lawyer pulled out a pipe, filled it with a most pleasant type of tobacco and lit it, puffing and exhaling. "I haven't heard a thing." He drew again on the pipe and looked over me. "I don't like this Simmons."

"Maybe the cops are trying to make the killer think that they know something so he'll panic and do something stupid."

"Maybe. It's been done before. In the meantime," he said, "I think you really need to take extra steps to ensure your safety." Here it comes, I thought. I had a flashback of the conversation on Mitch's boat. "Stay with Lillian or get that nice boy next door to stay with you and the dogs," said Weller.

Or get an exhausted, overworked, and often ill-tempered police detective to fall asleep on my couch. I wondered what Weller would say to that. Probably nothing. He'd just go on smoking, drawing deeply, with satisfaction, nodding and thinking.

I sighed, agreeing to look after myself, then settled back into Weller's couch to listen to what I was going to have to do legally with regard to Howard. The lawyer made a couple of notes, then looked over at me.

"So. Now, we get to why you made this appointment. Have you made a decision about Ray Tilghman's property yet?" His voice was kind, his eyes set back among folds of skin, concerned.

I swallowed. My mind flooded with odd bits of memories from last night: sitting in the car in the clearing and later, the sound of Lillian's anxious voice. I could almost see Zeke's brown eyes, the golden fleck spinning away from me. Ray Tilghman's house. And the responsibilities that went with it. Was I buying? We sat quietly for a couple of minutes, each lost in our own thoughts. A phone rang somewhere else in the office. Weller smoked quietly. I watched the rain drive sideways against his garden windows. I felt defensive, irritated, exhausted. I didn't want to make a decision in this state. And certainly not something which would not only affect just me but Lillian as well. My watch said 10:15. The rain was coming down harder, the thunder closer.

"Do you want me to go over the conditions of Ray's will again?" Weller asked gently. "Just to make sure you're clear?"

I shook my head. I knew them by heart: buying Ray Tilghman's property meant living in the cottage and caring for the dogs he had loved better than any person. It didn't mean living in New York and hiring Will or someone else to feed them. If I didn't buy the property I would have to move as soon as it was sold to the anonymous buyer. I felt a flash of temper. How dare someone put me through this? And how dare he stay anonymous? I took a deep breath, trying to quiet my racing thoughts.

"Weller," I said. "I just can't decide today. Can't you get me some more time?"

He was busy knocking ashes into an oversize ashtray. "You have two more days," he said, then looked up. "You know...you know the decision won't be any easier next week or next month than it is today?"

I nodded, then stood up. There was a knock on the door. Weller's secretary, an elegantly dressed woman at least as old as he, wobbled in and announced that I had a phone call. Weller pointed at the phone, then left, closing the door behind him to give me privacy. I picked up to hear Detective Clarke identify himself. Simmons was tied up in a meeting, he said. He would be happy to relay any information I had to him. I considered. What I had could hardly be called information. More of a collision of overworked brain cells and too much caffeine. No, I told Clarke, I didn't think so. Simmons could call me when he got a chance. I recited my phone numbers, thanked him, and hung up.

I left the lawyer on the front porch. I agreed again to have Will sleep on my couch. Or I would stay with Lillian. Or something, I thought impatiently. Tonight was far away. Weller would call me about the police statement. Nobody mentioned Ray Tilghman's property again.

The thunder and lightning had retreated, but the rain wet my hair and shirt. I didn't care. I ran the last few feet to the car. In a couple of minutes I was on my way to the office, ignoring the wet world on the other side of my windshield. I focused instead on corraling my skittering thoughts.

THIRTY-TWO

It took me thirty-five minutes to return to Pines on Magothy. I tried to order my drifting thoughts. No luck. My brainstorm was just out of reach, infuriatingly so. I was a prisoner of sensations without words, the kind that hung over you all day, infecting everything you do. Thinking doesn't shake them loose. Instead the day remained half in shadow, the dream more real than the road in front of the car.

Joe Lister had long ago suggested motion when the brain got stuck. Go for a drive, walk, run, or even ride the train, he would say. It didn't matter what. Your blood would flow, you might see new things, think new things. But today it wasn't working. I mentally treaded water, and still my mind wouldn't move.

I briefly toyed with the thought of going home, changing into sweats, and climbing onto the cross-country ski machine that I had inherited. Ben hadn't wanted it. Nor did I for that matter. But maybe hard exercise, something I hadn't done in a week, would help. Inertia won out. And I had a job, I reminded myself, however bad I was at it. I turned off Ritchie Highway onto Mountain Road.

The rain had let up some by the time I reached Weber Realty. I angled the BMW in beside Shirley Bodine's blue Chevrolet. The office smelled like wet dog. As did I. And the bottom of my pants legs were outlined in mud and my nicely starched shirt had long since gone limp. In New York, I'd have had a fresh blouse and an extra pair of shoes in my bottom desk drawer for days like these. I shook out my umbrella and jammed it into a tall bronze jar placed just inside the door, catching my fingernail on the uneven edge. Damn. I stuck my forefinger into my mouth, tasting blood. Looking closely, I discovered I'd torn it off almost down to the cuticle on one side. Blood seeped out in a thickening red line. I noticed that the rest of my nails didn't look so great either.

"You know a manicure place?" I asked Shirley, who grimaced when she saw my finger, then involuntarily glanced at her own nails.

"I use a woman at the mall. Wanda. She's always busy, but she'd probably squeeze you in if you tell her you know me." Shirley looked me over. "I heard about last night. Howard Lucas, of all people. I mean we all thought he was a little weird maybe, but a pervert? Who do you believe these days?" She shook her head.

The phone rang and Shirley grabbed it, pulling a pen out of a Snoopy mug on her desk and fishing around for her message pad. I headed for the bathroom. The stage lights over the sink made me look sick. Whatever had inspired Lillian to install these ghastly fixtures?

I studied my finger. The bleeding had slowed, but the nail wasn't pretty. Finding a Band-Aid in my bag, I wrapped it around my finger, then I leaned closer to the mirror and looked into my eyes. They appeared flat, tired. I applied bright lipstick, hoping it would help me feel better. Instead it reminded me of Leslie Ballard. I blotted my lips and leaned up close to the mirror again.

"Who killed Leslie Ballard?" I asked myself, hoping direct communication with the dreaming gray cells in my brain would yield something. Shirley had opened the door. I blushed, then turned. "Just talking to myself." She nodded politely, then stood next to me at the sink to wash something off her hands.

"Ink," she said, holding a mottled hand up for me to see. "Gaylin Realty pen. Serves me right, I suppose." She grinned, then efficiently grabbed a couple of paper towels and scrubbed off what was left of the blue smudges.

I studied her as she swiped at the sink with the crumbled towels, tossing them in the garbage. She had been Lillian's right hand for many years. She was also the tough survivor of a marriage to a husband incarcerated in Jessup for armed robbery. "Shirley," I said, "why do you think someone wanted to kill Leslie Ballard?"

"Because," she said, "Leslie probably knew something or saw something. Or somebody didn't want her to find out something. Just don't ask me what." She shook her head, making her dangling

earrings—large thunderbolts cast in silver—sway under a volu-
minous mane of graying hair. We both heard the phone ring. "It
wasn't random like some people are saying; not just somebody on
drugs choosing any old agent, then taking her cash and credit
cards. Far too much work for that, I should think," Shirley said,
heading for her desk. "It was stupid and cruel and senseless." She
turned back to look at me. "You know there's a teenage boy?"

I nodded. Together we left the bathroom. Two phone lines were
now lit up. Shirley skillfully got them both. "It's Lillian," she
said, putting my aunt on hold, then picking up the other line. I
walked to my desk and picked up the phone.

"Morning," she said. "I trust you got some sleep?"

"Yes. Not much, but I'm fine." I didn't mention Simmons.

"What really happened last night, Eve? With Howard?" Her
voice was distressed, as if she'd been trying to comprehend all
night how she could have been so wrong about a friend.

I again described the awful scene with Howard as succinctly as
possible, then what Simmons had reported in his statement on TV.
Lillian made little humming noises.

"Why on earth did Howard...?"

"No one knows, Lillian." I could practically see her shaking
her head, her thinning cap of hair not moving. Her eyes would be
puzzled and angry, trying to come to terms with it. "His problems
didn't happen overnight, Lillian."

"And he hid it well. Maybe, if we'd all taken a little more notice
of him once in a while..."

"No, don't start with that," I said. "There was absolutely nothing you or anyone at the church could have done."

"Well...okay, you're right, of course," she said. She would
move on, I thought. After weeping for Howard, my resilient aunt
would dry her tears, then let her natural optimism surface.

"Now, what are you doing about tonight?" she asked. "Where
will you stay?"

What followed was a repeat of Weller's earlier concern about
my safety. With the killer still out there. I again promised to ask
Will to stay with me. That seemed to satisfy her. At least she didn't
say anything more.

"Can we please talk about something else?" I asked.

"Okay. Actually, you may congratulate me," she said. "I've had a very good idea. Why doesn't Elizabeth rent Marianne Pinot's house until we can sell it? She wants to be out of here and settled into her own place. Marianne needs to get her house sold, but this way she won't have to accept a fire-sale price or carry two mortgages. Everybody wins."

I considered. "You think Elizabeth would want to live somewhere knowing that the house could be sold out from under her at any moment?" I could, I thought, tell her all about the down side of such an arrangement.

"That's the beauty part," said Lillian. "I think the chances of that happening are probably slim. And renting would buy her time, too. We'd write a year's lease. Maybe then her divorce from Hamm will be complete, so she will even have money to buy the place if she decides that's what she wants."

It was the first I'd heard my aunt mention divorce in such a casual tone. Lillian had apparently decided to accept that Hamm and Elizabeth were unlikely to reconcile. "Sounds great. But what does Elizabeth think?"

"That it's an interesting idea." My aunt was beginning to sound a touch annoyed that I was even questioning her scheme to fix everybody's life.

"And Marianne?"

"Loves the idea. Takes her off the hook. She knows the property will be well cared for," said Lillian. I could hear renewed enthusiasm in her voice. "It'll give her plenty of time to make repairs, maybe even install a new furnace and central air."

As usual, Lillian had thought of everything. "Well, okay, you're a genius," I said, getting ready to carry on as devil's advocate. "But has Elizabeth seen the property? It's lovely but inconvenient and hardly as comfortable as what she's used to."

My aunt snorted. "Nope, but she's on her way to the office right now to look at the pictures you took. Maybe you could show it to her later this afternoon, if she likes the pictures?"

"Okay."

I chatted with Lillian a minute more, then hung up, promising her I'd take Elizabeth to Hawk's Bay if she wanted to see Marianne's house. In the reception area, I could hear Shirley making and taking calls. The office hummed nicely.

I settled down to think. For the moment, I decided to give up chasing faint, sketchy dreams, or playing with possible motives I couldn't fathom. I needed to try to think in concrete terms. Had whoever wanted Leslie Ballard dead tried to put her eyes out? Had Leslie stepped back at just the right time, or moved sideways, causing her attacker to make marks on only one side of her face, only to then lose her balance and fall? I pushed away the revulsion the picture caused and made myself think about the self-defense workshop. Just going through some names might help jog my mind, I thought. And if it didn't, maybe that told me something, too: that maybe I was all wrong. Jack Hardwick and Hamm Hammett. Out of many ludicrous choices, they were the least ludicrous. Let Simmons interview the other hundred real estate agents. And Howard. After last night, it was still hard to be persuaded of his innocence.

Leaning back in my chair, I let my thoughts drift. Elizabeth had told me that the pastor had left for his cottage last Friday around noon. He'd told her he was going to have lunch, work on his sermon, and get the church's books ready for his meeting at Lillian's house later that evening. The parsonage—an updated bungalow—was separated from the church by a row of pines. He would presumably have walked home. Then what? Had he stayed there? Would anyone have seen him or his car? What about the neighbors on the other side of the parsonage? Were they home during the day?

I shoved the pad aside, slipped into my jacket, and looked at my watch. Where was Elizabeth? I was too edgy to sit there any longer. I needed to talk to Jack Hardwick. To ask him if he'd been home all afternoon. I picked up the photos of the Hawk's Bay house to leave at the front desk for Elizabeth.

"Mitch Gaylin, line four," said Shirley.

I sat back down, feeling a twinge of guilt. He'd called last night and I'd forgotten to phone back.

"Hi. Before you say anything, let me say that I'm sorry. I meant to call, but..."

"Don't apologize," he said. "You okay?"

"Yes. I gather you've been watching television like everyone else in Anne Arundel County?"

He grunted. I could hear someone talking to him in the background. "Sorry. Frantic around here this morning." Another insistent voice in the background. "I guess no one is going to let me talk with you just now. How about a late lunch? I mean very late."

"Today?"

"It would have to be... How about...?" I heard pages ruffling. Anxious voices. "I could meet you at your office about three p.m. That too late?"

"Pretty late, but sure, okay. Three." I hung up. From the front office, I heard Shirley speak to someone. Elizabeth's voice came in response. I took my jacket off and went out to meet her.

THIRTY-THREE

ELIZABETH WAS NOT the same woman I'd last seen sitting in Better Dresses, weepy and worried about her husband. She looked rested, her eyes less puffy, her skin pinker. The nightly vacuuming had stopped, Lillian had told me. And she had cut her hair, a sure sign of something. Maybe she was getting herself ready to finally be done with her marriage, emotionally and physically. I led her to my cubicle. She sat down, picking up the dozen or so pictures I'd taken of Marianne Pinot's house, and, of course, the usual shots of the cove itself: sailboats skimming, their sails trim and white against blue sky and water. She thumbed through them twice, then looked up.

"I think I'd like to see it," she said. Her voice was shy, the voice of someone who had never looked at property by herself. "I have a class this afternoon, but Lillian said maybe you could show it to me afterwards?"

"Sure." We agreed on 6:00 p.m., time enough for her to comfortably drive from College Park. There would still be plenty of light. Elizabeth looked at the listing as I called Marianne to make the appointment. I chatted a little with the shrink, playing for time, wondering how on earth I was going to tell Elizabeth about Hamm's whereabouts on the day of Leslie's murder. I'd toyed with not mentioning it, then discarded the idea. She deserved to know the truth. And just maybe, I thought, she'd have an idea about where he went before returning to the conference. I looked up to find her watching me.

"I heard about last night," she said. "And like everybody at church, I just can't believe it about Howard. Jack called to say he was going to go to the hospital to see him."

The picture of the timid pastor visiting Howard was an interesting one. What on earth did you say to someone who made dirty phone calls and was under arrest for sexual assault? That, I told myself, was why I wasn't in the helping professions. Elizabeth was again idly studying the pictures, flipping through them, her mind obviously on other things.

"Elizabeth," I began, "I...I know where Hamm was the morning before Leslie Ballard was killed." Her head came up, her eyes more curious than afraid. "He was with Leslie at Wildwood Bay. He took off his class ring and accidentally left it on the sink. I found it last night."

I didn't know what I expected her to do. She did nothing, said nothing, just sat shuffling the pictures. Finally, she looked up. "Did you tell the police?"

"I had to, Elizabeth. If I hadn't told them, I'd be an accessory." She nodded. I then explained about Hamm's absence from the conference for a couple of hours more, as confirmed by the parking attendant. With each detail, I was sorrier I'd ever gotten involved. The woman who had arrived this afternoon to take the next step toward a new life was beginning to dissolve again. I handed her a box of tissues. After everything, was she still in love with her husband? I could appreciate her dilemma: not wanting to be married and not wanting to be unmarried, just wanting the whole problem to go away. As I watched, she blew her nose, then tried to smile.

"Sorry. Every time I see you I'm crying."

"Doesn't matter. Elizabeth," I said, slowly, "Hamm lied about his whereabouts during the time of Leslie's death. And no one knows where he went after leaving the cottage at Wildwood. You have any ideas?"

"Maybe he just had lunch or something," she said. "You'll have to ask him."

Not me. Simmons, I thought. "Elizabeth," I began again, "there's something else I want to know. Why did Jack Hardwick really lie about your being together all afternoon? Was it just to protect you from a police investigation, as he said? Or was it something else?"

I leaned back in my chair. Was she going to tell me some sordid story of steamy afternoons in the parsonage, her revenge for

Hamm's philandering? Instead, she mopped her eyes and drew her chair closer to mine.

"I think Jack had an appointment that he didn't want anyone to know about," she said, quietly. "He was talking on the phone when I got to the church that morning. And he was very nervous. He was saying something about his options. He was quite secretive about it, clearly not wanting me to hear."

"What did he mean?"

"I don't have any idea. But I know that he was worried about getting the books ready for Lillian to go over that evening. After dinner they were going to go over...Well, you were there."

I had a mental flash of the uneaten dinner, the silent living room, the ledgers and checkbook lying forgotten on a nearby table as we all contemplated the horror of Leslie's death. Then Simmons' associate, Detective Clarke, had come by.

"Elizabeth, think back to that night. I wasn't paying much attention, but I was aware that Lillian was particularly annoyed with Jack. Is that normal?"

She nodded. "Well, he annoys her a little all of the time. I think it's because he's so...so sort of mumbly and clingy and timid. It's almost as if the harder Jack tries to please her, the less he does." She blew her nose a second time, her own problems forgotten for the time being. "But you know Lillian, she gives everybody the benefit of the doubt."

"But was her irritation with him worse that night?"

"Yes. He'd brought the wrong ledgers and checkbook."

"Were they arguing?"

"No. You know Lillian doesn't argue when she thinks she's right about something. But she was very irritated and Jack was very apologetic about his mistake. Like always."

"Do you think it was an honest mistake?"

"I don't really know. Maybe he was buying some time to get the books in order. The church isn't in great shape financially. Jack's outreach programs are ambitious and they've drained us. He's also kind of disorganized and he sometimes acts like the fund-raising is...is beneath him." She shook her head. "I think that is what gets Lillian's goat most of all."

"What do you mean, beneath him?"

"Well, not beneath him so much as he's not really interested, like he thinks it's the volunteers who should keep the money coming."

"What happened at dinner?"

"It was a little tense, what we ate of it." She was silent, remembering the evening. "Then...then we got the news about Leslie, and we left the table and just sat there in the living room thinking our thoughts. Then you came by. I had just sort of forgotten all this." She looked over at me. I waited.

"Why don't you ask Lillian about the church finances?"

"I will."

After glancing at her watch, Elizabeth stood up, anxious to be on her way to her class. I gave her instructions to Hawk's Bay and she left.

It was almost 12:30. I decided to go to the mall and try to get an appointment with Shirley's manicurist before I met Mitch for lunch. Earlier I'd added another bandage to keep the bleeding nail in check. Shirley was eating a container of microwaved soup at her desk, her mouth too full to respond when I said good-bye.

Shuffling my arms into my jacket, holding my handbag and briefcase with first one hand, then the other, I opened the office door to find a camera crew waiting on the tarmac. Signaling her cameraman to turn the tape on, the blonde reporter I'd watched interview Simmons this morning stuck a microphone in my face.

"Miss Elliott," she said. "Can we talk with you? About Howard Lucas? And whoever is killing real estate agents?" Damn. I ran for the BMW, feeling like some wretched slumlord or Medicare cheat in a *60 Minutes* exposé. The cameraman and blonde followed me around the car. "Miss Elliott, are you the member of the real estate community who gave the police the tip about the killer? Can you give us some idea of who that killer is?"

"If I knew anything, I'd tell the police."

I slid into the leather seat, shutting the door behind me, trying to look less angry than I felt. I wondered what protocol was called for in a time like this. I stifled the desire to get out of the car, knock the camera to the ground, and pull the blonde's hair. Instead, I merely put the car in reverse and backed out, leaving the reporter and her cameraman looking at me with even more interest.

I took a left onto Mountain Road and headed for Ritchie Highway and the mall, carefully checking my rearview mirror for the TV van. It apparently hadn't followed me. I parked my car in front of the South entrance and, looking around, grabbed my briefcase and went inside. I hoped I wouldn't have to wait for Wanda, but if I did, I might as well face the infernal pile of contracts.

I was in luck. In minutes, I was sitting on a small stool in front of a manicure table. A beautiful black woman, probably older than she looked, her hair upswept into large elaborate curls, tendrils dripping down, was gingerly removing the Band-Aids from my finger. We both looked down at the unappetizing mess. Her ornate curls shook back and forth. Then she dug around in a flat waist high drawer for more bandages.

"You wait, Hon, until I can do all ten. Get your money's worth." Two minutes later I was standing in the mall, my injured finger again securely wrapped and now throbbing, the other nine unimproved. I sat down on a bench not far from a potted ficus tree, its leaves falling. Beside me, a heavily made-up girl, maybe all of thirteen, was preoccupied by a nose-ringed and pimply boy standing behind her licking her neck. His hands explored as far as she'd let him. She giggled with pleasure as he came around to squeeze in between us. Soon they were deeply entangled, tongues exploring open mouths, unconcerned that I was inches away watching. I turned away, repulsed and amused, then reapplied my own lipstick, and got up to go. An idea suddenly scudded through my mind. I turned back to the couple, who'd come up for air. The boy was now openly examining the girl's belly. The idea was a long shot, but, hell, I thought, what did I have to lose?

A few yards away, I found a glass-encased layout map of the mall shops. I ran my eyes up and down, searching for men's clothiers. There were quite a few, so I set off to methodically canvass both floors before facing the large department stores that anchored the mall. Removing the Engineering Management Conference program from my briefcase, I folded it open at Hamm's picture.

Fifteen minutes and three stores later, I entered Shirts Unlimited to be greeted by a pointy-nosed salesman with greasy, slicked-back hair.

"Hi. I need some help, please. Could you tell me if this man bought anything from your store last week? Friday actually?"

The man took the program from my hand and studied it carefully, then handed it back. "I sold him a shirt. The one he had on was ruined."

"From lipstick?"

"Yeah, lots of it. Much redder shade than what you're wearing." I wondered if he thought redder lipstick might be the key to a more exciting marriage. "All over the back part of his collar. He bought a new shirt, blue with a white collar, then changed in the dressing room, and left the old one here."

"You still have it?"

"Of course I don't have it." He sounded insulted. "What would I want with some guy's shirt covered with lipstick?" He had a point there. It didn't matter. There would be a receipt or credit card slip somewhere if Hamm really needed an alibi.

I thanked the salesman and headed for the door. I was relieved and angry at Hamm for his stupid affair. Despite his obvious horror at seeing Leslie's body, it was no wonder he had been more worried about Elizabeth's involvement than his own. With the ferret-faced salesman and a credit slip to back him up, he had an alibi for the time of Leslie's death should he need it. There had been so much lying, I thought. Elizabeth, Hamm, Jack Hardwick, Howard: they had all lied. And someone was still lying.

Walking quickly back through the mall, I realized that I was lost. What entrance had I come in? Looking around, I decided it would be easier to get my bearings if I just went outside. I headed for the nearest exit. A security guard was sitting on a tall stool by the door. On a shelf nearby was a small black-and-white TV next to the security monitors. The guard appeared to be more interested in it than what was happening among the racks of clothes in the department store. I glanced at my watch. Almost one o'clock.

"To recap our top story. Regarding the recent brutal murders of two real estate agents in Anne Arundel County," said the anchor, "our Lisa Lyons is looking into a report that Anne Arundel

County Police believe that a member of the real estate community has new information.''

I was suddenly watching myself sprint around Shirley Bodine's blue car, stopping only to deny angrily that I knew anything. With difficulty, because of my bandaged finger, I had unlocked the door to the BMW and slid behind the wheel, all the while glowering. Behind me, the blonde nearly tripped over something. I watched as she stood with her microphone in hand, the cameraman videotaping the back of the BMW as I made my escape onto Mountain Road. So that's why the TV van hadn't followed me: they had wanted to make the noon news. A cold shiver fell down my shoulders. I sure as hell hoped the killer, whoever it was, didn't watch daytime TV.

THIRTY-FOUR

I WAS STARVING but there were two hours to kill before meeting Mitch. I hadn't heard from Weller Church. Or from Simmons, who must still be tied up. If he'd moved to Maryland to get away from stress, he must be kicking himself. I debated paging him again, but decided against it.

The thought of returning to the office and sitting in my cubicle made me claustrophobic. Besides, it wasn't as if I were actually doing anything except obsessing about the murders. Even the awful scene with Howard last night had paled.

The sky had cleared some and the sun was beginning to peek through the clouds, warming the air. I got into the BMW and sat thinking. Shoppers hurrying in all directions peered at me curiously. I stared back, my mind playing with what I had just learned. Hamm Hammett was off the hook. He'd been buying a new shirt when Leslie Ballard was killed, a shirt to replace the one covered with her lipstick. I could cross his name off my list. And it followed, I thought, that if I were right about the killer attending the self-defense workshop, that left only Jack Hardwick.

With an effort, I now pushed away intuition. I could almost hear Joe Lister's voice. When fresh ideas would not come, he had told me at the beginning of my advertising career, to look to the facts. Intuition, that most elusive source of inspiration, needed to be fed. Do research, learn more, he would say when I was stuck. Then let what you've learned mellow and ripen. It takes time and patience and trust, but the answers would come. And when they did, he had assured me, they would be a wondrous combination of fact and revelation.

I turned over the engine and slid out of the parking place and onto Ritchie Highway, heading east on Mountain Road. So research it was. In the form of talking to Lillian, something I wasn't

looking forward to. My aunt would give the pastor the benefit of
the doubt unless I could prove otherwise. Besides, what possible
motive could he have for murder? Opportunity, yes, but motive?
None that I could remotely think of. Research, I told myself.

Commercial areas along Mountain Road melted into stretches
of woods, broken here and there by small-town stores and gas
stations. Occasional side streets were lined with ranch-style houses
separated by chainlink fences. On the right side of the road, in
front of an antique store, a stocky woman was putting out a hand-
lettered sign announcing a sale. On my left, a garden center displayed flats of seedlings and an impressive row of shiny green
lawn tractors in descending order by size. A station wagon was
backed up to the double door and someone I couldn't see was
loading something into the hatch.

I turned right onto Lido Beach Road. Green creepers jutted out
over the road and the sweet spring smells were particularly pungent after the early-morning rain. Patches of blue peeped through
clouds that looked as if they still might have some role to play in
today's weather.

I slowed down as I drove through town, minding the thirty-
mile-an-hour limit. On my right, the Lido Beach Inn was doing
its normal lunchtime trade, its parking lot full. Across the way, at
the convenience store, a man in a too-tight suit was talking on an
outdoor pay phone. A flash hit me. Last Sunday, on the day of
the open house, Howard would have used the same phone to call.
The scene replayed in my mind. I had run out of the MacAfferty
house, locking the front door with trembling fingers and whistling
for Lancelot. Then, I had quickly backed out of the drive onto the
street, just in time to see Howard's old van coming toward me. It
had taken probably all of two minutes.

It angered me to think about it. I'd been so unnerved by the
call, I'd actually confided in the creep, told him all about it. That
must have really made his day. It had probably been so gratifying
that he was able to accept his disappointment about not seeing the
house then and there. I remembered how he'd made some stupid
little comforting noises, looked embarrassed, even asked if I'd
called the police and patted my shoulder. How could I have been

so dense? Well, Howard wasn't making any more calls just now and that was that.

I crept past the 7-Eleven, past the Church in the Pines. Next to it, separated by a row of heavy, graceful pines, I could see the parsonage. A typical 1940s bungalow, complete with front porch and louvered windows, it crouched a hundred feet from the street. The only vehicle in sight was a courier's van backing out of the narrow driveway and pulling away. The driver, a black man with an angelic face, waved and smiled.

On impulse, I turned into the drive and parked near the house, half wondering what I would say if Jack Hardwick suddenly appeared. Or Simmons. I decided the detective's likely comments didn't bear thinking about. I was just a neighbor, dropping by. It was broad daylight. Every passing car on Lido Beach Road could see me. I took a couple of deep breaths.

Climbing the three steps to the open porch, I rang the front bell, then listened to the echo. There were no steps inside. I rang again. Between the screen and the main door, on the floor, I could see the package left by the courier. It fell out when I opened the screen to pound on the door. Turning the label to me, I saw the return address: Hardwick Investment Services. Wilmington, Delaware. Above the preprinted label, someone had penned William Hardwick in neat black letters. I turned it over in my hand, then dropped it back behind the screened door. Jack's family was in investments? It didn't seem possible that the name was a coincidence.

Turning around, I saw that there were no nearby houses on the other side of the bungalow. No nosy neighbors to keep track of the pastor's comings and goings. Unsettled, I looked in the windows and was rewarded with a view of a modest living room, with oldish furniture and an upright piano. Probably came with the job.

I got back in the car and, squaring my shoulders, phoned Lillian. To my surprise, I got her answering machine. I called Shirley at the office.

"She's at the hospital for tests. For her ankle," she said. "Didn't she tell you that?"

"No. Maybe she forgot. Uh, who drove her?" Elizabeth was, I knew, in class at College Park.

"That pastor, I think."

A sudden gust of wind swept a loose piece of newspaper against the windshield. I thanked Shirley, told her I'd be in around 3:00 p.m. and backed onto the street. Suddenly sick of the whole mess, with time to kill, I decided to go home and change out of my mud-rimmed pants. In minutes, I was turning down the rutted road to Weller's Creek. Will's truck wasn't there, but Zeke and Lance greeted me joyously.

For once the answering machine was idle, no blinking red lights. I called the hospital and after a couple of minutes was referred to the orthopedic department. A cheery nurse informed me that I had just missed Lillian, who was on her way to X-ray. Call back in an hour or two, she said. Or three, since they were running late. I thanked her.

To hell with it. Resisting the temptation to turn on the television, I whistled for the dogs. Together we trotted down the wide path to Weller's Cove. After throwing a heavy stick far out in the creek for Lancelot to fetch, I sat down on the end of the dock, dangling my legs above the water to soak up the weak sun. Zeke ran excitedly along the shore, barking as Lance came ashore with the stick. The water lapped gently underneath me.

Who killed Leslie Ballard? My mind returned to the package in the pastor's screen door. William Hardwick. Of Hardwick Investment Services. The name seemed familiar, but I couldn't place it.

Forcing everything from my mind, I took myself back to the day of Leslie Ballard's death. Closing my eyes, I relived the surprise meeting with her at the Wildwood Bay cottage. I heard her laugh, then listened to her discouraging recital of all that was wrong in the real estate business. I saw the gold buttons on her dark dress reflect the sunlight as she got into her car a short time later.

Zeke rolled over onto me, dog feet sticking into the air. "Get off. You are hot and heavy," I said. He scrambled to his feet abruptly and shook himself out, then sat down, his back to me, to stare out across the creek. Was I getting anywhere? It certainly didn't feel that way.

Closing my eyes again, I pictured myself leaving the cottage, my irritation and frustration at full tilt. Back in Pines on Magothy, I had circled the Lido Beach Inn. The lot had been full of customers, so I'd parked on the street, then gone in to gossip with Marian and the locals, and eaten what passed for lunch.

Lunch. I opened my eyes and looked at my watch. I was going to be late meeting Mitch. The dogs romped by my legs as I hurried back to the cottage. Quickly changing my grubby slacks and shoes, I drove back to the office.

THE MEXICAN RESTAURANT was closed until dinner. Mitch banged on the door. After a muffled conversation I couldn't hear, with God only knows what financial inducements, a waiter led us to a table. A couple of minutes later a basket of multicolored chips and two kinds of salsa, one green and sweet, the other red-hot, appeared. Mitch ordered a couple of Dos Equis and two combination plates of cheese enchiladas with roasted vegetables. He leaned back in his chair, his face weary, the laugh wrinkles around his eyes caused by something other than mirth.

"It's been one long, ugly day," Mitch said. "And it's only three o'clock. Many hours for it to get uglier." He downed half his beer in one swallow, then turned the full force of his attention on me. "But who am I to talk? After last night you have the corner on ugly." I groaned. "You want to talk about it?"

From relief or exhaustion I didn't know which, I'd spewed out the whole mess from last evening. With all the details I hadn't confided to Lillian. I found that I now had some distance from the repulsive facts. I could almost objectively talk about how Howard had looked at me, my fear in the suffocating attic, the way his fingers had sounded when they snapped. Mitch drank quietly.

I also told him about Hamm's Friday lunchtime trip to the mall. About the blonde reporter and my new celebrity as the one person in Anne Arundel County who might know who the real estate agent killer was. A touch of fear nibbled around the edges of my mind. I was glad for the Mexican restaurant's bright decor.

"Okay, so that's the whole sordid story," I said. "Now tell me why you are having such a great day."

"Joyce. Among about ten other things. She came by this morning," he said. "Unannounced and contrite. She wanted her job back."

"What did you say?"

"I said no." He stopped fiddling with a salt shaker and turned toward me. "I can't run a business letting her insult people and make trouble for the other agents and the clients."

"You don't have to persuade me. How'd she take it?"

He put the salt shaker down. "It's hard to know. Angry, I think, but even more fearful and bewildered. I suppose she could have made a scene but she didn't. Just left. I told her I'd pay for her health insurance for the next six months if she would find herself a shrink."

He stared out the window, past the checkered café curtains, and out to a stand of tall, triangular pines planted to absorb the car fumes from Ritchie Highway.

The waiter appeared with our lunches. Mitch moved the chips and beer bottles to make room. We ate in silence. The food was remarkably good, and the beer cold. He signaled for another bottle. I shook my head when the waiter looked in my direction.

"Mitch, who is William Hardwick? Of Hardwick Investment Services?"

He looked up from his plate, mystified. "Isn't he the investment banker who was indicted a few years back? For insider trading or something? Along about the same time as Michael Milken and Ivan Boesky?" He finished eating and pushed his plate away. "He went to prison, I think. I remember because at the time, my wife was an analyst with..."

I sat still. This was news. For ten months, he'd acted as if he didn't have a past. And I hadn't asked questions.

"We divorced six years ago," he said. "She lives in New York with my daughter, Laura, who is nine." He smiled then, activating the sunbursts of wrinkles near his temples.

THIRTY-FIVE

THE RESTAURANT was quiet. Mitch fiddled with the flatware. The waiter put down his second beer. I pushed away my dishes.

"Why is William Hardwick important?" he asked, finally. "Other than you obviously think the name isn't a coincidence?" His voice was even.

"Jack got a package this morning. From Hardwick Investment Services. The courier who delivered it was just leaving when I stopped by his house." In a few words, I related my conversation with Elizabeth and described the scene at Lillian's house the night of Leslie's death. He listened intently.

"And so you think that the pastor has something to do with her murder?"

"Sounds crazy, doesn't it. I don't know what to think. But he was at the self-defense workshop, so he'd know how..." I stopped, not wanting to think about the way I believed someone had tried to kill Leslie. Mitch nodded, then backed his chair away from the table. It made an ugly scraping sound that echoed in the empty restaurant. "Look, I know this all sounds ridiculous," I said again. "And as for a motive, I don't remotely know what it would be. That's why I went to ask Jack himself where he was."

"You tell Simmons about all this?"

I held up my cell phone. "I'm trying."

Mitch drank the last of his beer. "Eve, maybe you need to talk to someone else. Clarke maybe. Not wait for Simmons."

"Okay, but I want to talk to Lillian first. About how the church came to hire Jack. Find out if it was one of those appointments that the congregation had no control over. Maybe she knows more than she's said." I leaned forward. "Besides, there's something else."

Mitch was now rotating a small bottle of hot sauce between his fingers. I could see a tiny picture of a happy-go-lucky devil on the label. "And that is?"

"Just before I fully woke up this morning, I knew who the killer was." I watched him carefully. But if he were amused, he had the good sense to keep it to himself. "Something just seemed to make sense to me. All the pieces fell into place. Then..." Why had I started this? "Then, I forgot."

"You forgot?"

"I forgot. It's just some little thing that nobody is paying any attention to. Some tiny incident or detail that seems innocent. Something I'm missing in the light of day. Maybe talking with Simmons will help bring it...oh, forget it."

"What makes you think that Simmons will be able to help you evoke your, er...brainstorm?" he asked. "He just doesn't seem like the kind of guy who deals in..." He looked away, not wanting to insult me but aware he was probably going to anyway.

"The last person I talked with before going to sleep was Simmons, so our conversation was in the front of my mind. I thought maybe...oh, I don't know." I felt whipped, defeated by the logic of it. "And there's another thing," I said, aware that I was trying too hard and unable to stop myself. "Because Simmons and I are both from New York, he seems inclined to cut me more slack than he does other people. He also fell asleep on my couch last night."

Mitch put the bottle down. "Oh." He pulled out his wallet when the bill came, handing an American Express card to the waiter.

I pushed back my chair and got up. "I'm going to call Lillian and find out what all she knows about Jack Hardwick."

Mitch drew a deep breath, letting it out as he signed the credit card slip. "I don't like any of this," he said.

HAWK'S BAY was looking mean and choppy. Two cars were parked on the grassy ledge above Marianne's property. I squeezed in nearby. Large drops hit the ground as I got out. My watch said 5:35. A cold gust made me shiver as I looked down at the fitful water, then scrambled down the crumbling stairs.

Marianne stood in the doorway laughing with a young woman,

her arm draped around her shoulder, friendly and affectionate. Then she saw me.

"Come in. I'll be right there." She looked up at the distant horizon, then encouraged the young woman to hurry while the rain still held off.

I walked through the door and into the dim sunroom. Before me was the watery panorama I had seen yesterday. There was a faint smell of cinnamon in the air, as if Marianne had known about the coming rain and baked something sweet to neutralize the darkening day. Maybe living high above the water made one more attentive to the whims of the weather, I thought. The Russian Blue rubbed my ankles.

"Elizabeth will be here shortly, I hope."

"Maybe. If the front doesn't come through first." She looked me over intently, her eyes turning to slits the better to imagine the inside of my head, I thought. "Well, you are all over the news today. You okay after last night?"

"It seems kind of far away, to tell you the truth. Like it didn't happen." I leaned down to stroke the cat.

"Your mind is taking care of things for you," she said. I raised my eyebrows. "Under great stress, people sometimes distance themselves from whatever is causing the stress. Put things out of their mind. Forget things. It's a defense mechanism."

"So how do you get stuff back? Other than self-hypnosis?"

"Well, time is one way. And sometimes it's healthy to forget. For the moment, anyway. But you eventually have to handle your emotions. Come to terms with them. And with what happened." She was still studying me like a bug on a pin. "It's okay to feel what you feel," she said. "And fear and anger would seem reasonable. Given the circumstances." She patted my arm. "I'll be out of your way in a few minutes." She glanced at a wall clock. "Less than a few minutes."

The phone rang. Marianne grabbed it. "That was Elizabeth. Because of the weather, there's been a bad pile-up on Route 50. She expects she'll probably be a few minutes late. Which means I'll probably be late, too. Along with all my students." She disappeared into the bedroom. I could hear her rumbling around.

"Make yourself at home," she yelled. "There's a television in that big cupboard across from you. And help yourself to whatever you can find in the kitchen. The coffee's moderately fresh."

In a couple of minutes, she returned, putting on a silly folding rain hat Lillian might have worn, and fishing an umbrella out of a ceramic stand shaped like a giraffe.

"Here goes nothing." Rain drove in the front door when she opened it. "Let me know what Elizabeth thinks. Oh, and I'm expecting a couple of calls. You can just let the machine take them." The door closed and I was alone. Then the door opened again. "Maybe," said Marianne, "you should deadbolt the door behind me. 'Bye."

The gray cat jumped onto a nearby bureau and began to nibble at a bunch of azaleas in a blue vase. Swollen drops of rain pelted the picture window, driven diagonally into the plateglass by the rising wind. Below me the dark water rolled tiny whitecaps up to the seawall.

I picked up the phone and dialed Lillian. My aunt picked it up just as her message tape began.

"Hold on," she said. I heard a series of clicks. "There."

"How's your ankle?"

"I have graduated to two canes. For what that's worth."

"Worth something, it seems to me." There was a snort. "Lillian, I have a question for you."

"Shoot."

"What do you really know about Jack Hardwick? And is something wrong with the church's finances...?"

"Eve, stop." Her voice had become serious and tired. "He told me everything."

I was astonished. "He did?"

I settled back in Marianne's desk chair. And for the next ten minutes listened as Lillian related a story of greed and family turmoil. The rain sprang out of the black sky and drove downward with some intensity now. I could hardly see the lawn and garden that separated house from water below me.

"After he was convicted, Jack's father went to jail for a few months," my aunt was saying. "About the same time that Jack went to the seminary. Against his father's wishes, I might add."

"And his family?"

"He has had no contact with them," said Lillian. "Not until last Friday. After he left Elizabeth at the church at noon, he told me he drove up to Wilmington to see his father. The first time in years."

I could guess what was in the courier envelope stuffed by the screen door: a cashier's check. "Jack somehow lost the church's money, didn't he?"

"Our whole endowment." Her voice was flat. "In fact, he even got a margin call that morning from the broker." The call he hadn't wanted Elizabeth to overhear, I thought. "So he went to his father for a loan."

"Lillian," I said, slowly, "I don't get it. Why did he risk investing the church's money?"

There was a long sigh. "Well, I'm not a shrink, but Jack's always tried too hard. Ever since he's been here. It's almost as if he wanted to impress me," she said. "As if I'm sort of a stand-in for his father." She coughed. "Oh, forget that I said that. I hate it when people play amateur psychologist."

"So he thought the way to impress you was to increase the church endowment?" I was trying to take it all in. How stupidly wrong I had been.

"Maybe. How do you know about all this, by the way? Or shouldn't I ask?"

I told her about seeing the overnight letter from Hardwick Investment Services, hoping she wouldn't ask what I was doing at the parsonage to begin with. She didn't. I stared out the window at the fading day. The rain was relenting some, turning into a dark spray against the fading sky.

Lillian sounded tired, I thought. The kind of tired a day of waiting for a five-minute X-ray at the hospital can make you. I promised to call her later after Elizabeth saw the house.

Six o'clock. I turned on the television just in time to see a repeat of the videotape of myself racing around the BMW and feverishly pawing my way into the car. Then the station cut to the blonde reporter.

"A wallet has been found near Grayson's Cove in Pines on Magothy," she said. "Sources tell us that it belonged to one of the murdered real estate agents, Rose Macklin. The police are not making further comment at this time except to say that an anonymous tip led them to it."

The gray cat had lost interest in the flowers and with a heavy jump landed in my lap. Marianne's phone rang four times. Then her answering machine clicked on. The police had found Rose's wallet? Because of an anonymous tip. So someone in the real estate community, as Simmons so coyly had put it, hadn't known anything. But someone else had. What was I missing? I struggled to get comfortable under fifteen pounds of purring cat. Sitting forward, I pulled a lumpy pillow from behind my back and slung it to the other end of the couch. The cat yowled in protest, then settled back as I stared at the pillow. On it were hand-stitched the words Practice Random Kindness and Senseless Acts of Beauty.

In the distance, a car engine idled, then turned quiet. I lifted the heavy cat off my lap, then fished Simmons' card out of my jacket. I dialed his private line. Busy. I dialed his pager and left Marianne's number.

There was a sharp rap on the door. In the distance, a dark echo of thunder warned of worse to come.

THIRTY-SIX

STEAM WAS FORMING on the windows of Marianne's house. Outside the rain continued, cold and blowy for May. The furnace kicked into life. Forced air whistled through ducts in the floor. The imbalance of temperatures created moving patterns of vapor that played around the edges of the windowpanes. I sat on the couch, my hands in my lap.

Joyce Nichols was sitting in Marianne's overstuffed chair. Her salt-and-pepper hair was slicked to her head, giving her a kind of monkish, tonsured look. She had shucked a black slicker-like rain poncho onto a chair near the door. A nearby table lamp illuminated the repertoire of emotions that flitted over her face. In her hand was a tiny gun. The minutes dragged. The cat rubbed against her legs, muttering. She shoved it away with her foot.

"You knew all along, didn't you?"

"No." I shook my head for emphasis. Across the room, on the cluttered desk, the phone rang. Simmons was returning my page.

"Let it ring," she said.

I sank back into Marianne's couch. On the fourth ring, again the answering machine clicked on.

"I saw you on television," Joyce said. "You were trying to get away from that television reporter. You knew about me and she knew it." Joyce fastened her eyes on me, her words hanging in the air. "That cretin Simmons had said as much earlier. I saw him."

Joyce shifted the gun from one hand to the other, then back, an uneasy gesture she'd been making since she'd burst through the door half an hour before. I moved slightly.

"Don't," she said.

"Joyce, why don't you put the gun down." I hoped I sounded soothing. "I will tell you what I know and don't know." Her eyebrows raised at that. I suddenly wondered if she had come with a plan in mind.

And what had the policewoman said about guns? If you planned to carry one, you damned well better be ready to use it. Did Joyce have the nerve? Could this sad, bulky woman really kill me? A cold little shiver reminded me that this was someone who had already killed two people. And not from a distance. She had tried to kill Leslie by putting her eyes out.

With an effort, I reined in my fear. Maybe if I could keep her talking, it would buy me some time. Maybe Simmons would try harder to return my call. Or Elizabeth... Oh, God, Elizabeth. She was going to walk right into this mess. And I was powerless to stop her.

"Joyce, I'm expecting someone," I said. "Elizabeth Hammett. I was going to show her this house."

"I know." She relaxed momentarily. "I wouldn't count on her turning up any time soon. An accident on Route 50. They've closed a good part of it."

The cat roamed restlessly, unable to find a suitable place to perch. A heavy wall clock ticked off the minutes. I thought about Joyce watching the video of me evading the reporters. It was as if in some awful way, we both knew this scene between us had to be played out. That it had been only a matter of time.

"How did you know I was here, anyway?" I tried to make my tone conversational and unthreatening.

"Shirley Bodine told me."

"You called my office?"

She grinned without malice. "Shirley thinks I am an old friend of yours who lost your phone number. She nicely volunteered that you were showing a waterfront property in Hawk's Bay. That was all I needed to know. I just looked for that expensive car of yours."

"You drove around in the rain?"

There was a loud snort. "There's about six blocks of waterfront in Hawk's Bay."

Outside, across the water, the day was dying, clouds helping the darkness along. I could see flickering pinpricks of light as residents, home from work, turned on lights in kitchens and screened porches. I could almost hear the comforting sounds of dinners begun, of dogs gently cursed for needing to be walked in the rain.

The clock ticked. The cat suddenly began to lick itself, one leg sticking up in the air like a big pork chop. He stopped momentarily, looked at me, the raised leg still in place. The rain came down harder.

Joyce didn't have a plan, I thought. Didn't know what to do anymore than I did. Where would we go from here? Where could we go? I looked around. Maybe if I ran for the door.

I focused on the gun. My eyes trailed up to her face. Hubris and indecision were fused together in an alarming marriage. I glanced at her save-the-rainforest T-shirt. And her old-lady jeans—elastic at the waist and sagging at the knees from heavy wear. What, I thought, after all, did she have left to lose? It was a frightening thought.

"Joyce? Why did you kill Rose? And Leslie?"

She twisted in Marianne's chair, releasing the wet dog scent of clothes damp from the rain. "Accidents. They were both accidents."

"But you tried to put Leslie's eyes out? How could that be an accident?"

"Well, it was." Suddenly, she seemed to take on new energy. When she spoke again, her voice was animated. "And you, of all people, should know about Rose. She stole your clients, too, and your sale." I started. The Round Bay house. This was about money? About unethical real estate practices? But then where did Leslie come in? "Well, didn't she? Didn't Rose Macklin steal your sale?" I nodded, slowly. "Well, she did that to me, too. More than once. Before I went to Gaylin. And do you know what that meant?" I shook my head. "No, you wouldn't, would you? You live in this insulated little world with the virtuous Lillian Weber. Everything all on the up and up. No need to meet quotas or compete with the Rose Macklins of the world."

"But everyone who sells real estate has tough times," I said. "Lillian, too."

"Not Rose Macklin."

"But what about Leslie? Where does she come in?"

My pager suddenly beeped, making my heart flutter. Joyce shook her head. There was quiet as one brief dart of lightning split the sky, illuminating the dark water spread out in front of Marianne's picture window.

"You were going to tell me about Leslie," I reminded her.

Remembering, her face grew congested. "She overheard me on the phone as I called Metro Crime Stoppers on Friday morning." She looked out as another quick dart of lightening hit. "I wanted the cops to think Rose's death had been a robbery that went wrong, so I took Rose's handbag." Joyce was motionless now, the gun pointing downward. "Leslie was in the next cubicle when I called. She overheard me tell them where to find Rose's wallet." Her voice turned hard. "Knew I was involved and she was going to turn me in." I wondered if Leslie had actually called the hot line with an anonymous tip about Joyce? Simmons had never said anything about it. But, then, how would he have known who had called? And there probably had been hundreds of tips to follow up. Consequently, the cops hadn't found Rose's wallet for days after Joyce called to tell them about it. Maybe Leslie hadn't even overheard her. Maybe this was Joyce's overheated imagination at work. But whatever it was, Leslie was dead because of it.

"Joyce," I said slowly, "I ran into Leslie that morning. I don't think she knew anything about you. If she overheard you, I don't think..."

I wasn't sure she was listening any longer. And the gun, I saw, was resting in her hand, as if she'd temporarily forgotten it. I could see her attention was flagging. The last week had not been kind. Her hair had dried, forming a thin, almost totally gray fringe that fluttered around her face. Her face looked older, too. And the wiseguy remarks were gone, replaced by a kind of dazed resignation. What did she want from me? What did she plan to do?

Whatever it was, it was better to keep her occupied. And she seemed to need to talk. My pager beeped for a second time. I swallowed, watching her hand with the gun closely. But she barely lifted it off her lap, closed off now in a world I couldn't begin to imagine. Was there relief for her to confess her terrible secrets? The way the Catholics promised?

"I didn't hate Leslie," she said, suddenly. "She wasn't a whore like Rose."

Keep her talking, I told myself. "How did you manage to cancel the appointment with Leslie's clients? To show them the Hammett house?" Her mind was clearly wandering now, I thought, maybe reliving the scene. Leslie's body lying broken and dead against the peeling blue of the swimming pool. "Joyce?"

With an effort, she drew herself back to the moment. "Her clients called and canceled. Nancy, the other receptionist, took a written message. So when I saw the pink slip in Leslie's mailbox, I took it. Just to screw her up. She didn't know they'd canceled."

"And you planned to go in their place?"

"No, not at first. But, then I began to think about it."

"And so you drove to the Pines around noon, left your car on the street by the Lido Beach Inn, and walked to the Hammett house?" I drew a deep breath, wondering if I was making things worse for myself.

"I didn't want anyone to see my car in their driveway." She roused herself then, looked at me directly. "How did you know about my car?"

"Your bumper sticker. 'Random Acts of Kindness,' or whatever it is. I parked behind you on the street that day. Went inside to get Marian Beall to notarize some things for me."

Her hand with the gun moved a little. "I didn't want to kill Leslie," she said, suddenly. "I just wanted to reason with her."

I nodded. Where the hell was Simmons? Surely, he must know something was up if I didn't answer my page twice. She wasn't going to talk forever.

"Joyce, tell me about Rose. Why did you want to get her out on that estate?"

"Because she wouldn't talk with me. She couldn't face me. She knew what she'd done. And she knew Mitch wouldn't have tolerated it. She treated me like I was scum. I didn't exist for Little Miss Frosted Hair." A glimmer of the old Joyce, I thought.

"So how did you arrange the appointment with her?" I kept my voice pleasant, interested.

"Just called her up at home. From a pay phone. Didn't give my real name. She never knew it was me."

A note of something had crept into her voice, something I really didn't like the sound of. Pride, I thought. She was trying not to sound proud of her scheme.

"But didn't Rose know it was you when you drove up in your car?"

Joyce laughed. "I made sure she got there first."

"What happened then, Joyce?"

She was no longer looking at me. Reliving, I guessed, that bright day on the estate overlooking the Chesapeake. "I found her on the patio. She cursed me," she said. "Refused to talk. Then she tried to walk away." A shadow passed over her face. "I...I took a brick. It was right there. She tried to walk away from me. So I took the brick and I..." She looked around, suddenly aware again of where she was. "Why are you asking me this?" Fear, then anger, sprayed over her face. She tried to make her features behave, clutching the gun tighter. "Well, it doesn't matter, does it? You're not going to tell anyone."

Had I just heard my death sentence? The very ease of choosing to pull the trigger suddenly hit me. What happened if Simmons didn't come?

"No. No, I'm not." I swallowed, hoping my voice was still soothing. "Never. Tell me what happened then, Joyce? After you, er, picked up the brick."

"I took her handbag to make it look like a robbery. That's what the police thought, wasn't it? That whoever did that to her did it for the money."

"Yes, I think so. Yes, I'm sure they did."

"Later, at home, I thought more about it. So I emptied her wallet, rubbed it clean, then went and dropped it in the woods near Grayson's Cove." Her pride was back. "Then I called the police with an anonymous tip. So they would believe it was robbery for sure."

Again, I tried to find some regret in this statement and couldn't.

And it had almost worked, I thought. If only Leslie hadn't been making calls in the next cubicle early Friday morning. If only the Fawcetts had been willing to leave a message on Leslie's voice mail rather than with the other receptionist.

There was a noise outside, from the direction of the water. The muscles of Joyce's neck and shoulders stiffened. She got up to look out the picture window.

"Joyce," I said, "why don't you sit down again. I have more questions. We can talk this out."

"Too late," she said. I could almost smell the odor coming off her. Suddenly, rage and impotency swirled through me. I couldn't just let myself get killed. I had to do something more, but what? From the corner of my eye, I saw the gray cat standing on the floor in front of a bookcase on the other side of the room. He was looking up. Oh, God, I thought, he was going to try to jump. Joyce followed my eyes, turning to look. At the same time, there was a resounding crash, as the cat fell back to the floor, then an explosion. The gun in her hand had inadvertently gone off.

I lunged toward her, grabbing it. Pulling it out of her hands, I threw it as hard as I could through the picture window. Rain and wind streamed in, covering Marianne's desk, wetting books and blowing papers. A cry went up, then Joyce was behind me, her hands fiercely clawing at me. I struggled, my breath coming harder. Suddenly, I felt a long hot stripe drag down my face. The scene in front of me blurred. There were only fingernails now, clawing again and again. In a motion born of fear, I threw my body toward hers, stamping my feet, and poking my fingers into her stomach. There was a grunt as I made contact with soft flesh. She went down.

It couldn't have taken more than a few seconds. Propelled by adrenaline, I raced for the door. Stumbling, I ran out of the house and turned left onto a narrow walkway. And still the rain came down, lighter than before, but making the ground muddy and the steps slippery. Behind me, I heard movement, then a slamming door. The walkway underneath my feet turned into a short flight of stairs to the seawall and dark water below. Suddenly, my right foot hit a patch of wet grass, sliding out from under me. Then I was falling.

THIRTY-SEVEN

I HEARD THE SIREN FIRST, its shriek piercing the distance, rapidly growing closer. A shadowy figure appeared high on the grassy margin of the road, then scrambled down the first flight of crumbling stairs. The siren grew louder. Barely able to see in the wet night, I watched as the shadow ran across the lawn. A second figure, chunky and backlit by the streetlight, stood poised at the top of the second set of stairs. Then there was a smothered cry as Joyce, surprised, her balance gone, fell forward down the steps, landing facedown and rolling onto her side near the seawall just yards from where I was lying. She made no sound. Only her eyes moved.

What had happened? My mind wouldn't focus.

"Miss Elliott, Eve, you okay?" Simmons took the wet stairs two at a time.

"Yes, I think so." Maybe. At least my legs and arms moved, I thought. Above us, the bit players were going through their parts in the rainy night. Flashing blue lights illuminated half a dozen figures half running, half sliding down Marianne's treacherous stairs. The sirens that had filled the air were replaced by the sound of radios and voices shouting.

Then I felt Simmons' arm around me, pulling me up and out of the way as several uniformed cops stumbled down the second flight to the seawall. Did they know whom to arrest? I wondered. Did they know about Joyce? The thought felt lazy, oddly detached.

I could feel water oozing in my shoes, my hair plastered to my head by the rain. My jacket was wet and useless. I wanted to peel it off, to go back inside Marianne's house and curl up on the couch with a blanket and the gray cat, to sit in peace and comfort looking out over the dark water. Then I remembered. By now the driving rain would have turned the desk by the broken picture window into an unrecognizable mass of pulpy paper.

I looked over at Simmons. His face was bloated from lack of sleep, from too much attention to the dead. And not enough on the living. The fuzz on the top of his head had flattened into little more than short, damp sprouts, its red color neutralized by the swirling blue lights of the police car beacons.

"You're very lucky," he said. "We weren't sure what we were going to find." He said something to a plainclothes cop behind him. Then he turned back to me. Below us the dark water pitched into small whitecaps. "I will need you to tell me what happened. When you can."

Above us, a floodlight suddenly illuminated the scene. Someone must have found the switch inside Marianne's house. Two cops crouched near Joyce's inert body. A shiver that had nothing to do with the cold rain slid down my spine. I could see her eyes, open and beyond pain—like that of an animal that doesn't understand what is happening—as they watched me. Was this crumpled body the same woman who had sat in Marianne's armchair just minutes ago, trying to justify what she had done? Two men with a stretcher made their way down the slippery descent toward her.

"Eve? You okay?"

"I guess so." The anxiety from what I had seen ran through me, my nerves firing, my heart pounding. And still her eyes followed me. I wanted only to be left alone to ponder what had happened, to make some sense of it.

Simmons shifted his weight slightly, waiting. Not once did he glance toward the house or the medics loading Joyce onto the stretcher. No one spoke. There was only the sound of the radios, of the medics.

"We can talk later," he said finally. "At your house."

"Just one thing. How did you know where I was?" Out of the corner of my eye, I could see Detective Clarke directing foot traffic at the top of the stairs near the house.

"When you didn't answer your page, I called your aunt, who gave me the address. She said you were meeting Mrs. Hammett here." He glanced upward, maybe to inspire me to get a move on out of the rain. "She's worried. You need to call her."

Spurred to action, I navigated the stairs in my sodden shoes, then looked around the lawn and into Marianne's brightly lit house. My fear had given way to a kind of emotional exhaustion. Oddly, I noticed the anger phase was missing. Behind me, Simmons' men were roping off the house.

"Someone needs to get in touch with Marianne Pinot," I said. "She's the owner. She's going to walk in on this mess when she gets home from College Park."

He nodded, then said something to one of his men. I slowly inched up the crumbly stairs to the main road, clinging to the pipe rail. Neighbors were crowded around, standing behind the police cars, murmuring among themselves. The ambulance carrying Joyce picked its way through the narrow streets, heading for the hospital. I walked to the BMW to call Lillian, then realized that the car keys were in my handbag in the house.

Suddenly aware of the cold, I sat down on the top step, not caring if I got any wetter. I'd have to wait for Simmons. He climbed the steps.

"Car keys," I said. "In my handbag. In the house." He nodded, his face mottled blue by the flashing lights, then turned to a uniformed cop. Another cop slogged past me up the steps, cradling in his arms a very scared and wet gray cat. He deposited it in the arms of one of Marianne's neighbors. For the first time, I noticed a slight cut on my arm that was oozing a little blood. And my shoulder ached where I'd landed on it.

In just over an hour I was home. I had called Lillian and Weller Church, then driven home with Simmons right behind me. My aunt and Weller had been waiting by the cottage in his old Lincoln. The clearing smelled fresh from the rain, full of ozone and fragrant with honeysuckle and pine. Simmons had parked on the wide path leading to Weller's Creek. I thought of another night, less than a week ago, when he had given me such a fright as I returned half-stoned from Will's house. I wondered again if he had known about the marijuana.

Hot soup revived me somewhat. And my damp clothes had

dried with blotchy scabs of mud. Simmons and I now sat across from each other in the small kitchen. He took notes and I talked between spoonfuls. Zeke and Lance lay ill at ease in the living room with Lillian and Weller. I heard Will come in. Someone said that Elizabeth had stayed the night in College Park.

My words came to me from a distance, unemotional words about what I had seen and heard tonight. There were no nightmares now, just my report of what Joyce had told me as she sat in Marianne's comfortable chair. My words seemed dry, distant, even to me. Blood and broken limbs, lost lives, and Joyce's tormented eyes seemed out of place in the kitchen.

In half an hour, Simmons was through with me for tonight. His red hair had dried back to its normal fuzz.

"We'll need to talk more tomorrow. I'll be in touch." He folded his notebook and got up heavily. There was one more thing I wanted to know.

"Did Leslie Ballard call in a tip? Explaining that she suspected Joyce Nichols of killing Rose Macklin?"

Simmons turned back, his eyes curious. "No." His voice was matter-of-fact. So Joyce *had* been wrong. Her guilt had distorted and magnified what Leslie had known. And then it had caused her death. Simmons walked from the kitchen and, after a word with Weller, left. I wondered if he would go home to sleep or go back to work.

I ran upstairs to change into clean corduroys and a sweater and thick socks. Returning downstairs, I found Lillian and Will falling over each other in Ray Tilghman's small kitchen fixing me hot chocolate laced with bourbon. Someone had lit a fire to take off the remaining chill. I collapsed on the couch. Across from me, Weller Church was drinking straight bourbon, having had the good sense to forgo the hot chocolate.

"Well, you've had quite a night," he said. I had given Lillian a synopsis of what had happened when I called her from Hawk's Bay. She in turn called Weller. Together they had filled in Will. "Two murders cleared up. We'll all sleep a little sounder for it."

I nodded, stroking Zeke's black head. Weller looked around, then cleared his throat. Before he could speak, I interrupted. "I'm going to buy the house.'' My words came to me from a distance, as if they had been spoken by somebody else. "I'll see about the money tomorrow.''

Weller took a deep drink from his glass, trying not to look too surprised. I was surprised myself. In some odd way, I thought, the events of the evening had made the decision easier for me. In the kitchen, Lillian's voice mingled with Will's as they banged pots and cups and saucers. Zeke jumped back onto the couch and nestled half on top of me, his brown eyes happy that I was home. Lance sat with his back to me, his head pointed up and looking back, having made sure he was near enough to the couch not to miss out on his share of the attention. I looked at the old lawyer across from me, his suit rumpled and his bowtie askew, the tumbler of bourbon more than half gone. He was smiling.

I closed my eyes for a minute. The scene in the muddy grass by the seawall below Marianne's house came rushing back. Surprised by the clarity of the image of Joyce's haunted eyes, I quickly snapped awake. Stay in the present, I told myself. Focus.

"I don't suppose you will now tell me who the other buyer is?'' Weller shook his head. "I didn't think so.''

"Are you going to tell Lillian about your decision?''

"Now?''

"No time like the present. She's worried, Eve. Her broken ankle scared her. She's got plenty of friends, but you're special to her.'' He took a deep gulp, then put the glass down on an end table. The fire spat out a stone. "For all the sadness of the Hammetts' separation, I think she was happy having Elizabeth around.''

"Yes,'' I said. Elizabeth vacuuming by night. Tomorrow, she and Hamm would know what had happened that sunny lunch hour a week ago, while Hamm changed his shirt at the mall and Elizabeth drove to her appointment with the divorce lawyer. I wondered if they would ever forgive each other. I turned back to Weller. "Okay, I'll tell her tonight.''

I pushed Zeke off the couch just as Will placed a steaming cup of chocolate in my hand. I sniffed it for booze, jumping back a little as the bourbon went up my nose. Lillian sat down heavily at the other end of the couch, her calf propped carefully on the couch so that no weight rested on her ankle. It was bothering her, I thought. Will swiveled the desk chair over for himself.

"I'm going to buy Ray's house," I said to no one in particular. Lillian looked at me, then reached across the sofa to hug me the best she could without getting up.

"I'm so glad," she said.

Both dogs struggled to their feet, looking first at me, then at the others around the room. I glanced over at Will, who hadn't said anything. If he was surprised, I wouldn't have known. Maybe he needed time to take it in, just the way I did.

Weller got to his feet. "Well, that's great news, but it's time to call it a day. Come on, Lil, Eve needs her rest and so do you and so do I. I'll take you home."

In a flurry of activity and kisses, Lillian and Weller were gone. Will and I stood on the porch steps looking at the crescent moon. The night air seemed too cool for the sweet green smells of May. Something broke through the water at the cove. Will followed me back into the house. Ray Tilghman's clock said almost midnight.

"My God, what about Marianne? Not only is her house destroyed, she won't be able to find her cat."

"Lillian called her. The police had already warned her. She's staying with friends near Washington. One of the neighbors boarded up that window."

"What perfectly lousy luck. Her house was in the wrong place at the wrong time. It's a mess." I looked over at him. "Thanks for everything." I swallowed. "Will, I want you to know that you're always welcome to the cottage."

"I know."

A tiny prickle of grief crept into my heart. The events of the evening, of the last week, already seemed ghastly and unreal. I was to get the dogs and a house and property that most people could only dream about, but Will might leave. If not right now, then later. He didn't have to say it. I watched as he moved the desk chair and then returned to stir out the fire. He was avoiding my eyes. Lance stood beside him as he knelt by the fireplace. Fatigue swept over me then like a wave.

"I think I'd better go home." I nodded. He hugged me tightly.

"You will call if you need something?" I nodded again. "We'll talk tomorrow." In his face was sadness. I felt as I were looking in a mirror.

"Maybe this friendship thing isn't so bad, Will, although it sure feels pretty bad. Maybe it's just the next step, that's all. And we can change our minds at any time, I suppose."

"I suppose," he said. But we wouldn't, I thought. With a final hug he left, closing the door carefully behind him, for the second night in a row. I didn't hear his truck. Maybe he'd walked. I took a deep breath, suddenly feeling free. We might care for each other, but for the long haul there would be someone else for each of us.

THIRTY-EIGHT

I AWOKE EARLY to a red sky spread out beyond the shutters. A pine bough brushed the window near the bed. Red sky in the morning, I thought, sailors take warning. Red sky at night, sailor's delight. Shifting positions among the warm, sleeping dogs, I turned away from the unearthly red light.

By the time I awoke again a few hours later, sweating from dreams I couldn't recall, the sky had turned a steely blue. I closed my eyes for a minute and let myself remember last night. The dark scene in the muddy grass by the seawall below Marianne's house came rushing back. Joyce Nichols had killed Rose Macklin and Leslie Ballard. It seemed less real than my dreams.

Beside me a friendly tongue licked my hand, then Zeke jumped from the bed, shook himself awake and joined Lancelot in the doorway.

It was after nine o'clock. My phone was ringing. I ignored it, wishing I had a newspaper or had awakened in time for the early-morning news. By the time I had dressed, made coffee, and fed and walked the dogs, there were two more red flashes. I sat down at the desk. The phone rang again.

"Hi. You okay this morning?" asked Lillian.

Her voice sounded as if she hadn't had any sleep or what she had was long ago. I reminded myself that she had had to cope with learning that someone she knew was a killer.

"Sort of. I should be asking the same of you." I took a sip from my second cup of coffee, wondering how long the chitchat could go on. "How's your ankle?"

"It's pretty much all right, I think. I just need to be careful not to use it too much."

"Lillian, you watch the news this morning?"

There was a long sigh on the other end of the phone. "Joyce

confessed.'' I could picture my aunt sitting at her desk, keeping up appearances: clothes, hair, and nails perfect, paperwork laid out in piles in front of her as if the world weren't turned upside down. "The whole thing is beyond belief. She was always a busybody and a little pushy, but..."

"But what?"

Lillian's voice grew quiet. "But nothing. This is what happens when someone gets pushed beyond their limits. It's what happens when you are alone and scared."

"Yes, but something was wrong with Joyce, Lillian. The seeds of this were there."

"Well, I can't imagine."

Remembering the scene at Hawk's Bay last night, I was afraid I could.

"Have you heard from Marianne this morning?"

"Yes. She's shocked, of course. Grateful that no one was hurt."

"The police let her into her house?"

"Later this morning. I'm going down with her and Elizabeth to assess the damage. We'll meet her insurance agent down there and see what needs immediate attention." I didn't ask her how she was going to navigate Marianne's steps.

"And Hamm and Elizabeth."

"Elizabeth wants the divorce, I'm afraid." Lillian's voice grew low and sad. "Though I think that Hamm would go for a reconciliation if only Elizabeth would agree to it."

I wondered if many marriages had enough goodwill and forgiveness to overcome such odds. Mine hadn't been able to deal with lesser issues. Lillian's long romance with my uncle Max was the exception, I thought, not the rule. My aunt was quiet on her end of the phone. I knew she was thinking of him.

"Well, maybe it's for the best, Lillian." What a bunch of crap, I thought. "I take that back. How in hell should I know what's for the best?"

She laughed then. "I am so happy that you are buying Ray's house."

"I'm happy, too. And glad to have made the decision." I

watched the red flashes on the answering machine, counting them silently to myself.

"You'll let Will stay in the cottage?"

"Of course I'll let him stay." I swallowed. Will. "Lillian, there are four red lights blinking away on this machine. Maybe I better go. I'll call you later."

I thought about Will then, wiry body clad in blue jeans and workshirt. I found myself happy and not happy, all at the same time. My finger pushed the button to listen to my messages.

Then my thoughts suddenly took off back to last night, to Joyce's indecision, her pride. I could almost feel her fingers raking down my face. But I'd been lucky. There was only a dim red line this morning. I started, then, realizing that the answering machine had turned itself off. Wearily, I listened as the tape replayed the messages.

Peter Fox asked me to call him. Simmons suggested strongly that I show up at his office later this afternoon. I was to call him to set up an appointment. And Weller wanted to discuss a few details about Ray Tilghman's estate. He added what I already knew: that Joyce had confessed, then added that she'd been charged with two counts of first-degree murder and was being held without bond. There was a big question of her competency to stand trial. I shivered, then with an effort I pushed thoughts of Joyce and murder from my mind.

The final message was from Mitch. "I heard about last night. It must have been terrible. If there's anything I can do, call me." As always, he gave his phone numbers. There was a tiny pause. "Actually, since I'm going to be in your neighborhood in a little while, maybe I'll drop by. If you're there, you're there. If not, I'll catch you later. I have some news about the house in Round Bay." I heard a car horn in the background. He was calling from the Jeep. "And congratulations on buying Ray Tilghman's house." The machine rewound and switched off.

I swiveled around in Ray Tilghman's old chair. News sure traveled fast. Not only had Mitch heard about the events of last night, he knew about Ray's house. Anne Arundel County was indeed a small place. I picked up the phone and made an appointment to meet with Simmons at one this afternoon. Weller would meet me there. We could talk afterwards. I'd call Peter later.

As I sat pondering whether I owed Lawrence Schoenfeld a call, somebody pulled up in the clearing. From the porch I watched as Mitch got out of the Jeep. He was carrying a paper bag from a local bagel bakery. I opened the door and let the dogs out.

"Hi. Get my message?"

"Yes. Just." The dogs were running in circles around him as he strode across the pine-needled clearing to the porch. He stopped once and picked up a stick for Lancelot to retrieve. Zeke didn't bother, preferring to stand waiting to be patted.

"Can I come in?"

"Yes. You want coffee?"

"Sure." He followed me into the kitchen, then handed me the bag. It contained assorted fresh bagels, still warm, and cream cheese with nuts and raisins. We took breakfast out to the porch.

"Simmons been to see you this morning? Since Joyce worked for you?"

He nodded, finished chewing. "About seven-thirty this morning. The guy doesn't sleep." He sipped coffee. "I'm very glad this is over. But Joyce, well..." For once, he was silent, looking out into the trees, the laugh crinkles nonexistent. "I don't know how I could have been so wrong about somebody," he said. "What exactly happened? I mean at Hawk's Bay? If you can stand to talk about it."

I found I didn't mind. And again I found he was a good listener. The thoughts that kept playing in my head were too poisonous to carry alone, thoughts of Joyce's tormented eyes. Her fear and self-loathing. Her guilt and pride. He sat drinking coffee and stroking Lancelot as I recited what had happened. When I was done, he shook his head.

"I'm glad it's over. And that you are safe. Seems your intuition was right about a lot." He finished his coffee.

"And wrong about a lot else." We sat peacefully together on the porch, listening to the sounds of chirps. "Mitch, what did

Leslie see in Hamm Hammett?" I asked suddenly. "The times we met, she seemed so vital, so much her own woman, not like someone who would be attracted to someone like Hamm."

He nodded, slowly. "I've been thinking about that and I think I know. Leslie once told me that she would do whatever it took to get Dennis—that's her teenage kid—into the Naval Academy. I think she thought Hamm could pull some strings."

"Actually, to tell you the truth, knowing that makes me feel a little better. At least she had a good reason," I said. "And who knows, maybe he can still help."

Mitch nodded. "You were right about something else."

"What?"

"The Canins. The contract on the house on Round Bay fell through late yesterday afternoon. It seems they are separating."

Everybody is separating, I thought, or getting divorced. Or already divorced. "What does my intuition have to do with it?"

"Richard Canin had apparently been having an affair with Rose Macklin. Another agent knew about it."

I stared at him. "That certainly goes a ways to explain why the Canins stopped taking my calls."

He glanced at his watch. "I have to meet someone in half an hour. Do you want to have dinner tonight? A real dinner?"

I looked around the small, unimproved cottage. It looked particularly dear to me this morning. Something was gnawing round the edges of my brain. "Mitch, how did you find out about my buying Ray Tilghman's property? I only told Lillian and Will and Weller last night. I didn't even know myself until then."

Mitch stood up. The dogs scrambled to their feet. For the second time in two days, I knew what I didn't want to know. I looked down at the dogs, then back at him. It had been right in front of me all the time.

"You. You wanted to buy this house. And you always have." He didn't say anything. "Ray himself threw you out, I heard, when you approached him about selling you the property." The laugh crinkles around Mitch's eyes had disappeared. His mouth was grave. "You were willing to put up with the dogs and try to drive me out just to make a few bucks?"

"No. No, it wasn't as an investment. Please don't think that." He sat back down, his head in his hands. "Look, Eve, I'm sorry. I...I don't really know what to say. Except that...except that."

"Except what?"

"I made a mistake." Then he grimaced and got to his feet for a second time. "I'm sorry. I didn't mean to make your life more complicated. I just thought that...that if I could sort of force your hand...I never planned to actually go through with actually buying."

I could hardly believe my ears. "Force my hand? Make me make a choice between New York and Maryland?"

He nodded. I thought about our evening on his boat. There'd been something between us since we'd met on Lillian's deck almost ten months ago. I could feel my anger rising.

"I'm sorry," he said. The screen door slammed behind him. I watched as he climbed into the Jeep, then sat for a moment staring straight ahead. Finally, he opened the door and ran back up the front steps, two at a time, to stand looking at me through the screen.

"I guess there's some other things I didn't say," he said. He stood on the top step, tense in casual slacks and shirt. "Look, Eve, I've had more than my share of success this last few years. But it's not all been wonderful. I guess that I'm...that I'm searching for something." He opened the door and came in a few steps. "This isn't about material success or things or houses," he said. "It's about something else. I keep moving on, looking and not finding. Making more and more money. After my wife and daughter left..." He stopped, his lips pulled back. I didn't know this man, I thought. "I really need to go," he said. With a quick glance at me, he left again. I watched as the Jeep turned and took off up the driveway to Weller's Creek Road.

I had already had enough surprises for one day. Calling the dogs, I walked down to the water and stood on the dock. Last night's rain had cleared the air. Birds I couldn't name sang for a fine spring morning. Running and barking, the dogs raced into the water. I threw stick after stick, until they slumped panting at my feet to rest.

The sun was rising in the sky as the dogs and I walked up the path to the cottage in the pine clearing. And today, unlike yesterday, it was home.

THE LAZARUS HOTEL

JO BANNISTER

AND THEN THERE WERE NONE...

A group of six strangers meets for a weekend therapy retreat at London's newest but incomplete luxury hotel. The six quickly discover that no one is there by accident. They have been sought out by someone whose identity is unknown and whose intentions they can't predict.

But terror closes in as the phones and the elevators go out, trapping the group from the outside world. Then accidents begin to happen. One by one, they are being hunted. By one among them who is a killer.

Available March 1999 at your favorite retail outlet.

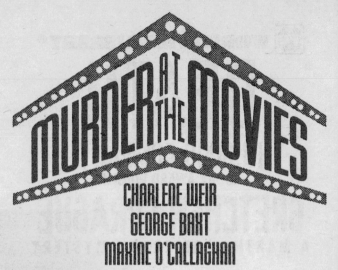

MURDER AT THE MOVIES

CHARLENE WEIR
GEORGE BAXT
MAXINE O'CALLAGHAN

MURDER TAKE TWO
by Charlene Weir

Hollywood comes to Hampstead, Kansas, with the filming of a
new picture starring sexy actress Laura Edwards. But murder
steals the scene when a stunt double is impaled on a pitchfork.

THE HUMPHREY BOGART MURDER CASE
by George Baxt

Hollywood in its heyday is brought to life in this witty caper
featuring a surprise sleuth—Humphrey Bogart. While filming
The Maltese Falcon, he searches for a real-life treasure, dodging
a killer on a murder trail through Hollywood.

SOMEWHERE SOUTH OF MELROSE
by Maxine O'Callaghan

P.I. Delilah West is hired to search for an old high school
classmate. The path takes her through the underbelly of broken
dreams and into the caprices of fate, where secrets are born and
sometimes kept....

Available March 1999 at your favorite retail outlet.